～THE～
LAST DOGS
JOURNEY'S END

by
CHRISTOPHER HOLT

illustrated by Allen Douglas

LITTLE, BROWN AND COMPANY
NEW YORK   BOSTON

Text copyright © 2014 by The Inkhouse

INKHOUSE

Illustrations copyright © 2014 by Allen Douglas

Little, Brown and Company

Hachette Book Group
237 Park Avenue, New York, NY 10017
Visit our website at lb-kids.com

Little, Brown and Company is a division of Hachette Book Group, Inc.
The Little, Brown name and logo are trademarks of Hachette Book Group, Inc.

The publisher is not responsible for websites (or their content) that are not owned by the publisher.

First Edition: June 2014

Library of Congress Cataloging-in-Publication Data
Holt, Christopher, 1980–
Journey's end / by Christopher Holt ; illustrated by Allen Douglas.—First edition.
pages cm.—(The last dogs ; [4])
Summary: "Canine heroes Max, Rocky, and Gizmo journey deep into the desert, intent on reaching the silver wall that separates them from their families, helped along the way by a ragtag group of friendly animals, and coming snout-to-snout with wolf pack leader Dolph for a final showdown"—Provided by publisher.
ISBN 978-0-316-20007-3 (hardcover)—ISBN 978-0-316-27969-7 (ebook)—
ISBN 978-0-316-27968-0 (library edition ebook) [1. Dogs—Fiction. 2. Adventure and adventurers—Fiction. 3. Science fiction.] I. Douglas, Allen, 1972– illustrator. II. Title.
PZ7.H7388Las 2014 [Fic]—dc23 2013034218

10 9 8 7 6 5 4 3 2 1

RRD-C

Printed in the United States of America

For a dog named Kobe,
since he didn't get a cameo.
— Christopher Holt

In Memory of Katahdin
2003–2013
— Allen Douglas

THE SILVER WALL

———◆———

Max was running through a vast and dusty desert.

The sky above was a pale, milky blue, and the sun was fat and overwhelming. The heat was intense, baking the ground beneath Max's paws and drying his tawny fur to a crisp. The few skinny, leafless trees were burned black.

On the horizon was an endless wall of silver. It glared bright and harsh, reflecting the giant sun and searing Max's eyes.

Gusts of wind swirled behind Max, and he yelped at the sudden cold. Still running, he looked back—and saw an enormous, inky cloud that swelled like a stormy ocean in the sky. It billowed toward Max, ready to envelop him.

Max turned away from the cloud as he urged himself to run faster.

A voice rose over the wind. *Hello, Maxie.* The speaker was female, canine, and older. The words hadn't been spoken aloud, but they echoed in Max's head, as though the speaker was right next to him.

And then she was.

An elderly Labrador ran at Max's side, her eyes sparkling and her tongue lolling free. Her fur was as dark as the night sky, flecked with white. Around her neck hung a golden collar with three rings connected in a row.

The dog was his dear friend Madame Curie.

"Madame!" Max barked, his tail wagging. "There's something on the horizon, and I don't know what it is."

I do, Madame said, though her mouth did not move. *I'll show you.*

She ran ahead at a speed Max hadn't thought was possible for his old companion. He tore after her, sending up a cloud of desert dust in his wake. The huge silver wall towered above them, taller than any building Max had ever seen, stretching endlessly in either direction.

It's time, Madame said as they neared the wall. *This is the end—and the beginning.*

Max slowed his pace. "I don't understand. How am I supposed to get past it?" Glancing back, he shivered. "The darkness is almost here."

Madame wagged her tail once more. *It's easy, Maxie. All you have to do is jump.*

Before Max could question her, Madame bunched her hind legs and leaped into the air.

She soared up toward the sky, higher and higher. Then, at the very top of her jump, she arced over the wall and disappeared.

"Madame!" Max barked. "Come back!" Frantic, he jumped but only managed to rise a few feet.

"Madame!" Max cried once more, scrabbling in the cracked earth. The wind roared and screamed around him. No matter how deep he dug, there was still more wall.

Make the right choice, Maxie, Madame's voice cried.

"Please help me!" Max barked over the storm. "The darkness is here! Rocky? Gizmo? Where are you?"

If you want to find your people, Madame said, her voice distant, *you have to choose the right path.*

"I don't understand," Max said. "What path?"

But even though he couldn't see her, he could feel that Madame was gone.

Max was alone.

CHAPTER 1

SNAKE IN THE GRASS

Max awoke to find something wet and leathery pressing against his nose.

He barked in surprise and jerked away.

"Aah!" the creature yelped, rearing back—and Max realized it was his friend Rocky. The Dachshund had been sitting snout-to-snout with Max in the overgrown grass, intently watching him sleep.

"What are you doing?" Max asked.

"Just making sure you're okay," Rocky said as he hopped onto Max's back, as if he hadn't just startled the both of them. "Gizmo asked me to stay and watch over you."

"Why wouldn't I be okay?" Max asked.

The little Dachshund leaped off Max's shoulder and landed in the grass in front of him.

"You were growling and kicking in your sleep, like you were battling dream wolves again, buddy," he said. "We all know how your dreams can get to you sometimes."

Max remembered glinting silver, intense heat, and black clouds. He shivered.

"What did you dream about, anyway?" Rocky asked, cocking his head. "Nothing too horrible, right?"

"Nothing horrible," Max said as he rose on all fours. "I'm fine—don't worry."

It was morning, and the sun was still low in the sky. They'd spent the night beside the highway, near a row of hay bales and some scrubby brush. The day before, they'd come through a mostly empty town. In the past, they might have taken a night or two to rest in one of the abandoned houses, rather than sleep outside.

But they couldn't risk stopping any more than necessary these days. There was a pack of angry wolves on their trail, led by the vicious Dolph, and although the three of them had come a long way, they still had a lot of ground to cover before they could be reunited with their people.

Max had insisted the dogs stop only briefly to scavenge for food and water in the empty town. Then they'd continued down the highway until they were so tired they'd had to rest.

"Where is Gizmo?" Max asked as he started toward the highway.

6

"She went for a walk," Rocky said. Max could barely see the Dachshund as they waded through the overgrown grass and weeds. "I think she had a bad dream, too. Me? I dreamed I was in a land of kibble, big guy. We're talking roads paved with kibble, and sausage trees, and...a river full of gravy! You ever had gravy?" The smaller dog's tongue dangled from his pointed snout, and he drooled. "My pack leader poured some into my food dish once. Oh, man, it was great."

Gurgling sounded from Rocky's stomach, and he looked up at Max. "I think I'm just a little hungry," he said.

In response, Max licked his friend's black forehead reassuringly. "Don't worry. I'm sure we'll reach a town soon. Then we can find something to eat."

In another minute, they could see the highway up ahead. It wasn't a huge road, just a couple of two-lane streets divided by a grassy median. Beyond it was another open field bordered by towering trees, but no houses or barns.

Gizmo looked up from a puddle as Max and Rocky approached. She offered them a brief, halfhearted wag of her tail.

"Good morning, boys," the Yorkshire Terrier said. "I found this puddle. It's a little muddy, but it's not too bad."

Max nodded at her and took a few laps of water. She was right—it was gritty with dirt, but Max's mouth and throat were parched, and he needed to drink.

While Rocky drank his fill, Max studied Gizmo. "You took a walk by yourself?" he asked her. "You've got to be careful. The wolves are still following us."

Gizmo's ears drooped, and she looked away. "I know," she said. "I had a dream about Belle—a nightmare, really. It made me sad, so I wanted to chase away the thoughts."

Belle was a Collie whom Max and his friends had been asked to seek out by an old Australian Shepherd named Boss. Boss had heroically given his life to save many other dogs, and it was his last wish to let Belle know he hadn't abandoned her. They'd found Belle, half mad from loneliness, in a filthy, decaying mansion in a city called Baton Rouge. It took everything they had to persuade her to leave her home and make a new life with other dogs.

"She has friends now," Max said. "Georgie and Fletcher and Whitey. She's not alone. And besides, Dr. Lynn said the people will come home soon, remember?"

"I know," Gizmo said. "But what happens if Belle's people decide not to go back? Or if they find her, what happens to her friends?" She ducked her fuzzy head, looking sad. "Everything has been so different since the humans left. More changes might be hard for Belle."

Smacking his lips, Rocky stepped away from the puddle. "You two sure are gloomy today. Where's my chipper, energetic Gizmo? And our fearless, tireless leader, Max?" Running onto the highway, he looked back at his friends and barked. "No more moping, guys! Let's get a move on!"

Max barked, and Gizmo's short tail wagged itself into a blur. They galloped after Rocky, following the road west, away from the rising sun.

"You're right," Gizmo said as the dogs slowed their pace. "It's a nice day for a walk, isn't it? I wonder if we'll meet someone new today. I hope we do."

Rocky trotted at Gizmo's side. "You know these long walks aren't my favorite, but as long as I'm with you, it's time well spent."

"Aww!" Gizmo said. She nudged his side with her head and offered him an appreciative lick.

Rocky was right, Max thought. Though their travels were often exhausting, having his two friends beside him was a help.

Just ahead, Max noticed a car in the median. It was partially hidden by the tall grass and covered with dirt and leaves. Max was used to seeing these rusting, empty signs of humanity now.

Their journey had started months ago, when Max found himself locked in a kennel. Not long after Max had run out of food and water, Rocky had freed him. That was when Max learned that all the humans had disappeared, leaving their pets behind. The birds had disappeared, too.

Max knew his human family—his pack leaders, Charlie and Emma, and their parents—wouldn't have left

him if they'd had a choice. He had decided he would do anything to find them.

It was then that Max and Rocky had first faced off with Dolph. When Max protected Rocky from one wolf in Dolph's pack who was trying to steal the Dachshund's food, the vicious gray wolf vowed to track Max down and make him pay.

The three friends had traveled across half the country, and still Dolph tailed them.

Now, silent and watchful, Max padded down the highway behind Rocky and Gizmo, who were deep in a friendly conversation. He raised his snout high and inhaled. Pollen. Grass and weeds. Damp earth. Moss and fungus and mold, and the tangy scent of hidden squirrels and rabbits.

No wolves. So far.

Still, Max had to stay alert. Dolph always showed up eventually.

"Hey, look!" Gizmo barked.

Max glanced past her down the road—and saw the beacon.

It was an amber light attached to the top of a small traffic barricade painted with orange and white stripes. More beacons like this had been placed along the other roads the three friends had traveled, marking a trail they were meant to follow.

"Yes!" Rocky ran around in an excited circle. "We're heading in the right direction! Maybe we don't need to be wearing these collars after all."

"I think your red collar looks very handsome," Gizmo said.

Rocky wagged his tail. "Thank you! That green collar brings out your eyes."

Gizmo's eyes widened. "It does?"

"Sure," Max said. "You both look good. Well, as good as any of us can look at this point."

Rocky groaned. "Don't remind me. Remember that day with Dr. Lynn? When we were all pampered and clean?" He sighed. "That was the best."

"It was," Max agreed as he took the lead and began walking once more. "We'll be with her again soon. We'll follow her trail while she tracks our path, and we'll find each other in the middle!"

The tag on his collar jingled softly. Just when Max forgot it was there, the collar would rub his neck or get caught on a branch, and he would remember all over again. He hadn't worn a collar in the past—if Max had ever gotten lost, he had a little electronic chip planted under his skin that a vet could scan to find out his name and who his pack leaders were. But these new collars were special. They contained trackers that would help Dr. Lynn locate Max, Rocky, and Gizmo once it was safe for them to be reunited with the humans.

Dr. Lynn was a scientist and a veterinarian. She had been the pack leader of Max's old friend Madame Curie, a fellow Labrador. Near the start of their journey, Madame had urged Max to follow a three-ringed symbol to find the doctor, who would reunite Max with his people.

Tracking the symbol had led Max, Rocky, and Gizmo to a laboratory. It turned out that the symbol represented Praxis, a virus that was meant to help people with mental illnesses or brain injuries but had infected animals instead. The virus was harmless to pets and wildlife, but it had mutated to become dangerous to humans, which meant they couldn't be around their pets. And so all the people had left.

It was a pig named Gertrude who had blasted the dogs with electricity. The electricity had triggered the Praxis virus, which transformed the dogs' minds and made them so smart they could read and understand human speech. The pig had told them to follow the orange-and-white barricades with the flashing beacons, which led the dogs farther south. Eventually, they'd found Dr. Lynn, a kind older woman who wore a big straw hat over her white hair.

Dr. Lynn had bathed them, fed them, and loved them, and when she discovered they were smart enough to understand her, she explained that she was working to find a cure so that all the people could return home. Once the virus had been triggered, Max, Rocky, and Gizmo were no longer infectious to humans, so before Dr. Lynn left, she gave them their new tracking collars and promised that she would come back for them soon.

Without her, the dogs walked on, exhausted and

hungry and aching all over, but determined to be reunited with their families.

Now, as the sun rose higher in the sky and the day grew warmer, Gizmo stopped in the middle of the road, her whole body rigid, her tufted ears perked up.

Rocky came to a stop next to her, his head darting frantically from side to side. "What is it?" he whispered anxiously. "Is it Dolph? Is it food? Is it Dolph eating food?"

"Is everything okay?" Max asked.

"Shh," Gizmo said. Dropping to her belly, she inched toward the grassy median. "Be very, very quiet."

Confused, Max sat next to Rocky and watched as Gizmo crept near the weeds in the center of the highway. She stopped as she came to the edge of the asphalt and raised her paw—then let it swing down to slap the dirt.

What looked like a long, slender stick darted out of the grass and onto the road, slithering quickly away from Gizmo.

"What is *that*?" Rocky asked nervously.

Gizmo jumped up to all fours, her tail wagging ferociously. "A garter snake! I *love* garter snakes." She turned to look back at Rocky and Gizmo. "Come on, let's chase it!"

"What?" Rocky asked again. He looked at Max. "Why would we want to chase a snake?"

But Max was caught up in vivid memories of his days on the farm, when he was just a puppy and life was simple. He'd bounded through the fields at dusk, chasing the harmless snakes through the grass, catching and releasing them, and occasionally delivering them, squirming, to his squealing pack leaders.

"Who wouldn't want to chase one?" Max barked at Rocky as he leaped up and raced after Gizmo. "Come on!"

The garter snake wound down the center of the road just ahead of Gizmo, its stripes standing out stark and white against the dark asphalt. Gizmo jumped forward to bat at its tail.

"Don't be afraid," she yipped after the fleeing snake. "We just want to play!"

The snake did not respond, but it flicked out its tongue and slithered forward.

Max quickly gained on Gizmo. Leaping over her, he landed in front of the fleeing snake, darted his head down, and carefully snatched it up in his jaws. The creature squirmed helplessly, its tail curling around Max's snout.

Holding his head up high, Max pranced in a big, triumphant circle.

Gizmo jumped up and down. "Aw! You beat me to it," she said. "But that was so fun! I bet if you let it go, I'll get it first."

Snout scrunched in disgust, Rocky approached the other two dogs. "Max, buddy, did you really put that thing in your mouth? You don't know where it's been!"

Max gently set the garter snake on the ground and let it slither away toward the grass.

"I can't believe you've never chased a snake before," Max said to Rocky. "It's like trying to catch a living stick!"

"You two are crazy," Rocky said.

Gizmo butted him playfully with her head, then started after the snake again. "You're just saying that because you know you'll never catch it!"

"Oh, yeah?" Rocky said. "Well, watch out, 'cause here I come!"

Max barked happily as Gizmo ran up behind the snake once more, and all three dogs gave chase. Worries about Dolph and their missing people faded for a few joyful moments—until, captured in Rocky's jaws, the snake flicked out its tongue and hissed, "Friendsss, thisss hasss been entertaining."

Startled, Rocky dropped the snake, yipped, and leaped back.

Raising its head, the snake nodded at the dogs. "Really, it hasss been a blassst. But haven't you noticed? The weather hasss turned. I mussst go."

Max looked up to find that the snake was right.

Clouds had mounded in the sky, fluffy and white in front, then swelling with dark gray. The wind rose in heavy gusts. The air felt thick and charged, tingling Max's fur and skin.

"Nice to meet you!" Gizmo said to the snake. "Thank you for being a good sport."

The snake responded with a final flick of its tongue, then wiggled off toward a nearby field.

"Don't tell me it's going to rain," Rocky moaned, glancing up at the darkening sky. "I'm not in the mood to get wet."

"Maybe we can take cover in the forest?" Gizmo asked, looking to Max for approval.

Max shook his head. "No, we have to keep moving. Dolph is still behind us. A little water won't hurt us. Besides, I think I see a town up ahead."

Max's stomach twisted, and he realized just how hungry he was. If the rain was bad enough, surely Dolph would take shelter, too. Maybe they had time to search for someplace dry and scrounge for food.

As if reading Max's thoughts, Rocky said, "Okay, just as long as we find some grub soon. I'm feeling a little woozy."

Max opened his snout to answer, but before he could say anything, thunder rumbled across the sky.

At first, Max thought it was from the oncoming storm. But the rumbling didn't stop. Instead, it grew louder and louder. He saw shadows flooding the streets in front of them, dust billowing in their wake.

Max remembered the massive clouds of darkness from his dream.

As the thunder rose to a roar and the ground trembled beneath his paws, Max barked as loudly as he could, "*Run!*"

CHAPTER 2

STAMPEDE

They had only seconds to hide.

The shadowy figures were rumbling toward them, filling the air with terror. Panicked, Rocky turned in circles, yipping, "Where do we go?" while Gizmo started toward the nearby fields, until she realized that Rocky was no longer behind her.

Nipping at Rocky's side, Max barked, "Into the ditch, hurry!"

Yowling in fear, the Dachshund stopped spinning. Then he raced through the untamed grass and dove headfirst into a dip in the ground. Max let Gizmo dart ahead of him next to Rocky, then flung himself on top of his two small friends to protect them.

The ground trembled and vibrated as though it

would break apart, and Max's heart pounded, punching at his chest.

He dared to look up at the surging darkness.

And saw a stampede.

The shadows weren't the cloud from his dream after all. They were dozens upon dozens of *horses*, galloping as though their lives depended on it. The front of the line was dominated by giant steeds with sleek brown, white, and black coats. Their manes and tails flew behind them, some tangled and ratty, others appearing as though they'd once been groomed. As they ran, dust from the road kicked out around them, filling the air and making it hard to see clearly.

"Hey!" Max barked loudly over the sound of hooves slamming against dirt and asphalt. "Stop!"

But none of the horses heard him.

Closing his eyes, Max pressed himself down into the narrow ditch.

And the horses were upon them.

The earth above the dogs erupted as hooves slammed into the dirt and grass, flinging pebbles and soil into Max's fur. The wind and noise were tremendous, like hail smacking against a tin shed during a storm.

The steeds neighed and whinnied, frantically urging one another on as they galloped past the three dogs.

"Don't let the storm reach us!"

"We must get back to the wild!"

"Never return to the wall!"

At that, Max opened his eyes in surprise—just as a stallion's hoof slammed dangerously close to his head.

"Please! Watch out!" he barked again.

A tan mare heard Max as she raced toward him. Eyes wide with panic, she reared back on her hind legs, then spun away from Max moments before she would have stepped on the three dogs.

Another horse, a brown colt, also pulled away from the herd, snorting and blinking at the dust kicked up by the stampede.

And then it was over.

The horses had raced past, continuing down the highway, still neighing as they galloped away from whatever danger had them so horribly spooked.

Max lay atop Rocky and Gizmo, not daring to move, his heart still thudding. His ears rang, and all around him dust hung heavy in the air.

"Is it over?" Gizmo asked from underneath Max, her voice muffled.

"I think so," Max whispered.

"Can't...breathe..." Rocky gasped. "Get off...big guy..."

"Oh!" Max jumped to his feet. "Sorry!"

Rocky and Gizmo gulped for air as they emerged from the shallow dip in the grass. "What happened?" Gizmo asked.

"Horses," Max said, panting. "Lots and lots of horses."

Rocky exhaled. "I'll say."

All around them, the tall grass and barbed weeds were trampled and torn to pieces.

Clopping hooves echoed nearby, and the three dogs turned to see the mare and colt who had veered off from the other horses.

The mare nickered a hello as she approached, her ears tilted toward Max and her brown eyes soft and kind. She was mostly tan, save for a large splotch of white on her side. There was something regal about her, and gentle at the same time.

Her companion seemed more wary. The colt was slightly smaller than the mare, and something about his shaggy dark brown coat and the length of his mane gave Max the impression that it had been a long time since he'd been groomed—if he ever had. He flicked his long tail and stared at Max.

The two horses stopped at the edge of the highway, towering over the three dogs. They were *big*. Rocky and Gizmo barely came up past their fetlocks, and even Max felt dwarfed by the giant beasts. Their heads and snouts were as long as Max was tall.

"Sorry for nearly trampling you," the mare said, shaking out her mane. "I was so caught up in the panic I almost didn't notice you."

Max made his way over to the horses, his tail wagging slowly as he looked up at them. "I'm glad you stopped. I'm Max, by the way. These two are Rocky and Gizmo."

The colt snorted and flicked his ears. "Are those your puppies? They don't look anything like you."

Gizmo wiggled her hindquarters, amused. "No, he was protecting us, but we're not puppies—we're just on the small side!"

"Oh," the colt said, snorting a second time.

The mare sighed. "Don't mind Duskborn," she said, peering down at the dogs. "He is young and was raised in the wild. He's still learning things we riding horses picked up on our farms and in the stables. I'm Savannah Rose, though my friends call me Rosy."

"Oh!" Gizmo said. "Rosy! That's such a pretty name."

Rosy clopped a hoof against the road. "Thank you. Gizmo is also a very nice name."

A whoosh of wind rose from the west, and Max shivered. Looking around, he saw that the clouds had grown darker. The trees on either side of the highway danced back and forth, their branches lashing.

Duskborn stomped backward, away from the dogs, thrashing his head. "We have to go, Rosy. We'll lose the others."

"Wait," Max said. "Why is everyone so scared? Where are you running to?"

Rosy's tail flicked as she eyed her younger companion. "Not so fast, Duskborn. We have to warn these dogs."

Duskborn whinnied. "They're just dogs—"

"Hush!" Rosy said. "We're all family now—all of us animals. Big or small." She turned her head to the dogs. "A great storm is coming. We're aiming to outrun it." She paused. "You should, too, if you can."

Rocky plopped down. "You're going to try to outrun a storm? That's impossible."

"Maybe for *you*," Duskborn neighed. "But we horses are made for running."

"We're faster than we look," Gizmo said as she came to sit next to Rocky. "Anyway, wouldn't it be easier to find shelter and ride out the storm indoors?"

Rosy opened her long muzzle to say something, then hesitated. Muscles rippled beneath her sleek, shiny coat as she turned her whole body toward Duskborn. "Go over there and graze for a moment."

"But—" the colt started to say.

Rosy stamped a hoof. Suddenly she didn't look so gentle anymore. *"Now."*

Duskborn clomped off toward the other side of the road and started yanking up stalks of grass with his big yellow teeth. While he did, Rosy lowered her head close to Max, Rocky, and Gizmo. Her breath smelled of hay.

"It's not just the storm we're running from. There's also the wall," she whispered, her large, bright eyes fearful.

"A wall?" Rocky asked.

"*The wall*," Max said softly. Last night's dream

came back to him in bits and pieces: a giant silver wall. Madame leaping over it with ease. The darkness pinning him until he was surrounded.

"That's right. The only thing at the end of this road is a big silver wall," Rosy said. "It's much too high to jump over—trust me, I'm an award-winning show jumper." She swished her long tail with pride. "And any animal who strays too close gets a nasty shock."

"Has the wall always been there?" Gizmo asked.

Rosy shook her great head, sending her mane cascading. "It's new. The humans put it there to keep us all out."

Clopping hooves sounded behind Rosy, and Duskborn approached, chomping on a mouthful of grass.

"Are you telling them about the wall?" he asked.

Rosy nodded. "They deserve to know."

Duskborn's nostrils flared wide. "That place is full of awful humans! I heard they've got a slaughterhouse back there. They're planning to turn us into meat!"

Max shuddered. "I don't believe that. We're their pets. They love us!"

Rosy shoved Duskborn away with her head, then looked down at the dogs. "Whatever the people want, it's a mystery to me. Truth is, none of us knows what's behind that wall. We just know animals and humans aren't on the best of terms these days."

Another gust of wind washed over the animals, and

flashes of lightning arced through the dark clouds. Max looked down the highway to the west, imagining the great band of silver beyond the trees. It hadn't shocked him when he'd touched it in his dream, but it *had* clearly been made to keep him away from whatever was on the other side.

Dr. Lynn had warned them that some humans were afraid of animals and might not react kindly to their presence. But Max pictured the sweet, laughing faces of Charlie and Emma as they ran their sticky hands through his fur and scratched his belly. He couldn't imagine them hurting him. Ever.

"That's not true, though, Rosy," Duskborn said. "Someone *does* know what's over the wall. Remember?"

"You're right," the mare said, her enormous head bobbing. "I remember now. From a few towns back, that peculiar fellow. Stripes, was it?"

"I'm pretty sure it was Spots," Duskborn said.

"I'm almost positive it was Stripes."

"And *I'm* almost positive it was Spots."

Rocky jumped to his feet and barked, "Whoa, whoa, take it easy. Stripes or Spots, Lines or Dots, whatever the name is—is this guy a dog? 'Cause if he knows something, we need to talk to him."

"All I know is Stripes is most certainly not a horse," Rosy said. "He's some sort of small creature, like you. But why would you want to try to get past the wall? It's dangerous."

"There could be kibble!" Rocky said.

"Or people," Max said. "I had a dream about a silver wall. I think it's where we're supposed to go."

"A dream?" Duskborn asked, then snorted. "You're chasing a dream? You dogs sure are silly."

"Hey!" Gizmo said, baring her teeth. "You'd be surprised. Max's dreams are special!"

At that moment, a great flash of white light flared out of the clouds. The horses whinnied and reared back on their hind legs.

Seconds later, a cracking boom rumbled through the sky.

"We have to go!" Duskborn neighed, already trotting down the highway to the east, away from the approaching storm.

"Sorry, but we must leave," Rosy said as she followed him. "For your own sake, turn back. You don't want to go that way!"

"Wait!" Max barked. He climbed onto the asphalt and started to chase after them. "We need to know more about Stripes. I mean Spots. I mean . . ."

It was too late.

The two horses had sped into a full gallop, and there was no way Max could catch up to them. A few seconds later, they were distant shadows.

Panting, Max returned to his friends, who were huddled together in the center of the road. The wind was now a steady, constant rush of air that twisted and tangled their fur. Cold drops of water fell into Max's eyes, just a few at first, then more and more.

"Come on," Max said as he passed his two friends and quickened his pace, heading west toward the nearby town.

"Are you sure we should be going in this direction?" Gizmo raced to Max's side, her tiny legs a blur. "If the wall is as dangerous as it sounds, maybe we should turn back."

Max raised his snout as the rain grew heavier. "No, Dr. Lynn's beacons want us to go this way. We're supposed to follow them to that wall."

"Besides," Rocky added as he ran next to Gizmo, "we're not fraidy-cats like those horses. I mean, who's scared of a little wall or a silly storm?"

"Weren't you just complaining about getting your fur wet?" Gizmo asked.

Before Rocky could answer, another flash of lightning blazed up ahead, and thunder exploded in their ears. The sky was now a sickly greenish gray, and the rain had turned from a few tiny droplets to a watery onslaught.

"Okay!" Rocky yipped. "Maybe I'm a little afraid!"

Lightning arced above them once more, this time touching down in the field to their right, close enough that they could practically feel the heat. The noise was tremendous, so loud that Max's ears rang and buzzed.

Despite the heavy rain, flames licked at the grass where the lightning had landed.

Running wildly ahead, Rocky howled in fear. "Make that *a lot* afraid!"

Max didn't respond. Instead, he lowered his head and barreled forward. His fur was soaked, and he could barely see. The wind was so strong that it felt as if someone were trying to shove him backward.

The horses were right to be afraid, he realized. This wasn't just any old storm.

This was a hurricane.

CHAPTER 3

TEMPEST

The wind screamed and roared as it flung the rainwater sideways. Sticky, shredded leaves and broken branches swirled through the air. Above, the clouds mounded thick and black, as if night had fallen early.

"Keep running!" Max barked over the howling winds.

"Where are we running to?" Gizmo barked back.

Max didn't answer. He lifted his head as he sprinted down the center of the highway, his eyes narrowed to avoid the icy rain.

The trees near the road thrashed from side to side, creaking and groaning. There was a group of trailer homes almost hidden behind tree trunks, rocking on their foundations as shutters slammed against their painted metal siding. As Max watched, the wind lifted a pink plastic flamingo from a yard and tossed it into the sky.

Then, up ahead, he saw a big green sign with white lettering: SHOPPING MALL—NEXT RIGHT.

"There's a mall nearby!" Max bellowed. "It will be safe!"

Neither Rocky nor Gizmo answered. Both were too busy panting, their small legs pounding on the road, their fur slick with rainwater. It was hard enough for Max to run against the wind—he could only imagine how much harder it was for them.

Up ahead, Max saw traffic lights dangling from power lines. They flashed red as they were flung back and forth by the winds. Then Max heard Rocky bark a warning.

"Watch out, big guy!"

Max skidded to a stop as a flash of white and orange flew across the road in front of him. Blinking away the rain, he saw one of Dr. Lynn's traffic barricades go tumbling into the trees. The beacon on top of it blinked twice before it crunched against the ground and shattered.

"Oh, no," Max said quietly.

The storm was blowing away their trail.

Max shook his head. He couldn't think about that now. He had to get his friends to shelter.

"This way!" he barked as he veered onto the road that led to the mall. It wasn't long before the three dogs were racing through a flooded parking lot toward the large, dark shopping center.

The dogs splashed forward as the wind sent waves crashing against their sides. Rain came at them from every direction. Abandoned shopping carts slammed into sidewalks and lampposts.

Ahead, Max saw heavy glass doors below a glowing green sign that read ENTRANCE. Checking that Rocky and Gizmo were still behind him, he raced toward the doors.

He stepped onto the rubber mat in front of the entrance, panting for breath. For a moment, Max thought the doors might not open, that he'd led his friends astray.

But then Rocky and Gizmo collapsed upon the mat, and the doors wheezed open.

The three dogs jumped through the doorway, the storm practically shoving them inside as it, too, tried to enter the mall. Then the doors squealed shut, and, finally, the wind and rain stopped.

Max, Rocky, and Gizmo dropped to their bellies on the cold tiled floor, soaking wet and panting. Max's whole body trembled from the cold. He shook his fur and a spray of water flew off.

"Remind me never to question a horse ever again," Rocky said. "Them brutes have good instincts."

Gizmo rolled onto her side, licking one of her paws. "I'm so cold, Max."

"Me, too," Max said. "But we're safe now."

"Safe?" Rocky said. "Ha! *Soaked* is more like it. Anyway"—he glanced around—"where are we?"

The glass windows rattled. Thudding raindrops and whooshing wind echoed through the dim halls. High above, domed skylights showed off the gray-green sky.

The storm was getting worse by the second.

Groaning, Max climbed to all fours. "We're in a mall, Rocky," Max said. "And malls have food, don't they? Let's get away from these windows and see if we can find something to eat."

Rocky jumped up. "Yes! It's bad enough being soaked without being hungry, too. I sure hope this place has a pet store."

While Rocky and Gizmo shook themselves dry, Max studied their surroundings. Most of the lights were dark, but high above, a few fluorescent bulbs were lit a dim blue. Their glow barely cut through the gloom. Dust coated the fake trees, the tiled floor, and the benches in the center of the hall. The stores on either side of them were drenched in shadow, their entrances blocked off by metal gates.

"Let's see if we can find a map of this place," Max said as their steps echoed through the empty hall. They'd been in big, abandoned buildings before, but Max never quite got over the uneasy feeling of being somewhere dogs didn't belong.

"Creepy," Rocky whispered as they walked.

"Shh!" Gizmo said.

They had barely made it halfway down the corridor when something sputtered and crackled from the walls above.

Max stopped midstep, his ears alert and his tail raised. Beside him, Rocky and Gizmo went still.

"What was that?" Rocky whispered.

"Was it the doors opening?" Gizmo asked. "Did someone follow us in out of the storm?"

Max slowly craned his head back and forth, studying the dusky hall. High above, rain and stray branches slammed against the skylights. But that was not the source of the noise.

There it was again. A crackling of something electric. A sizzling pop and a distant squeal from somewhere up ahead.

Then a single voice boomed from above.

"Go away!"

Rocky went rigid and lowered his body flat against the tile. "What was that?" he yelped.

"Leave now," the voice bellowed. *"You do not belong here."*

A single word flashed through Max's mind: *Dolph.*

Could the wolves have gotten here first? Was their unrelenting pack leader lying in wait, deep within the mall?

At that moment, logic overwhelmed instinct in Max's

Praxis-enhanced brain, like a bolt of lightning zapping his mind awake.

Of course it wasn't Dolph. For one thing, the beast would never announce his presence. He'd just attack.

So the voice was something else.

Max stepped forward, sniffing. Behind him, Rocky and Gizmo huddled together.

"Listen at once!" the voice cried. *"WE—I MEAN I—SAID TO GO AWAY! GO!"*

"Do you know what's happening?" Gizmo asked. "Is it some sort of alarm?"

"I don't think so," Max said as he sniffed at the air. The smell of wet dog fur overwhelmed his nostrils, mixed with musty clothing and the stench of rotting food.

But there was something else, too—something consistently foul—tingeing every scent: acrid animal droppings and musky fur.

The smell was familiar, almost like that of the rats they'd encountered in a junkyard outside Baton Rouge. But it wasn't the same—not exactly. In fact, it reminded Max of smells on his farm.

Mice.

There were mice!

Max's tail wagged excitedly as he spun to face his friends. "There aren't any large animals here at all," he said. "Smell!"

35

Rocky scrunched his snout. "I only smell you, big guy. And I guess some mice."

As he said the word, the patter of the storm gave way to a rush of whispers in the darkened stores. The voices spoke over one another, a waterfall of unintelligible words.

"Oh!" Gizmo said. "It's mice!"

"And *lots* of them," Max said, narrowing his eyes to see if he could spot any of the tiny critters.

A loud squeal and a screech sounded from above.

"*Make no attempt to come farther into the mall,*" the voice said. "*There are no mice here. Just a big, scary, superstrong monster who will devour you!*"

"Oh, yeah?" Rocky howled, his snout raised high. "If you're so eager to eat dogs, why do you want us to leave?"

"*Umm... uh... I guess... I am not hungry at the moment. I ate a whole bunch of dogs right before you arrived. They were delicious!*"

Gizmo looked at Rocky and Max as if to say, *Let me handle this one.* "Oh, that means we're probably safe for now," Gizmo said. "I'm always sluggish when I eat too much, so this monster probably wouldn't be able to chase us."

"*No! I am full of energy! I could chase you. I just don't want to.*"

Gizmo pranced ahead. "Come on," she called. "Let's go see what's up there."

Max and Rocky trotted after her. Max expected the

speaker to shout at them again, but after a final electronic crackle, it fell silent.

Instead, the mall echoed with what sounded like thousands of tiny feet scrabbling over carpet and tile. At first, Max thought it was just the din of the storm. But through the metal gates, he could see black and gray and white bodies undulating as mice swarmed over one another, following the dogs.

The mice whispered and hissed. They watched the dogs with eyes that glowed in the dim light. Max couldn't make out what they were saying—all he heard was a constant *psst psst psst*, like a trickling waterfall.

Gizmo led Max and Rocky past kiosks stocked with sunglasses and calendars, steering clear of trash cans that obviously hadn't been emptied since before the humans left.

The hall opened into a grand plaza, illuminated in hazy, misty light from a massive glass dome high above. In the center of the plaza was a big, open booth next to a map and a sign that read INFORMATION.

A line of mice snaked its way from a storefront filled with gleaming gold necklaces and jeweled rings. The mice raised their tiny paws and whispered, as though passing along messages.

Gizmo slowed to a stop, and Max took the lead once more as they approached the information booth. Mice swarmed the counter, surrounding a silver microphone with a big black button set into its base. A white mouse with red-rimmed eyes, the largest of the creatures, stood next to the microphone.

As Max watched, amused, the white mouse pressed both paws down on the button. Hidden speakers crackled to life.

The mouse spoke into the microphone, in a frightening voice: "*Pay no attention to the mice inside the booth!*"

"That's what made that big sound?" Gizmo said. "But he's so...so...small."

"Pay no attention?" Rocky said. "Then why is he talking so loudly?"

The mouse stared directly at them. He opened his mouth, exposing a set of miniature, razor-sharp teeth, and hissed. *"You don't want to find out."*

CHAPTER 4

THE INFESTED MALL

Wagging his tail, Max padded softly toward the booth. As he drew near, several of the mice on the desk squealed, scattering in every direction.

The big white mouse didn't run. Instead, he pressed the microphone's button one more time. "*Don't come any closer!*" he said, his amplified voice now a terrified squeak. "*The mice are—are—they're my snacks for later! I'm big! Once I'm hungry again I'll—*"

Max jumped up onto his hind legs and set his front paws on the counter so he could look at the mouse snout-to-snout.

"Eeeeek!" the mouse squealed as he fell backward off the microphone.

"Don't be afraid," Max said. "We're not going to hurt you."

The mouse sat up on his hind legs and flailed with his front paws. "You lie! You want to trick us into feeling safe so you can eat us, just like all the other strays that pass through this mall."

"Is that why you're trying to scare us?" Gizmo asked. "You're afraid we'll eat you?"

"Who's that?" the mouse asked. Skittering to the edge of the counter, he peered down at Gizmo and Rocky.

"Are you cats?" he asked.

Gizmo wagged her stubby tail. "No, silly. We're just small dogs."

"We *are* hungry," Rocky said from next to her. "But I'd never eat a mouse. I bet you'd just taste...gooey."

Warily, the mouse scooted backward.

Inside the booth, Max could see tiny heads slowly emerge from the dark shelves. He glanced to the right and spotted more mice outside the shops. Several were in the jewelry store's display cases, resting on red velvet amid the glittering gems.

The big mouse sniffed at Max's nose. "You smell *wet*," he said.

Max gestured at the big dome overhead. "It's storming outside. We barely managed to make it in here."

The mouse looked up at the leaves plastering the

glass and the waves of water rolling down the dome. Though slightly muffled, the wind could still be heard high above.

"Huh," the mouse said. "I hadn't noticed." Looking back at Max, he added, "I'm Samson."

"Nice to meet you, Samson," Max said. "These are Rocky and Gizmo, and I'm Max."

Samson flicked his long, skinny tail. "And you're *sure* none of you wants to eat us? Like, positive?"

Rocky groaned, and Max glanced down to see the Dachshund flop onto his side. "We're starving," Rocky said. "But we're not wild. If you could just show us to the kibble, that would be great."

"Samson!" one of the mice hissed from inside the booth.

Max peered into the shadows and saw a slender brown mouse crawl off a shelf and onto the floor. Whiskers twitching, she sat on her hind legs and looked up at the fat white mouse.

"Samson!" the brown mouse repeated more loudly. "Are you sure we should trust them? You vowed to protect us and our children, and our children's children, and our children's children's children, and—"

"Yeah, yeah," Samson said with a dismissive wave of his paw. "I get it, Lilah. But I think we can trust these dogs. Anyway, if we feed them, they're less likely to eat any of us."

"Are you the leader here?" Gizmo asked.

Samson twitched his nose. "I'm sort of a big deal." Then, turning back to Max, he said, "When the people stopped coming, a whole mess of dogs and cats raided the pet store down the hall. We let them have at it until the cats turned mean and tried to hunt us. That's when I scared them off with the speakers." He whipped his slender tail. "Funny how they believed me so easily, but you three figured it out."

"We're smarter than the average dog," Rocky said from below. "And definitely smarter than any cat."

"I guess so. Anyway, they left behind some bags of those pebbles you dogs eat. I can show you where to go."

In a flash, the big mouse leaped onto Max's snout, then scampered up his forehead to rest between his floppy ears. Max felt the small creature grasp two tufts of fur in his tiny paws.

"Down, boy!" Samson squeaked.

Trying not to yelp, Max dropped to the floor. Samson tugged with his left fist, so Max turned to head down the hallway leading left.

Rocky tore ahead, skidding slightly over the tile. His spiky tail was a blur as he yipped, "Kibble time! It's time for kibble!" Closing his eyes, he raised his snout toward the high ceiling and half howled, half sang, "I won't take just a nibble! My jaws ain't gonna dribble! I've gotta gobble up that delicious, scrumptious, supermeaty *kibble*!"

Gizmo chased after him, the two small dogs racing

around each other. Max let out a happy bark, and from atop his head Samson squeaked.

"You dogs sure are weird, you know that?" the mouse asked.

"I do," Max said, glancing at Rocky and Gizmo. It was true—the three of them were far from normal. "But that's why we're a family."

Samson cleared his throat and said, "So, what brings you through these parts? Other than the storm."

"We're on our way to find our families," Max replied.

"Ah," Samson said. "I respect that. I'm a family man myself. I have a hundred and sixty-seven children, each more precious than the last."

Max was so shocked he almost stopped walking. "That's a lot of babies!"

"I'll say!" Gizmo chimed in.

"Go big or go home—that's my motto," Samson said.

Squeaking laughter rose behind him, and Max turned to discover that they hadn't been traveling down the hall alone. The floor behind them was covered storefront to storefront with mice. There had to be thousands of the creatures.

"These aren't all mine," Samson said. "A lot of mice from around the town and countryside decided to band together here. It's our cozy little place of safety in this new, wild world, especially once we figured out the microphone can scare off predators. Plus the humans left behind lots of rotting food for us to eat."

"It sounds like the mall is the perfect place for you," Max said. He nodded cordially at the army of mice and offered a friendly wag of his tail.

"Hey, what's the holdup?" Rocky barked, looking back. "We're wasting away up here!"

Samson yanked on Max's fur, and Max turned away from the other mice and continued down the hall. Max thought the mice didn't need to use microphone tricks to scare away intruders. As many as there were, they could swarm almost any beast that might come through.

Not that he was going to tell Samson that.

Trailed by the legion of rodents, Max let Samson lead him past a foul-smelling food court. It was clear from the stench that any real food had long since rotted into moldy mush. The tables and booths were littered with trash, and clouds of flies buzzed around the over-flowing garbage cans.

"Almost there," Samson said.

Quiet voices echoed from behind a glass wall, and Max saw a TV on display in a store filled with electronics. He hadn't seen any human broadcasts since he first left his home to start this journey, and he wanted to take a look—but then a new smell met his nose.

Kibble.

Beefy, crumbly kibble. The scent wafted from the store across from the electronics shop, and Max saw that its gate was wide open. Inside were rows of glowing blue aquariums, shelves with litter boxes, and walls hung with leashes on hooks. Most of the toys and other pet treats were gone. Littering the aisles were scraps of torn paper bags that had once contained pet food. Crumbs were all that remained.

But Max could smell that, somewhere nearby, more kibble awaited.

Rocky and Gizmo were already running full speed toward a back storeroom. "Whoa!" Samson squealed from atop Max's head as he hung on for his life.

Max ignored the tiny mouse. The store was dark save for the glow of the empty aquariums, but he didn't need to see—his nose told him where he needed to go.

Joining Rocky and Gizmo in the storeroom, Max saw they'd already ripped a hole in one of the few remaining bags and had dived headfirst into the resulting avalanche of kibble.

"Ohhh," Rocky moaned as he came up briefly for air. "So good. So, so good."

Gizmo, her jaws full, mumbled to Max, "Come getsh shome."

Max didn't have to be told twice. He snatched up a mouthful of the meaty pebbles and was ducking his head for more before he'd fully swallowed the first bite.

Still clinging to Max's fur, Samson hummed absentmindedly while the dogs crunched and munched. "You dogs seem like you haven't eaten for days...no, weeks!"

he cried, but the dogs ignored him and focused on filling their bellies.

"You'd think I'd be bored with kibble by now," Rocky said later as they made their way back through the ransacked pet store. "But I'll always love a good, old-fashioned, classic meal."

Max barked in agreement. "You're going to get so pudgy when we find the humans again. I can see it now."

"You bet!" Rocky said. "Once we're back home, I'm never, ever running away. I'm just gonna eat and sleep and get petted." Nudging Gizmo with his snout, he asked, "How about you? You going to let your pack leaders pamper you until you're fat and happy?"

Gizmo's pointed ears drooped, and she lowered her tail. "I don't know," she said softly. "I try not to think about that too much."

It was a strangely sad thing for Gizmo to say, and Max was going to ask her if anything was wrong, but Samson interrupted.

"Wait a second," the mouse asked, still perched between Max's ears. "You telling me you're actually going to look for humans?"

"Of course," Max said as they stepped out of the pet store. "Like I said, we're searching for our families."

Max stiffened in surprise as Samson leaped to the tiled floor. "I thought you were talking about your dog families!" the mouse squeaked, thrusting his paw in the direction of the army of mice. "Like my family. Of mice. Who are just like me."

"I have a family of dogs, too," Max said. "You're looking at them."

"Aw," Gizmo said, wagging her stubby tail. "Thanks, Max."

Max wagged back at her, then continued. "But we've come all the way from the far north to find our people. Our *humans*. We intend to help them all come back."

Gasps and murmurs rose from the shadows. The mice huddled together, glaring at Max.

"I don't know why you'd wanna do a thing like that," Samson said. "We've got a good setup here. A whole mall to ourselves, no one shooing us out into the wild, where all those owls and hawks are waiting to swoop down and steal our babies."

"Actually, now that you mention it, all the birds are gone," Max said.

Samson didn't seem to hear him. He paced back and forth, still ranting. "Or worse, humans who set out traps and lace our food with poison. Humans are awful! I hope they stay away forever! Besides, they look happy enough to me."

Rocky came forward to stand next to Max. "What do you mean? How do you know how the humans look?"

Samson pointed his tiny snout at the TV on display behind the glass window of the electronics store. "See for yourself. I can't understand any of the words, but I know a happy face when I see one."

Max looked up at the screen, Gizmo and Rocky flanking him. In the mad dash to find kibble, he'd forgotten about the television, but now he was captivated by the flickering images.

A woman holding a microphone appeared on the screen, walking past dozens and dozens of tents. Sad-looking humans—children and parents, young and old—sat on plastic coolers and lawn chairs around smoking grills. Their faces were worn and weary...and certainly *not* happy.

The woman spoke gravely into the microphone: "The mood here in East Texas Tent City remains grim, even with rumors coming in of a possible cure. Former Alabama resident Guy Jackson told me why."

The image cut to a bearded man wearing a ratty baseball cap.

"Everything was supposed to be fixed right when all this started," he said into the microphone. "The next thing you know, we're being escorted across the country to live like bums. Not a week's gone by without a rumor about some new serum that's gonna fix this mess. Been a lot of weeks, and we ain't seen that magic medicine."

The image cut back to the reporter, now strolling in front of a big silver wall.

"The wall," Max said, remembering his dream.

"Many people here have told me that as the weeks

and months go by, the quarantine seems less likely to be temporary." The reporter raised a hand and gestured at the wall behind her. "And with the building of the Great Wall of Texas, their living arrangement is seeming more and more permanent."

The picture changed to an older woman. "With that Hurricane Ruth heading through our cities and no one there to prepare them for the storm, we don't even know if we'll have homes to go back to," the woman said.

The image returned to the reporter, once more walking past the tents.

"Just an hour ago, Dr. Lynn Sadler, the scientist whom many deem responsible for the Praxis virus, gave a statement outside her mobile laboratory on the safe side of the wall. She confirmed the rumor about the impending cure, claiming that she will have one within weeks, if not days."

At this, Gizmo let out a loud bark. "Dr. Lynn!"

"Who?" Samson said. "What? Where—"

"Shh," Max said, turning his attention back to the TV.

"But even if Dr. Sadler's claims prove true," the reporter continued, "with so many cities overwhelmed by storms or destroyed by the evacuations, it seems unlikely that life as we knew it will ever return to normal." She nodded at the camera. "Back to you, Bryan."

The screen flipped over to a man in a suit sitting behind a desk, but Max was no longer interested in the broadcast. Instead, he looked down at Samson.

"You think the humans looked happy there?" he

asked, bewildered. "They're all cramped together! Living in tents!"

"Exactly!" Samson squeaked. "I know that when I'm not with the rest of my tribe, I get anxious."

"But humans aren't like mice," Gizmo said. "They're supposed to have space, and live in houses."

Samson flicked his tail. "Not my problem."

Rocky paced back and forth beneath the glass window, eyes still on the TV screen.

"Is that the wall you dreamed about, buddy?" he asked.

Max wasn't sure, but it seemed possible. "It could be." He thought of Charlie and Emma, living like all those other people, and knew that it was more important than ever that he find them.

"What wall?" Samson asked.

Before Max could reply, Rocky said, "We ran into some horses who described a wall with all the humans on the other side. Some animal named Spots or Stripes is supposed to know more about it."

A rush of murmurs sounded from the mice. "Stripes?" Samson asked. "Spots?"

"You know him?" Max asked.

Samson rubbed his paws together, whiskers twitching. "Them," he said. "It's two different animals. We heard about them from some of the strays we scared off. They live down the railroad tracks in a place called DeQuincy."

Max felt a burst of excitement rush through his body. He hadn't led Rocky and Gizmo astray after all! Because

51

they had taken shelter in this mall, they had found Samson. Now Samson was going to lead them to Stripes and Spots, who would lead them to the wall, which was where they would find their people. *Finally.*

Max spun in a circle. "Then that's where we need to go!" he said. "We'll follow these tracks, find those dogs, and they'll tell us how to get past that wall and into the city of tents." Lowering his voice, Max met Rocky's and Gizmo's eyes and added, "Besides, even with the storm we shouldn't stay in one place too long."

"I suppose you could follow those tracks," Samson squeaked. "It's just..."

Rocky snorted and waddled back to Max's side. "Yeah, yeah, we get it, pip-squeak; you don't want to risk losing your new digs when we find the humans."

"It's not that," Samson said with a slight twitch.

"Then what?" Gizmo asked, cocking her fuzzy head.

The other mice hushed as Samson peered left and right down the dim hall. Leaning in close to Max's lowered snout, Samson whispered, "The tracks lead into a tunnel, you see."

The sea of mice trembled. Softly at first, then louder and louder, their voices rose in a chorus of fearful "Ooooooohs." The sound was so eerie and unsettling that Max's heart started to beat faster.

Samson blinked—his red-rimmed eyes looked fiercer than ever. "And no one who's gone into the tunnel has ever come back out."

CHAPTER 5

DARK PASSAGE

Rocky stepped forward, his head high and defiant. "We aren't afraid of some tunnel," he barked over the frightened squeaks. "We've been in plenty. Take us there!"

Gizmo scrambled to Rocky's side. "Are you sure?"

"Yeah," Rocky whispered back. "If a train track goes through that tunnel, I bet you anything the reason no one comes back is 'cause they went out the other side!"

Max gulped, relieved. Of course Rocky was right.

The large white mouse rubbed his paws together. "Well, if you insist on going, I won't stop you. Lower your snout, Max, and I'll hop back on."

Max lowered his head so that his nose rested against

the cold, dusty tile. Samson climbed back up between Max's ears and grabbed two tufts of fur.

The mouse led Max, Rocky, and Gizmo farther down the main hall, trailed by a small group of curious mice. There were no skylights at this end of the mall, and all the lights were off.

"That door," Samson said as an exit sign appeared up ahead. "Push that big metal bar."

Max could barely make out another sign on the door. Squinting, he read to himself, " 'Employees Only. Improper entry will sound alarm.' "

"Are you sure this is the right way?" Max asked. "If I open that door, it might make a loud noise."

"Yeah, don't worry about that," Samson said. "We chewed through the wires that make the noise ages ago. Behind the door, there's a hallway that leads to where the big trucks used to deliver stuff. You can get out the back of the mall there. Then just run across the parking lot to the train tracks and the tunnel."

"All right, then, hold on!"

Max leaped back on his hind legs and pressed his front paws against the metal bar. With a click, the door swung outward into blackness.

Max shoved himself against the door to hold it open, then looked back to see Gizmo and Rocky huddled together, nervously eyeing the dark hallway.

None of the mice seemed concerned. They skittered past the dogs, disappearing into the darkness ahead.

The hall echoed with the clicking of their tiny claws against concrete.

"What's the holdup?" Samson squeaked. "You wanted to see the tunnel, and this is the fastest way to get to it." He puffed out his tiny white chest. "I can't stay with you dogs all day, you know. I have a hundred and sixty-seven mouths to feed."

Rocky backed away from the doorway. "Maybe we should wait until the storm is over and leave from the front of the mall. I mean, there's all that kibble back in the pet store. We shouldn't let it go to waste."

"No," Max said, "we can't stay in one place too long. We should at least check out this exit. Meanwhile, the rain will wash away our scent so that our, uh, old friend won't be able to find us."

"You mean Dolph?" Gizmo asked.

"Who's Dolph?" Samson replied.

"No one you need to worry about," Rocky said. To Max, he said, "But, big guy, what about the beacons Dr. Lynn left?"

Max's tail drooped. "We saw one fly by earlier, remember? I have a bad feeling the storm might have blown away the trail she left for us. But on the TV, they said Dr. Lynn was working behind the wall, so that's where we need to go. And we know the animals at the end of the train tracks can help us get there."

"All right, all right!" Rocky said, already waddling into the hallway. "I give up."

"I'm sure we'll be fine," Gizmo said, following Rocky. "Samson wouldn't lead us the wrong way." Glancing up at him, she added, "Would you?"

In spite of Gizmo's chipper expression, Max could sense a subtle growl in her voice, an unspoken *Because if you do, you'll have to answer to me.*

Samson seemed to sense that, too. "Yeah, of course you can trust me."

"Then let's go!" Gizmo said as she bounded forward.

Max padded through the doorway after his friends.

With a slam and a click, the door shut, thrusting them into blackness.

Max stopped walking. There were no windows, and no light leaked from under the door. He could sense the ceiling above him, and the concrete floor was hard beneath his paws. But he still felt lost in nothingness.

Max heard his friends moving slowly forward. It was strange to be unsure of each step he took. At the same time, the musk of the rodents was stronger than ever in Max's nostrils, and each step pinged loudly in his ears, making them twitch.

"Hey," Samson chirped, "watch out for—"

"Whoa!" Rocky yelped.

"Rocky!" Gizmo barked.

Samson yanked back on Max's fur to signal him to stop. "Yeah, there's a step there," he said.

Chittering laughter came from unseen mice. Some

were so close Max wondered how he hadn't stepped on the tiny creatures.

"You could have told me," Rocky growled.

"I tried!" Samson said. "Anyway, there are steps down to a landing, then more steps leading to another door."

"Are you all right, Rocky?" Max asked.

"Yeah, yeah," Rocky answered. "Just surprised me, is all."

"Be careful," Gizmo said. "Both of you."

Thumps echoed as the two small dogs plopped down the concrete steps.

"There's another door here!" Rocky called up.

Max carefully made his way to the bottom step. From there, he could hear the muffled *hush hush* of the storm, and cold radiated from the metal door in front of him. Beyond it, Max could swear he heard waves crashing against rocks. Why would there be a lake under the mall?

Leaping up once more, Max reached out with his front legs. They landed heavily against a metal bar, and the door flung open.

Through a haze of gray-green light, he saw a vast room that seemed to be under the mall. Great gusts of wind swelled over him, splashing his fur with water. Samson squeaked, and Max felt the mouse press himself flat onto his head.

Blinking, Max stepped out of the dark stairwell and onto a wide concrete platform that overlooked a pool. The ceiling high above was crisscrossed with pipes and metal grates—the underside of the mall. The stairs had taken them to an area that shoppers never saw.

To Max's left, yellow stairs led into the water. Next to that, a waterfall cascaded down a wide asphalt ramp into the strange little lake. High on the walls were white doors, like the doors on garages.

This room wasn't meant to be a lake at all, Max realized. It was some sort of loading dock. Before the humans left, trucks must have backed down the ramp to the white doors so that their contents could be unloaded into the mall.

Max vaguely heard the squeals of mice behind him, but he couldn't understand what they were saying over the wind.

"Max!" Gizmo barked loudly. "Can't you hear the mice? Shut the door before they all get blown away!"

"Oh, sorry," Max said. He stepped away from the door and let it swing shut behind him.

It closed with a heavy, solid thunk. Max turned to see that there was no handle on this side of the door, just a keyhole.

"Hey!" Max barked, his hackles raised. "How are we supposed to get back in?"

"Sorry!" Samson squealed over the wind. "Can't hear you!" He tugged with his left paw. "Tunnel is thataway, and let's make it snappy."

Rocky spun around in a frantic circle. "Did we just get locked out? What if the storm is so bad we can't get to that tunnel?"

Gizmo growled and flattened her ears. "We trusted you, Samson."

The white mouse said, "If it's necessary, I'll find a way to get you back in, all right? Excuse me for wanting to help some human-loving dogs leave my home. I didn't have to come with you—remember? I'm the good guy here!"

Max fought back his own growl. "Come on," he said, padding toward the yellow stairs. "We're outside; we might as well check it out."

He hesitated at the edge of the top step. Turbulent black water filled the loading bay and had already swallowed the bottom few steps. There was no way his two small friends would be able to wade through it.

"What's wrong?" Gizmo asked.

Max saw a narrow concrete ledge along the wall above the exit ramp.

"Nothing," he said, veering left. "This way."

The three dogs walked single file along the ledge, Samson still clinging to Max's head. It was easy enough for Rocky and Gizmo, but Max had to hug the wall, fighting the wind, and he worried he'd fall off at any moment.

Reaching the end of the ledge, he craned his head around the corner—and was met with a faceful of icy rainwater.

"Hey!" Samson squeaked. He scrambled down Max's spine, then leaped over Rocky and Gizmo onto the ledge.

Ignoring the rodent, Max studied the parking lot, the rain soaking his fur.

Just as in front of the mall, the back lot was under a half foot of water. There were big semitrucks parked back there, as well as several huge metal containers. To Max's right, streetlamps lit the parking lot. On the other side of the lot, the tall lamps were off, leaving the area as dark as night under the heavy clouds.

Beyond the parking lot was a road, and behind that road was an overgrown field, where grass was tossing back and forth in the heavy winds. Barely visible through the weeds was a metal railroad track that disappeared into the face of a cliff.

"What's it look like, big guy?" Rocky asked. "Think we can make a run for it?"

Max shook his head to fling off the water and turned back to his friends.

"I don't know," he said. "The storm is still pretty bad."

Gizmo rounded on Samson. "You have to let us back inside," she demanded. "We were nice to you, and we promised not to hurt anyone. We'll have to wait out the storm—then we'll leave."

Samson twitched his whiskers. "Fine, fine. Follow me. I think one of those big white doors may be open enough for you to slip under." He scrabbled ahead, and Gizmo and Rocky trotted after him, the wind gusting at their backs. But there was no way for Max to turn around on the narrow ledge. Instead, he moved slowly and carefully backward, one step at a time.

He was halfway to the main platform when he heard

the mice squeal in distress. Rocky yelped, and then both he and Gizmo began to bark, sounding frantic.

"What is it?" Max called back over his shoulder. "What's wrong? Are the mice swarming you?"

The patter of paws sounded on the ledge behind him. Panting, Gizmo and Rocky came to a stop behind Max's hind legs.

"The mice saw more animals in the mall," Gizmo said. "Their speaker trick didn't work, and now they're being hunted!"

"Do they want our help?" Max asked.

"No!" Rocky said. "They came to warn us, Max. The animals—they're not dogs or cats."

"The mice are afraid," Gizmo said. "And they think we should be, too."

"What should we do, big guy?" Rocky asked.

Before Max had time to answer, they heard muffled howls from behind the closed bay doors.

Then more howls came from outside the mall, loud enough to be heard clearly over the raging storm.

Despite the hurricane, despite how far they'd traveled since their last encounter in Baton Rouge, Max recognized those howls.

"It's *wolves*," Gizmo yipped.

Dolph and his pack had found them.

CHAPTER 6

THE TUNNEL

Squealing at the top of his tiny lungs, Samson scampered across the ledge toward the three dogs. He was trailed by the slender brown mouse Max had seen earlier—Lilah.

"I told you!" Lilah squeaked. "We shouldn't have trusted these dogs. My babies are going to get eaten!"

Samson squeaked furiously, "You didn't tell us there were wolves after you. You have to get out of here so they'll follow you and leave us alone!"

Gizmo's pointed ears flattened, and she growled. "Stop accusing Max. It's not his fault."

Spinning so fast she was a brown blur, Lilah squealed, "My babies! I need to save my babies!"

Samson pounded Max's foot with his paw. "You

better leave now. I'll go on the speaker and tell those wolves that you're outside. Then they'll scoot out there and leave us alone!"

Eyes wide, Rocky whimpered. "You're going to tell them where we are? Why would you do that?"

"Do what you have to do, Samson," Max said. "But at least give us a head start."

"Fine!" Samson said, already racing back toward the main platform with Lilah. "You better hurry!"

More howls pierced the air, slicing through the torrent of rain and wind. Because of the storm, Max couldn't smell the wolves searching for them outside, but from the sound of their howls, they were getting close.

"Storm or not, we have to make a run for it," he told Rocky and Gizmo. "Are you ready?"

Gizmo bared her teeth, gathering her courage. "We could always stay here and face Dolph. I wouldn't mind giving him a good talking-to."

"Uh," Rocky said, "between a pack of angry wolves and a hurricane, I'm gonna take my chances with the hurricane."

"I agree," Max said. "We'll face Dolph on our own terms, not when we're cornered." Once again, he crept forward carefully on the narrow ledge. "Stick close—both of you."

Lowering his head, Max took in a deep breath, then rounded the corner. A wave of rainwater plastered his fur to his skin. Shivering, he leaped down onto the parking lot, running through the icy sheets of water.

He veered left and crawled underneath one of the delivery trucks. Crouching low, he turned to find Rocky and Gizmo beside him, shaking themselves dry.

They peered out toward the train tracks, which were obscured by the lashing grass. Even though it was still daytime, the storm clouds cast the world in deep midnight shadow.

"That's where we're running to, right?" Gizmo asked, snout pointed at the tracks. "There's not a lot of places to hide between here and there."

"Oh, no," Rocky whispered, looking back the way they'd come. "I think I see wolves!"

Lowering himself so he was partly submerged in the water, Max crawled up next to Rocky. Though it was hard to see in the gray-green darkness, there were several large shadows stalking slowly in their direction. The figures pawed at a door to the mall, testing to see if it would open. One wolf raised his snout high just as lightning flashed behind him, illuminating the dark gray sky.

Thunder boomed almost immediately, and Max heard an angry, defiant howl, one he'd heard many times before. *Dolph.* But there were too few wolves with him to be the whole pack; the others must still be inside. And they hadn't spotted Max and his friends—yet.

Turning awkwardly, Max crawled toward Gizmo. "We have to go right now and hope they don't see us." He licked Gizmo's forehead. "Ready?"

"I think so," she said.

Rocky stood next to Max, trembling from the cold. "Some days, I wish I'd just given those stupid wolves my kibble back at Vet's office. Maybe then Dolph wouldn't have gotten so mad that he'd come after us even in a hurricane." He sighed. "Okay, I'm ready, too."

"Then let's go," Max said.

With a deep, steeling breath, Max darted out from underneath the delivery truck. Immediately he was swallowed by the storm. Wind swirled the rain around him and buffeted his chest, threatening to shove him backward.

"Are you still with me?" he barked.

"Yes," Gizmo panted as she splashed behind him. "But watch out for that—"

Max looked up and yelped. He dodged to the left just in time to keep from running directly into a burned-out streetlamp.

"—light." Gizmo finished her warning.

"Thanks!" Max said.

The parking lot seemed like an endless black ocean, and his whole body shouted at him to turn back, to stop fighting.

But more howls rose over the storm, and Max forced himself to continue.

Grass slapped his face and then surrounded him, and Max realized he'd run out of the parking lot and into the overgrown field. Mud squelched beneath his paws, coating them in slime.

Rocky and Gizmo had disappeared into the tall grass. All Max could see of them was the rustling of the stalks as the dogs made their way across the field.

Then the mud gave way to tiny sharp stones, and he saw metal and damp wood up ahead. They had reached the train tracks.

"Go left!" Max cried as he headed west, in the direction of the cliff.

He bounded over the tracks, the pads of his feet landing on icy steel and rotted wooden beams. He narrowly avoided stepping on shattered glass. A plastic shopping bag slapped against one of Max's front legs, clinging as though desperate to be free from the wind. Max awkwardly shook his leg until the bag tore free and flew into the sky.

This didn't feel right, thought Max. These rails must have been falling apart since before the humans left.

"We're almost there!" Rocky barked from behind Max.

Max peered through the rain and saw the entrance to the tunnel. There was a shelf of rock above it, casting a dark shadow. Then Max realized that what looked like a giant black opening in the hillside wasn't an opening at all.

The entrance was completely boarded up.

Max slowed to a stop. The tall cliff provided some shelter from the rain and wind. He looked back to see if they were being followed, but there was no sign of the wolves, at least not yet.

Gizmo darted forward and sniffed at the boards. "These smell really old," she said.

"They *look* old, too," Rocky said.

Max could make out the tall, wide concrete arch above the tunnel. Long strips of rotting wood ran across it almost all the way to the top. A few boards lay on the ground, where they'd fallen from the arch.

Attached to the front of the barricade was a white sign with bright red lettering. Though the message was coated with streaks of mud, he saw the words WARNING: UNSAFE CONDITIONS.

Maybe Samson hadn't been wrong about animals going in and not coming back.

"What do we do?" Rocky asked, pacing in an anxious circle. "I don't think those wolves outside the mall saw us, or they'd be here by now, but any second that mouse might rat us out and tell Dolph exactly where we went."

Gizmo dug under the bottom board, but the wet rocks were packed too tightly for her to shift them.

Giving up, she trotted to the left edge of the board. "Maybe we can bite it off?"

"That sounds like a good way to yank out your teeth," Max said. "The humans must have used really strong nails to attach this."

Gizmo cocked her head, looking up at the opening at the top of the barricade. "Hmm, I guess there's no easy way to climb up there."

Wind whistled on Max's side, and he looked over to see a big, rusted barrel sitting in front of the right side of the arch. He padded toward it.

"You see something, big guy?" Rocky asked as he and Gizmo followed.

"No," Max said, "but I hear something."

Sticking his head around the back of the barrel, he felt a gush of wind coming past the boards, carrying with it a strong, pungent stench that burned the inside of his nostrils. He reared away, startled.

Rocky dropped to his belly. "What is it? What did you see?"

"It's a smell, actually," Max said. "Animal droppings, I think. Mixed with something...awful."

Gizmo went forward for a sniff, disappearing around the side of the barrel. A moment later, she leaped back, her eyes watering.

"What could be causing that terrible smell?" she asked, then sneezed. "But Max, did you see the opening?"

Max's tail wagged. "There's an opening?"

"Yes!" Gizmo said. "The barrel is hiding it, but it looks like someone tore away the end of the bottom boards. It's a tight squeeze, but I bet we could all fit!"

Rocky turned away from Max and Gizmo. "Nope, not doing it," he said. "Someone blocked this tunnel off for a reason. We need to find somewhere safe to lie low and hide until this stupid storm is over. Someplace dry, with smells that aren't terrible."

A long, low howl rose through the slamming rain, over the roar of the wind.

It sounded close.

Tail tucked, Rocky yelped, then spun around. "On second thought," he said, "I'll take whatever's in there over all those wolves."

Gizmo followed him, and the two small dogs vanished into the shadows behind the rusted barrel. Rocky's muffled barks of disgust echoed through the barricade.

Holding his breath, Max shoved himself at the barrel, moving it just enough for him to slip behind. Just as Gizmo had said, the ends of three boards had been wrenched free, revealing a dark jagged opening.

Dropping down, Max crawled forward. The edge of the boards scraped at his sides, and he held back a yelp, focused on getting out of the storm and away from the wolves.

With one last shove of his hind legs, Max was past the barricade and crawling on concrete. He climbed to his feet and shook himself, sending water flying, and then took a deep breath.

The stench of animal droppings nearly smothered him.

Hacking, Max shook his head back and forth and closed his eyes.

"You get used to it after a few moments," Gizmo said, her barks echoing through the vast tunnel.

"Lies," Rocky said between whimpers. "This smell *hurts* me. I feel hurt."

"I know, Rocky," Max said. "But we have to deal with it for now."

Max opened his watering eyes to study the tunnel. A small amount of gray light streamed through the top of the barricade, brightening the center of the wide passage, so he could see the train tracks that ran along the floor. Everything was concrete and steel, with metal beams supporting the ceiling high above. There were unlit lamps attached to posts along the wall. Farther down the tunnel, a few lamps cast a meager orange glow.

Buffeted by the storm, the boards behind them rattled, and the wind whistled and whined. The hurricane was mostly muffled now, though pings of dripping water were all around them, and Max thought he could hear the faint rushing of a river.

Despite the awful smell, nothing looked dangerous. Holding his tail high to reassure his small friends, Max trotted forward along the right side of the tracks.

"Let's get moving," he said as Rocky and Gizmo fell in line behind him. "The faster we reach the other side, the faster we get away from these wolves."

"And the faster we get some fresh air!" Gizmo added.

They made their way quickly past the first bend, the stench growing stronger by the minute. Aside from the awful smell, Max couldn't figure out why the tracks had been abandoned.

A gentle breeze blew over Max's damp fur. He turned

to look for its source and got his first glimpse of something wrong.

On the other side of the tracks, one of the steel beams had buckled, and the concrete wall had collapsed into a pile of wet rubble. The opening revealed some sort of cavern.

"How do you think *that* happened?" Rocky asked.

"I have no idea," Max said.

Gizmo's pink tongue lolled free. "I wonder how far down the cavern goes."

Rocky nudged Gizmo's side, urging her forward. "I don't think we have time to find out. We can visit spooky deep caves another day."

"I hope so," Gizmo said with a wag of her tail.

Max quickened his pace as the tunnel straightened out. He had no idea how far they'd come. All he knew was that the fetid smell was stronger than ever. The source became evident as they trotted forward—the floor and the tracks were littered with mounds of black droppings.

"Oh, yuck," Rocky said as he carefully stepped around the pellets. "This. Is. Gross."

Something rustled high overhead.

"Shh," Max whispered to his friends as he looked up.

He expected to see more of the crisscrossing metal supports, but the dim lamps revealed a ceiling coated with what looked like fuzzy dark brown mold dangling from the beams.

One of the fuzzy things moved slightly, twitching a leathery wing.

Max felt his heart nearly jump out of his ribs.

"What is it?" Gizmo asked.

"Bats," Max whispered. "Thousands of them." Looking back at his friends, he added, "And if we wake them up, we'll be swarmed."

CHAPTER 7

THE SLUMBERING SWARM

"Bats?" Rocky yipped.

Gizmo shushed him and, more quietly, Rocky said, "Please tell me you mean baseball bats, buddy. My pack leader loved to play baseball out in the fields behind Vet's house."

"I'm afraid not," Max whispered, glancing back up at the winged creatures. "These bats are the kind that can fly."

"No wonder the smell is so bad," Gizmo said in a hushed voice, carefully stepping between mounds of droppings. "Maybe they're friendly? I've heard stories of bats that drink blood from other animals, but any I've ever seen were only going after bugs and fruit."

Tail tucked, Rocky took a few steps forward. "I'm not

gonna wake them up and find out," he said in the quietest voice Max had ever heard the Dachshund use. "Bad enough we have wolves after us; no need to make other animals angry."

Max followed him. "The exit can't be too much farther if all the bats are hanging here," he said. "They wouldn't want to fly very far to go hunting."

The bats continued to rustle their wings in the darkness above. A few chirped in their sleep, but none seemed to wake up.

As the dogs crept slowly and carefully down the tracks, Max realized the bats had infested most of the abandoned tunnel. They hung from the ledges, covering every surface above their heads.

Even in slumber, their pellets rained down, plinking on the concrete floor. Some landed on Max's back, and he shook himself to fling them off.

He was beginning to miss the raging hurricane.

The soft shushing of a river came from ahead, and the track appeared to veer suddenly to an opening on the right. It was a far tighter turn than Max imagined a big train would be able to make.

Rocky slowed to a stop. "Uh, I think we just found out why the tunnel was all boarded up."

"What is it?" Gizmo asked as she came to sit at Rocky's side. "Oh," she said.

Illuminated by a shaft of hazy light was a large pile of debris. Chunks of broken concrete and rocks, twisted metal, and mounds of mud covered the tracks and filled the space from floor to ceiling.

The tunnel had caved in.

Max saw a jagged hole to the right, revealing another large cavern. Gushes of fresh air came from the other side of the opening, chasing away some of the horrible stench.

"Looks like there's only one way to go," Max said.

Rocky let out a whine. "You think these bats are bad. But do you know what lives in *caves*? Bears and lions and tigers. Not to mention wolves." He trotted sadly after Max. "This just isn't our day."

"Cheer up, Rocky," Gizmo said, then licked his side. "I don't think lions or tigers live anywhere near here."

"Great," Rocky said, his ears drooping.

Max stopped at the opening, where rough concrete gave way to a smooth, damp, rocky ledge.

Max said to Rocky, "If any bears cause you trouble, I'll fight them off. And just think, once we're out of here, we won't have to deal with that awful smell anymore."

"True." Rocky tentatively wagged his tail. "All right, I can do this!"

"Glad to hear it," Max said. "Now, stay behind me. I'll make sure the ground is stable so you don't fall."

The stone ledge was cold and damp beneath Max's paws. He looked up to see long, spiky stalactites hanging from above—and bats, too, still apparently asleep.

Max peered over the ledge. Deep below was the river he'd heard, probably fat with rainwater.

Turning to the left, he followed the ledge in the direction the tracks had been leading. He heard Rocky and Gizmo stepping cautiously behind him, and he could see dim daylight.

"We're close!" Max said, his voice echoing throughout the cavern.

Both Rocky and Gizmo hissed for him to be quiet.

"Sorry," Max whispered. "But there's light up ahead, and the stone feels solid. We're almost free."

A howl.

Max stopped in place, his body rigid. The howl had come from behind them in the tunnel.

The wolves had followed them.

Worse—the howl had been *loud*, which meant the beasts didn't know about the slumbering bats.

The crinkle of wings came from just beyond the cavern entrance. One bat squealed, then another.

They were waking up.

"We need to move," Max barked, already galloping forward along the ledge. "Stay close to the wall!"

"Max," Gizmo panted as she and Rocky raced after him. "Be careful! The rocks are slick!"

"Don't worry. Just keep running!"

Max's pulse pounded, and a surge of panicked energy flooded his limbs. He bounded forward, veering around outcroppings and leaping over fallen rocks, his eyes focused on the light ahead.

Behind him came more howls and bat screeches. Rocky whimpered.

Then the cavern exit loomed in front of them, a gray gap offering a glimpse of a rain-soaked world. Clouds of water droplets whirled in through the opening, tugging at Max's fur and making the stone beneath his paws slick and dangerous. He ducked his head and slowed his gait as he reached the exit.

Outside, the three dogs were immediately enveloped by the hurricane. They found themselves standing on a narrow precipice at the edge of a deep, jagged gorge. A large river surged at the bottom of the gorge, cresting in angry white waves.

Looking to the left, Max saw the train tracks emerging from another concrete arch built into the rocky hillside, the exit also covered with boards. The tracks spanned the gorge on a trestle, a high bridge over the empty air, reaching solid ground on the other side. It must have once been a sturdy construction of iron and timber. But now, the metal was twisted and rusted; the wooden railroad ties underneath the tracks looked as if they were rotted and moldering.

Max felt Rocky and Gizmo huddle behind him as he looked around, desperate for some other way across, but the gorge seemed to stretch forever in either direction.

"We need to get across those tracks," Max barked. "It's the only way to escape the wolves."

"That doesn't look too sturdy, Max," Rocky said. "A good gust of wind could blow us right off!"

"Max won't let anything happen to us," Gizmo said confidently. She crawled under Max's belly and onto another ledge outside the cavern, a narrow strip of stone that led to the tracks.

The wind tangled her fur and forced her to keep her eyes half closed, but she kept walking toward the bridge.

Max followed her carefully. Each step was slippery, treacherous. Cold, wet fur plastered his skin, and he shivered.

Gizmo and Max reached the boarded-up archway and stopped to catch their breath. From here, the tracks spanning the gorge seemed even less sturdy. The trestle swayed back and forth in the wind, creaking and rattling.

But the three dogs had no choice. The wolves were behind them, and there was nowhere else to go. They had to try to cross.

"Rocky, are you ready?" Max said, turning his head to look back at his friend.

The Dachshund was still huddled at the jagged entrance to the cavern, trembling with fear.

"What are you doing, Rocky?" Gizmo barked. "Dolph is coming!"

"I'm acting as lookout," Rocky said, sounding unsteady. "You two start crossing, and I'll come right along."

Up above, the dark sky flashed as lightning crackled between the clouds. The thunder made the ground tremble beneath Max's paws.

Max nudged Gizmo with his nose. "Start crossing. Be very careful. I'll be right behind you."

"But what about Rocky?" Gizmo asked.

"He'll follow us once he works up the nerve. He always does."

Gizmo tucked her tail low as she took a tentative step onto the first wooden railroad tie, then jumped to the next. One more—and she found herself standing on the last beam still supported by solid ground.

The next one hung over empty space. And it didn't look the least bit stable.

Baring her teeth in defiance, Gizmo jumped onto the next tie. It squeaked, and the trestle shuddered in the wind.

But it held.

More confident now, she continued forward. Soon she was a third of the way across the unsupported tracks.

With one last look at the terrified Rocky, Max spread his legs wide and awkwardly waddled forward. He tried to keep his paws as close to the metal tracks as he could, where the wooden ties met the steel supports. Unlike tiny Gizmo, he didn't trust the wood to hold his weight, not the way it was quaking in the wind.

It was achingly slow going. Max followed Gizmo over the gorge, the tracks rocking beneath him, rain and wind surrounding him on all sides. He tried not to look down, but there was no escaping the sound of the river deep below, crashing against jagged rocks.

A piercing howl met Max's ears, but he couldn't tell if it was the wind or if the wolves were closing in. Then a yelp echoed from behind him, and Max dared a look back to see Rocky scrabbling over the stone ledge toward the boarded-up arch.

With a creak and a whine, a great shudder quaked through the elevated tracks. Gizmo yipped and Max barked in fear, but the tracks did not collapse. Even with the hurricane trying to twist it free, the metal held.

"Are you all right?" Rocky barked from behind them.

"Yes!" Max barked, though he was so frightened he couldn't stop shivering.

"No," Gizmo said, whimpering.

Max looked ahead to see the terrier standing, frozen, on one of the wooden railroad ties. The ties that had been behind and ahead of her had come loose, and Max heard a splash as the rotten boards fell into the river below.

The gap between the board where Gizmo stood and the next one was too far for her to jump. And as Max watched, the board that held her started to pull free from the tracks.

She was going to fall.

In that moment, Max forgot entirely about the raging storm, the tracks swaying in the wind, and the wolves who might be moments away from bursting out of the cavern.

He took a deep breath and bounded forward.

Max raced across the rotting boards, some of them breaking free from the twisted tracks and tumbling down below.

Reaching the last wooden tie before the gap that lay between him and Gizmo, Max made a wild jump. As he flew through the air, he snatched up Gizmo in his jaws by the scruff of her neck, then leaped once more.

There was no stopping now. Max landed on another wooden tie and ran as fast as his legs could carry him until finally, mercifully, he and Gizmo were on solid land once more.

Max carefully set Gizmo down in the grass next to the tracks, panting to catch his breath.

"Oh, thank you, Max," Gizmo said, huddling up to his side and licking his fur in gratitude. "You saved me."

Max looked back at the bridge—horrified to see that nearly all the boards had broken free from the tracks. "You were brave enough to go first, Gizmo. Thank *you*."

"Oh, no," Gizmo cried. "Rocky!"

Rocky still stood on the opposite side of the gorge, in front of the tunnel entrance, staring wide-eyed and frightened at his two friends.

"How am I supposed to get across now?" Rocky barked over the roar of the storm.

"Don't try!" Max barked back. "It's too dangerous. With the wind and rain, you'll fall."

Rocky paced in an anxious circle. "What am I gonna do?"

Huddling next to Max, Gizmo shouted, "We'll walk south. There has to be another way across somewhere."

Suddenly, growls echoed from the cavern.

Looking across the gorge at the craggy opening in the rock, Max saw several shapes creeping out, barely visible through the downpour.

But Max didn't have to see the creatures to know who they were.

Dolph and his wolves had arrived.

And Rocky was mere feet from the whole pack, all alone, with nowhere to run.

CHAPTER 8

LEAP OF FAITH

While the dogs stood watching, shaking with fear, the rain suddenly softened from a torrent into a gentle shower, as though the storm itself had been scared away by the wolf pack. The howling wind became a strong breeze, and a few of the sickly clouds parted to reveal shafts of late afternoon light.

But there wasn't any time to enjoy the end of the storm.

Wolves filled the cavern entrance, eight in total. Half were large with gray-and-white fur, the other half slightly smaller and a reddish brown, including one who seemed familiar. All were skinny and scarred from battle, especially Dolph, who had angry-looking scratch marks on his snout and scorched patches in his gray fur.

The wolves flattened their ears and bared their teeth, growling at Max from across the gorge.

They hadn't seen Rocky by the boarded-up tunnel entrance.

Yet.

Max nudged Gizmo with his front paw. "We need to distract them," he whispered.

Mimicking the wolves, Gizmo flattened her own pointed ears and showed her teeth. Yipping at the top of her lungs, she raced back and forth on the cliff edge.

"Go away!" she barked. "You leave us alone! No one wants you here, you big mean wolves!"

While Gizmo had their attention, Max caught Rocky's eye and gestured with his snout toward the trestle. It would be dangerous, but there were still enough wooden railroad ties attached to the track bed that Rocky *might* be able to leap over the gaps—if he was careful.

Rocky dropped to his belly and backed away from the edge of the gorge until his hind legs hit the plywood barricade. He shook his head wildly, his whole body trembling.

From the cavern entrance, Dolph howled over the patter of the rain and the surging river. "I do not care what you want, meat," he said to Gizmo. "Max knew this day was coming."

He jerked his snout at Max and said, "Face me, mutt. I gave you a head start for feeding my pack, and again because I did not want that crazy mongrel at the garbage house to destroy you before I was able to. You get no more chances to escape."

Hackles raised, Max bounded away from the track and through the weeds. He skidded to a stop next to Gizmo on the smooth ledge, sending tiny pebbles tumbling into the gorge.

"Give up, Dolph," Max growled. "You have no way across, unless you want to hurt yourself more than you have already. Still got that limp?"

One of the smaller red wolves came to Dolph's side, his fur also raised. "He runs like the wind, meat! We will leap over this gorge and rip out your throats!"

Max recognized the wolf as Rudd, who had tried to attack him once before. He didn't doubt the angry creature would try to jump the gap, no matter how wide it was.

"We will get across," Dolph said with a snarl. "You and your puny friends can try to run, but—" He stopped speaking, and his ears perked up as he scanned the cliff face.

"Where is your little sausage-shaped follower?" Dolph called.

Lowering her front end against the slick ground, Gizmo growled, "He ran ahead. We have friends the next town over. They'll be here any second to take you on!"

One of the gray-and-white wolves slunk out of the cavern and took a few steps toward the boarded-up archway. She sniffed the ground, then jerked up her head.

"They lie!" she howled. "I smell the small one. He is this way!"

Frantic, Max backed away from the cliff edge, then raced toward the tracks. "Rocky, run!" he barked. "Run right now, as fast as you can!"

Rocky seemed to have another idea.

As Max watched in horror, the small black Dachshund bounded out of the archway—toward the cavern full of wolves.

Barking wildly, he held his tail in the air as he neared the gray wolf who'd caught his scent. His yips echoed through the gorge, drowning out the retreating storm.

"What is he doing?" Gizmo asked, pacing helplessly back and forth.

The gray wolf yelped in surprise as Rocky leaped toward her, a small black blur. She padded backward, her tail tucked and her paws skidding over the wet rock.

"Yeah, you better run!" Rocky cried. "I'll nip you all over!"

Dolph shoved himself past his wolves, Rudd at his heel. "You think you can take me on, little meat?"

Rocky stopped mere feet from the cavern entrance. The wolf pack leader was so close that with one quick lunge he could snatch the small dog in his jaws.

Max's heart pounded so fast it hurt his chest. Maybe he could find some way to distract the wolves.

Gizmo butted Max's hind leg with her head. "We have to do something, Max!"

"I know," Max said, panting. "I'm thinking!"

On the opposite ledge, Rocky stood firm, even as his

tail drooped and his body trembled. Pointing his snout toward the tunnel, the tiny dog barked louder than Max had ever heard him bark before.

"I sure hope there aren't any *bats* around who got *woken up* by these *loud, mean, ugly wolves*! *Aaaroooooo oooooooooooooo!!!*"

Dolph spat out a laugh. "Now I am meant to be afraid of flying rats?"

"Uh, Dolph," Rudd said from behind him.

All the wolves craned their necks to look back into the depths of the cavern.

Then Max heard it, too.

The sound was soft at first, but it quickly rose louder and louder.

It was the flapping of hundreds upon hundreds of wide, leathery wings. The chittering squeaks and squeals of a thousand angry bats who'd been woken abruptly from their slumber.

In a furious, furry brown cloud, the bats swarmed through the cavern exit—directly toward the wolves.

Rocky half ran, half leaped back to the barricaded archway. Dolph and Rudd followed, howling in distress.

The rest of the wolves weren't so lucky.

The throng of bats slammed into the wolf pack. Two wolves fell off the cliff edge, scratching desperately at the muddy walls as they slid and tumbled down the slope toward the whitecapped river.

The other wolves howled and ran in blind circles

as tiny bat claws scraped at their backs and heads, and leather wings slapped their snouts. High-pitched shrieks tore into their ears. Four more wolves slipped off the ledge, following the first two down into the gorge.

As the swarm of bats billowed up into the gray sky, the wolves dragged themselves to the narrow river-bank far below, where they huddled together, wet and frightened.

Up above, by the cavern entrance, Dolph and Rudd held themselves flat as the bats flittered around them. By the tunnel, Rocky did the same, making himself as small as possible.

Soon the cloud of brown bats headed west, disappearing into the trees. Their squeals faded as they flew off toward the setting sun.

From across the gorge, Gizmo jumped up and down. "Rocky!" she yipped. "Come on, Rocky, while they're distracted!"

Dolph and Rudd were so overwhelmed by the sudden arrival of the bats that they didn't seem to hear Gizmo. But Rocky did. He raised his head and blinked his big brown eyes. Seeing the two wolves nearby, he jumped up and ran forward onto the tracks—stopping at the last board before the big gap.

He trembled, his eyes on the swollen river far, far below. The larger, stronger wolves had barely managed to escape its torrential waves. If Rocky fell, he'd be swept away.

"I don't know if I can make the jump," Rocky barked at his two friends. "It's a long way down."

Visions of the tiny dog tumbling to his doom flitted through Max's brain, but he couldn't show his fear. He shouted to Rocky, "You can do it! Just leap from board to board."

Rocky's tongue lolled free as he panted for breath. He scratched with each hind leg and shook his backside.

Then he leaped into the air with a "Hiiii-YAH!"

Max went still as he watched his friend's black figure soar through the air.

Rocky landed with a heavy, wet thud atop the next damp, rotting board. It creaked beneath him.

"I did it!" he yipped in surprise. Meeting Max's eyes, he wagged his spiky tail. "I actually did it!"

"That was amazing!" Gizmo said.

Down below, the wolves leaped against the cliff face, scrabbling with their claws, eyeing the dogs.

"The bats are gone!" one of them howled. "The meat is getting away!"

In front of the boarded-up tunnel, Dolph raised his head, and Rudd climbed to all four paws. Snarling, he stalked toward the tracks.

"You will not escape!" Rudd howled.

Gizmo spun in a panicked circle. "Keep going, Rocky!"

Rocky dared a glance behind him, then yipped at the sight of the red wolf's dripping fangs.

"Don't have to tell me twice!" Bunching his legs, Rocky made another wild leap, and once more landed safely on one of the remaining boards. Another leap, another solid landing.

Groaning, Dolph climbed to his feet. The big, scarred wolf scanned the trestle, then growled at Rudd.

"Get back here," he said. "You want to fall into the river, too?"

But Rudd ignored him.

The wiry, angry red wolf howled as he jumped from the ledge onto the trestle. He landed heavily, sprawling across the tracks so that his hind legs dangled over the metal support and his chest thumped against a rotting railroad tie.

The track rattled and quaked, screeching in protest. Rocky clung to his board, shivering.

"Keep going," Gizmo barked. "You're over halfway there!"

"You can do it!" Max shouted.

Behind Rocky, Rudd kicked his hind legs, trying to hoist them back onto the track.

"You will not escape!" he howled.

Rocky peered ahead, clinging to the narrow railroad tie. Then, taking a deep breath, he jumped over the gap.

And fell short, smacking against the next board with his chest.

"No!" Gizmo cried.

Rocky clung to the damp wood with his front paws, his long body and hind legs dangling in the air. Max could see the Dachshund slipping down, losing his grip.

"I can't hold on!" Rocky yipped, his voice high-pitched and terrified.

Max wanted to jump across, to snag Rocky in his jaws, just as he had done for Gizmo. But there was nowhere for him to land. No way for him to crawl back across the swaying trestle.

Then, several things happened at once:

Rudd managed to climb onto the surface of the bridge, and he flung himself forward, frothing wildly at the mouth. As he did, the tracks bounced.

The sudden drop and rise of the tracks hefted Rocky's hind legs into the air, and he managed to land with all four paws on the wooden beam.

The twisted tracks groaned as they started to pull free from the ledge in front of the tunnel entrance.

Rocky leaped to the next beam and the next, landing on solid ground with one final jump. Gizmo tackled him in relief, wagging her tail and licking his face. Rocky barked as he tumbled to the ground.

"You did it!" Gizmo said between licks.

"Of course I did," Rocky said, wiggling on his back. "I was never afraid, not once!"

Boards creaked and metal screeched. Max looked past his friends to see Rudd standing in the center of the bridge.

The red wolf opened his jaws and roared. "I am coming for you, meat!"

From the safety of the ledge outside the tunnel entrance, Dolph watched silently.

Rudd placed one leg atop the metal rail, then struggled as the track swayed beneath him. Unable to support his weight, the rotten beam sagged beneath his front paws.

Just as he was about to jump, the board beneath his feet snapped, and Rudd was pitched headfirst off the trestle. He howled as he tumbled through the misty air, until he landed with a splash far below.

Max, Rocky, and Gizmo looked over the edge of the cliff. For a moment, all they could see was the rushing, surging water.

Then Rudd's head popped up from beneath the waves. The wolf fought for air as he paddled toward the bank where the rest of his pack still huddled—all except Dolph.

"Serves him right." Gizmo leaned into Rocky's side.

Max licked them both between their ears. "I'm glad we're all okay. We should hurry and move on, though. The storm has died down, and night is coming. We need to find someplace safe to stay before Dolph and his pack can recover."

Groaning, Rocky got to his feet. "You think they'll be able to get out of that gorge anytime soon?"

Max looked down at the soaking wet, enraged wolves pacing by the river, then up at Dolph.

The big wolf stood stock-still on the narrow ledge outside the boarded-up tunnel. He did not bare his teeth, or raise his hackles, or flatten his ears.

He just glared directly at Max. Max could almost taste the wolf's anger.

"I don't know," Max said to Rocky as he turned away and followed him and Gizmo down the old tracks and through a wide field. "But I do know that nothing will stop Dolph from coming after us."

With one last look back at the wolf leader, Max said, "We need to get to the people before those wolves get to us."

CHAPTER 9

AN ODIOUS STENCH

Night came swiftly as gusts of wind rose, chasing the main storm.

Max, Rocky, and Gizmo ran beside the tracks, fleeing the gorge and putting as much distance as they could between themselves and the wolves.

Behind the dogs, in the distant east, thunder still rumbled, and the night blazed with flashes of lightning. It was almost as if the humans had come back to send up fireworks, just like they always did in the summertime.

"Max," Rocky said as he scrambled over a tree that had fallen across the tracks, "I don't know if I can run any more."

Max slowed down, then stopped entirely. His whole body ached, and his limbs were trembling.

Rocky and Gizmo rolled onto their sides on the wet, leaf-covered grass, panting, their tongues hanging free.

"Do you think we've run far enough?" Gizmo asked. "Have we lost them?"

Max looked back. They were in the middle of a narrow field with tall trees on either side. Raising his snout, Max huffed at the air. It smelled of fresh, clean grass and hidden bush animals, but there was no scent of wolf. The pack must have had to travel a long distance to escape the gorge before they could resume following Max and his friends.

Which meant the three dogs had a few hours of freedom.

"I think we have some time to rest," Max said as he turned in a circle, scanning the dark trees. "We just need shelter."

Rocky sat up and pointed with his snout at the tree line just north of the tracks. "What's that?"

In the distance, Max saw a shed that had been blown against the trees. It must have once been beside the tracks, but the storm had torn it free.

"Come on," Max said.

The three dogs padded softly through the tall, wet grass until they reached the wooden shed, which leaned at an angle. Sniffing, they crawled through an opening in the side.

The shed's interior smelled of dust and mold—but

it was dry. Some of the night sky showed through slits in the wood, and Max could even see a few stars. Rocky paced in a circle, then plopped onto the wooden floor. "This works for me, big guy."

Cuddling up next to him, Gizmo said, "Me, too."

Max lay down, his eyes already halfway shut. "You were both so brave today," he said.

"Ah, it wasn't nothing, buddy," Rocky said.

Gizmo nuzzled close to the Dachshund. "No, it was really something," she said softly. "I don't know what I'd do without you two."

"Don't worry," Rocky said. "You'll never have to find out."

Max's tail thumped happily against the floor of the dark shed. And then sleep came, and he drifted off into dreams.

Max was back in the desert.

Wolves howled in the dark clouds that surrounded him. But they weren't the only shapes in the blackness.

The clouds twisted and ballooned into familiar figures. Rocky and Gizmo appeared first, staring at him before disappearing.

Then he saw Charlie and Emma, clinging to each other.

And then the clouds were clouds again, a swirling funnel that kept Max stuck in place on his little patch of scorched desert. Wolves howled, the noise rising out of the screeching winds.

You are not as trapped as you feel, Madame's voice said.

Max turned to find the old black Labrador standing behind him. She wagged her tail—and the clouds behind her parted, revealing the towering wall of silver.

Max ran past Madame, toward the wall.

Make the leap, Max, Madame barked.

And he did.

He jumped with all his might, soaring into the blue-and-white sky high above him.

The three dogs woke with the rising sun.

They snuck out of the tattered shed and blinked at the morning. Everything looked brighter and fresher than it had yesterday. After the storm, it was easy to find a puddle deep enough to drink from, though their stomachs growled with hunger. The kibble they'd devoured at the mall was a distant memory.

Gnawing on a stick next to the half-collapsed shed, Rocky said, "You think we'll reach that town soon?"

"I hope so," Max said, leading his small friends back to the tracks. Renewed from sleep, they continued trotting west toward the town the mice had spoken about, in search of the mysterious Stripes and Spots, who could lead them to the wall.

Dawn's rays revealed a pink-and-blue sky, and a gentle breeze carried a fresh, dewy scent to Max's nostrils. But daylight also exposed the full aftermath of the hurricane's rampage.

The train tracks led Max and his friends through wilderness. The storm had felled many trees, cracking some in half and uprooting others. The grasslands were swampy and overflowing with water. Broken branches and torn leaves littered the ground.

"This stuff is not pretty," Rocky said. "No sirree."

Occasionally, the forest to the north would thin out to reveal a highway that ran parallel to the old, decaying tracks. Some of the big green signs had fallen free of their supports, the metal poles bent in half as though they were straw.

There was no way Dr. Lynn's beacons had survived the storm. The dogs' only hope of reaching the wall, and their people, was to find Stripes and Spots.

By midmorning, the sun was so warm that Max's fur was dry and tangled. Up ahead, he saw the train tracks cross a four-lane road running north and south.

"Hold up, guys." Max slowed to a stop in the center of the intersection and looked down the road both ways. Rocky and Gizmo collapsed next to him on the heated asphalt.

"Are we there yet?" Rocky moaned as he lay on his back, letting the sun warm his belly.

Just to the south was a large, single-story brick building with a big sign that read DEQUINCY SHOPPING CENTER.

Tail wagging, Max barked, "We *are* here, Rocky! DeQuincy—just like Samson told us. Now we have to find those two dogs."

Max headed north, where most of the animal scents were coming from. They passed houses with shattered windows and shutters torn free. A utility pole had fallen onto one of the houses, collapsing its roof.

Seeing the storm's destruction, Max was actually glad the humans hadn't been at home.

Other than the sounds he and his friends made, the town was eerily quiet. Most of the places they'd traveled through on their journey had at least *some* animals, either abandoned pets or wild scavengers. That must have been true here, as Max could clearly pick up their scents.

But the streets were empty.

As they walked, one animal smell grew much stronger than the rest.

They had just passed a grand two-story home when Rocky scrunched his snout.

"Something is rotten in the state of DeQuincy," he muttered.

"What's that?" Max asked.

Rocky shook his head, flapping his ears. "Nothing. There's just some bad scent around here. Can't you smell it, big guy?"

Max inhaled. Rocky was right. Among the musk and

tang of assorted animals was something weirdly oily, a smell like burning rubber.

Gizmo sniffed, her nose twitching, then said, "Oh, I smell it, too! It's not as bad as the bat pellets, though."

"That's not saying much," Rocky said.

"I'm sure it's nothing," Max said. "Probably just garbage left behind when all the humans went away."

"Nope!" Rocky suddenly backed away from his friends. "I don't trust places that don't smell right, big guy. And this place smells like nasty, stinking garbage. Remember Belle's mansion?"

"Yes," Max said. "But we *have* to keep going, Rocky. Dolph is after us, and Dr. Lynn's trail is gone. This is the only way we're going to find her."

Gizmo wagged her tail. "Plus, just yesterday you stared down a whole pack of wolves, Rocky! You can't be afraid."

Rocky paced back and forth, growling softly. "I'm not afraid. It just smells bad!"

From somewhere nearby, a high voice shouted, "*You* smell bad!"

All three dogs stiffened. Max slowly turned in a circle, searching for the animal who had spoken.

He saw a gas station off to his left, its windows dark. Atop the bright red awning that shaded the pumps sat a small, striped creature. She had pointed ears and a strip of black fur over her eyes, like a mask. She looked like a cross between a fox and a bear, with a bit of squirrel thrown in for good measure.

A raccoon.

Rocky stomped forward, his eyes on the creature. "What did you say about how I smell?"

The raccoon sat back on her hind legs. Her claws were almost like tiny human hands.

"You heard me," she said, sniffing. "You stink." She leaned over and picked up a branch, then fanned herself with the leaves. "You're probably just smelling yourself."

"Hey!" Rocky yipped. "I don't smell any worse than any other dog."

The raccoon flipped the branch back over her shoulder, then dropped to all fours. Imitating Rocky, she hefted up her backside and stiffened her fuzzy, gray-and-black-striped tail. "Hey! I am the stinkiest dog who ever lived! They call me the King of Garbage, because that's what I smell like!" She looked up. "In case you didn't understand, I was pretending to be you." She laughed—a tiny cackle.

Letting out a noise halfway between a growl and a whine, Rocky turned to Max. "Are you gonna let her talk about me that way, big guy?"

From above, in a near-perfect imitation of Rocky's voice, the raccoon said, "Are you gonna sit there like a big, doofy mutt, big guy?"

Max padded over to the sidewalk in front of the

gas station. Tilting his head back, he met the raccoon's beady eyes.

"Maybe you can help us," he said. "Can you come down here?"

"You can help yourself," the raccoon said, her voice a mocking squeal. "*You* come up *here*."

Max cocked his head. "And how am I supposed to do that?"

The raccoon twitched her whiskers. "Well, *I* had no problem."

Rocky dropped to his belly, his tail sagging. "Of course you didn't," he grumbled. "Rodents like you can climb anywhere."

"Hey!" The raccoon tossed down another branch, narrowly missing Rocky. "I am not a rodent."

Rocky jumped to his feet and bared his teeth. "You sure look like one!"

"*You* look like one!"

Gizmo nudged past Rocky and Max, wagging her tail. "Hello!" she barked. "Hi! I think we might have gotten off on the wrong paw. I'm Gizmo, and these are Rocky and Max. We're actually looking for some animals who live here."

Raising her snout in the air, the raccoon said, "That's nice." She leaped down to a trash can and sniffed inside, then jumped to the ground and waddled down the road.

Gizmo looked back at Max and Rocky, bewildered. "How...how *rude*!"

Rocky licked Gizmo's fur. "I don't care if it smells awful around here," he declared. "I'm not gonna let her get away with talking to you like that."

Ears slightly flattened, Gizmo said, "Me neither. Let's go after her."

The two small dogs didn't give Max a chance to chime in. They darted forward, chasing the young raccoon. Max followed.

"Excuse me!" Gizmo said as she raced to walk on one side of the raccoon. "Miss...um...raccoon?"

"We weren't done talking," Rocky said as he trotted up on the animal's other side.

Despite being outnumbered, the raccoon seemed unconcerned.

"Quit following me," she said, holding her ringed tail high. "I don't want to pass out from your funk."

There was definitely a funk in the air, but it was not from the dogs or the raccoon. It was so acrid, so pungent, that Max could almost taste it.

Max quickened his pace to catch up to the others. "We're looking for two animals named Stripes and Spots." Sniffing the raccoon's tail, he said, "You wouldn't happen to be Stripes, would you? Since your tail is—"

The raccoon spun around and smacked Max on his nose with her tail. He was so stunned that he stood there on the sidewalk, silent.

"Ew!" the raccoon squealed. "No, of course not. Stripes is such a stupid name."

Gizmo growled at the raccoon. "Don't hit him! You're being really mean. And for no reason!"

Crossing her arms, the raccoon glared at Gizmo. "I'm just trying to do you a favor. If you knew who Stripes was, you'd know why you're the one being mean."

"Well, we don't know who Stripes is," Rocky said. "That's why we're asking!"

The raccoon looked from Rocky to Gizmo to Max. She scratched her chin. Then she scrabbled up the trunk of a nearby tree and nimbly raced across a long, thick branch to the eaves of an abandoned coffee shop.

"Wait!" Max called out. "We really need your help. We're searching for our families...and we need to talk to Stripes. Or Spots. Maybe even both of them. Can you help us? *Please?*"

The raccoon peered down at the dogs and called, "Trust me, if you think what you're smelling is bad now, you really can't handle meeting Stripes."

"Should we take that as a *no?*" Rocky asked.

As her small head disappeared from view, the raccoon cried out one last warning.

"You'd better turn tail and leave town. Or else Stripes will turn her tail on *you!*"

CHAPTER 10

STRIPES AND THE SILVER BANDIT

Despite the rude little raccoon's claim that she didn't want to be bothered, she continued to taunt the three dogs.

While they scrounged for food in a corner market, its windows blown out by the hurricane, the raccoon draped herself against the cash register. "I'm telling you, if you lay one eye on Stripes, she'll squirt you square in the face!"

When they were lapping up rainwater from a pool whose tall sides had collapsed during the storm, she curled up on the grate of a rusty barbecue grill, warning them, "Stripes is feared for miles around! Even the bears are scared of her!"

And when they huddled together on a porch, shading themselves from the sun for a brief rest, she squealed, "Stripes will make you wish you'd never been born!"

Each time Max tried to confront her, to find out where he and Rocky and Gizmo needed to go, the raccoon pointed her muzzle into the air and waddled off, as though *they* were bothering *her.*

Max had no idea why the raccoon kept trying to get rid of them, but he found it hard to take her warnings seriously. It was early afternoon by the time Max, Rocky, and Gizmo found themselves wandering through the center of the town. They couldn't leave until they'd located Stripes, and if the shifty raccoon wasn't going to help them, they would have to search for the animal themselves.

It was a modest town, this DeQuincy, its small houses surrounded by fields and trees.

It must have been a nice place to live once, but the storm had taken its toll. Street signs lay flattened against sidewalks. Abandoned trucks were crushed by fallen trees. Plastic bags and scraps of wet paper littered the streets and mounded in the gutters, the hurricane having upended Dumpsters and trash cans.

The horrible smell wasn't from the trash, though. As pungent as it was, yesterday's storm would have washed it away—so it must be fresh. Someone had worked this very morning to make DeQuincy as off-putting as possible.

"I'm really, really tired of this!" Rocky yowled, shaking

his head. "Every time I try to sniff out where some dogs might be, this stupid stench gets in the way."

From a building on the nearby corner, the raccoon's high voice cried out, "You're just smelling your own breath after eating all that dog food. Everyone knows you're supposed to wash your food before you eat it!"

Rocky growled, but Gizmo nuzzled him. "Just ignore her."

The building the raccoon sat on was painted with red and white stripes and had big open windows. Inside, the dogs could see colored booths and a yellow menu on the wall that showed pictures of food. The sign out front read RANDY'S DINER.

A bright burst of wind came from around the diner, and with it a quick breath of fresh air. For a brief moment, Max smelled musky dog and cat fur.

Quickly, he veered toward the road on the other side of the diner. "This way!" he barked to his friends. Max sensed the raccoon watching them eagerly from above, but he took Gizmo's advice and ignored her.

As Max rounded the diner and trotted onto the new street, the stench once again smothered every other smell. And now he could see why: Standing in the center of the road, all alone under the high, hot sun, was the source of the odor.

The creature was smaller than Rocky or Gizmo, with a wide, fat body held low to the ground. Its head was tiny, the size and shape of a squirrel's. It had four squat legs and a thick, flat, fuzzy tail. The tremendous stench wafted off the creature's backside, and Max wondered what the thing could possibly have eaten to make such a smell.

Max, Rocky, and Gizmo stood still in the street, silent and wary. A dry, warm breeze rose, swirling dust and dead leaves.

The creature flicked its tail to the side, cocking it with warning.

From atop the diner, the raccoon squeaked in glee. "Oh, now you're going to get it! I *tried* to warn you, but you didn't listen." She clapped her small hands together. "Ooh, this is gonna be good!"

Max took a tentative step forward. "Hello?" he barked.

Rocky nipped at Max's heel. "Are you crazy, big guy? Don't go talking to it. We don't even know what it is!"

"I think I do," Gizmo said. "I met one before, but the smell wasn't anywhere near this bad."

"What is it?" Rocky asked.

The animal walked forward on its short, squat legs. As it came closer, Max could make out two stripes of white fur that ran all along its black body, from the top of its head to the tip of its upraised tail.

"It's a skunk!" Gizmo said.

The raccoon raced back and forth, her paws clanging on the diner's metal roof. "Get 'em, Stripes! Spray 'em good!"

Max had heard woeful tales of skunks before. Other

dogs at the kennel had told stories of sniffing out a new friend, only to be met with a faceful of an awful, smelly spray that clung to every piece of fur and made their eyes and nose and mouth burn. Even after a bath, they *still* smelled horrible.

Warily, Max backed away from the approaching skunk. At the first sign that it was going to turn tail on him and his friends, he was ready to run.

But despite the raccoon's warnings, when the skunk approached, she merely said, "Hello!"

Wagging her tail, Gizmo trotted over to the skunk and sniffed her carefully. Doing her best not to show her disgust, Gizmo said, "Hi! You must be Stripes. We've been looking for you."

"Have you?" the skunk said. "Well, I'm glad you're just dogs, then. I heard a rumor of wolves nearby, so I've been spraying the whole town to try to scare them off." She ducked her head. "Sorry about the smell. It's only supposed to be used to defend myself. I don't like making friendly animals feel sick."

"Aw!" the raccoon cried from above. "Why are you *talking*? Spray them! Make 'em run away howling! Show 'em who's boss!"

Stripes sat back on her hind legs and turned to look up at the raccoon. "Tiffany, what have I told you about trying to scare off guests?" Stripes squeaked. "Predators, sure, but I can tell these dogs are good folk."

Shaking a tiny fist in the air, the raccoon squealed,

"And what did I tell *you* about calling me Tiffany? I'm the Silver Bandit! I scavenge treasure where none dare go!"

To the dogs, Stripes whispered, "She means the garbage dump."

Tiffany didn't hear her. From the corrugated roof, she cried out, "I am a nimble thief! A shadow in the night! I sneak past bobcats and coyotes without them even knowing I was there!" She leaned back on her squat hind legs once more and smacked herself on the chest with a tiny paw. "Tiffany was my baby name. I'm nearly six months old now, and I demand to be called by my grown-up name: the Silver Bandit!"

Sighing, Stripes turned back to Max, Rocky, and Gizmo.

"I have no idea where she gets this stuff," the skunk said. "I'm sure she doesn't even know what a bobcat is."

"I do too!" Tiffany squealed. "A bobcat is just like a normal cat, only its head is too big for its body, so it bobs like a chicken when it walks! I saw one just yesterday, and I snuck past its stupid big head and stole one of its eggs. Then I escaped without it even waking up!"

"I'm pretty sure cats don't lay eggs," Max said.

Tiffany scrambled to the edge of the roof, then leaped down into a row of overgrown bushes. In a moment, her masked face popped up through the leaves.

"You're pretty sure cats don't lay eggs, huh?" Tiffany said. "Well, *I'm* pretty sure I know what I saw, and that was a whole herd of bobcats, bobbing their heads, laying eggs as they walked, just leaving them behind to be taken by a master thief like myself."

"But if they were doing that, why would they care if you took one?" Rocky asked. "Anyway, I thought you said the bobcat was asleep!"

Gizmo nuzzled him, saying, "Don't think too hard about it, Rocky."

Tiffany twitched her ears and said, "I'm pretty sure thinking too hard isn't something we need to worry about with this guy."

"Hey!" Rocky barked.

But in a flurry of leaves and branches, Tiffany disappeared behind the bushes.

Stripes sighed and lowered her tail. "Follow me while we talk," she said. "I only sprayed the outskirts of the town, so the farther in we go, the easier it'll be on your poor noses." She lowered her head. "Really, if I had any other way to scare off predators..."

Gizmo ran up to trot at Stripes's side. "It's all right! You're a skunk, so it's only natural."

Whispering to Max, Rocky said, "There's nothing natural about the stench wafting from her backside, if you ask me."

Max's tail wagged in amusement, but he didn't want to risk insulting the friendly skunk. He quickened his pace to walk on her other side. "I'm Max, by the way," he said. "And these are Gizmo and Rocky."

"Good to meet you," Stripes said. "You said you were looking for me?"

"It's kind of a long story," Max said as they passed more small stores and homes with broken windows and rain-soaked yards. "But before that storm came through—"

"Such a dreadful storm," Stripes replied with a shake of her head. "Most of the damage was on the east side of town. Luckily it's not so bad farther in."

"That's good to hear," Max said. "Anyway, yesterday morning a herd of horses almost ran us off the road, and one of them told us they were trying to outrun the storm. They also wanted to get away from an electric wall. When I tried to find out more, she mentioned your name—is there someone here named Spots, too?"

Stripes stopped in the middle of an intersection. Despite the hot sun, she shivered.

"Oh, I remember those horses, all right," she said. "Those big, clomping hooves of theirs did a number on the lawns a few days back. Of course, now you can't tell the difference between the damage they did and what the storm tore up."

Max followed her gaze to a nearby cluster of houses whose windows were all blown out. An ancient tree had been uprooted, its coiled roots dangling in the air, its trunk collapsed across the lawn.

"Why were the horses here?" Rocky asked.

Stripes turned to look at the Dachshund.

"A few were from the stables in town," she said. "The rest of them had been traveling all over the countryside, and some had been to the wall you talked about. When they weren't stamping around like they owned the place, they were nattering on about humans coming to electrocute us all."

Waddling close to the other animals, she lowered her voice and said, "We know the humans aren't ever coming back, and that's just fine by me. Some of the house pets aren't too thrilled about it, but I rather like having the freedom to roam the streets, don't you?"

Rocky looked at the skunk, bewildered. He started to speak, but Gizmo got there first.

"It is nice being with other animals," the little terrier said. "Sometimes I miss my pack leaders—my human family—but I don't know if I'll ever see them again."

Stripes's black-and-white head darted back and forth as she studied the dogs. "Oh, I didn't notice those collars you're wearing. You're pets, too." Turning away from them, the skunk continued down the road in the direction of the afternoon sun. "You seem so familiar with the wilderness that I just assumed you were feral."

First the mice they met preferred the world without humans, and now this skunk was saying the same thing. Max wanted to defend his human family, but he didn't want to argue with Stripes, at least not before finding out more.

"So about the wall," Max said, following the skunk. "The horses made it sound like you might know something about it."

"Not me, no way," Stripes said with a swish of her tail. "I haven't been out of this town since I was born, and I don't ever plan to leave. Anyway, I would never go poking around a wall put up by humans."

"So is it Spots, then?" Rocky asked. "The horses said one of you had been on the other side of this mysterious wall."

The skunk twitched her big, bushy tail for a second time. "Oh, it was definitely Spots. He's a crazy old Bluetick Coonhound, though he wasn't always so crazy. Or so old, for that matter. He likes to be called the Train Dog."

"Do you know where we can find him?" Max asked.

Off the side of the road, branches rustled in a tall, spindly tree. The three dogs and the skunk stopped to look at the commotion. For a moment, Max thought it might be birds, returned from wherever they had flown off to.

Instead, the dogs saw Tiffany scrabbling onto a wide branch above their heads.

"First," the little raccoon bandit declared, "I present to you a one-of-a-kind, genuine bobcat egg. So there." In her tiny hands, she held up a smooth gray stone.

Spinning in a circle, Rocky yipped, "That's a rock!"

Tiffany ignored him. Setting the stone carefully on the branch, she twitched her furry tail. "Second, where do you *think* you'd find some mutt calling himself the Train Dog?" she said. "Maybe by some *trains*?"

Max's ears perked up. "Are there any trains around here?" he asked Stripes. "The tracks we were following seemed abandoned."

Stripes sat back on her haunches and rubbed her paws together. "There is another set of tracks that runs through town and goes by the old railroad museum. More days than not, that's where you'll find Spots. He's a creature of habit."

"Can you take us to the museum?" Gizmo asked.

The smooth, polished stone flew down onto the street, cracking against the asphalt.

"Never!" Tiffany cried, shaking a tiny fist. "Only the animals of DeQuincy are allowed there! The Silver Bandit forbids you, Stripes, to lead them to our museum!"

Raising her tail, Stripes hefted up her backside and aimed it at the raccoon. "If you don't stop it right this instant, Tiffany, I'm going to spray you! You know what your mother will say if I do!"

"Not my mother!" Tiffany squeaked, and disappeared into the foliage.

With a sigh, Stripes lowered her tail and met Max's eyes. "I'll take you to see Spots," she said. "But be warned: The Train Dog who went to the wall is not the same Train Dog who came back. And he's not going to take very kindly to strangers poking in his business." She shivered. "Not one bit."

CHAPTER 11

THE TRAIN MUSEUM

Stripes was right about the markings she'd made—the farther into the center of town she led Max, Rocky, and Gizmo, the more the odor faded. Finally, Max was able to inhale without swallowing a mouthful of burning gas.

"And I thought *I* was gassy," Rocky muttered to Max. "Remind me not to make a habit of hanging out with skunks."

"Be nice," Max whispered. "Stripes is helping us— and besides, it doesn't smell *that* bad anymore."

The skunk led them off the main street and down a dusty road made of packed dirt. Old brick buildings were on either side, surrounded by yellow fields. The breeze rose, carrying downy white dandelion seeds and dry, broken blades of grass.

Ahead of Max and Rocky—who stayed a safe distance from Stripes's bushy tail—Gizmo kept pace with the skunk. "How did you come to know Spots?" she asked as they walked. "I've met some skunks before who were nice to me, though I do tend to get along with most animals. But I've heard from other dogs that if you even go near a skunk they'll spray you."

"I almost did spray Spots when we first met," Stripes said. "I was a kit at the time, hiding under his pack leader's porch, all alone, when his big head burst into the darkness. All I saw was a giant snout huffing and slobbering, and I was scared out of my mind. I didn't even think—I turned around, raised my tail, and got ready to spray."

The skunk ducked her small head. "I'm ashamed of it now, but I was orphaned and alone, and all I knew how to do was spray and run. But Spots caught scent of what I was, and before I could do anything, he howled, begging me to wait. No dog—heck, no other animal at all—had ever tried talking to me, so I was surprised enough to listen."

"Lucky Spots," Rocky said.

Stripes chuckled. "Very."

In front of them, a small tree that had been torn up by the storm lay across the road. Stripes carefully led the dogs around it, then resumed course.

"Anyway," the skunk went on, "Spots asked me why I was there by myself, and I managed to squeak out an answer. He promised to be my friend and help me, so long as I never perfumed anyone without good cause. I trusted him, and soon he and his brother were bringing me food and keeping me a secret from their humans so I wouldn't get chased away."

"Spots has a brother?" Max asked. "Is he around somewhere, too?"

"His brother's name is Dots," Stripes said. "He's not here anymore, though. He—" She looked away from Max, whiskers twitching. "Honestly, it's not my story to tell. I'll let Spots explain."

"Fair enough," Max said.

The group continued on in silence. Something had clearly happened to Dots, and Stripes seemed upset about it.

"How did Spots come to be the Train Dog?" Gizmo asked. "It's such a regal name."

"Oh, he'd been calling himself that long before I ever met him, since the day he took his first trip aboard a steam engine," Stripes said, staring at the horizon. "I still remember the first time I saw him ride. Dots carried me through the fields on his back so we could watch the train come down the tracks, all decked out with colorful lights." Stripes was clearly enjoying telling this story. "It was wintertime," she continued, "and Spots's pack leader was in the locomotive—that's the big car at the very front—wearing his blue-and-white-striped cap, waving out the window. And hanging his head out that same window was Spots, having the time of his life.

"He always spent a lot of time at the museum with his pack leader. Spots was the mascot of the place. He told me plenty of stories when he came to see me." Stripes sighed—the kind of sigh that was full of memories. "It wasn't long before I became too big to live under the porch, so I moved out to the field behind their house. I still had to stay hidden, but we remained friends, even though Spots spent most of his time at the museum." Stripes glanced at the empty train tracks. "When the humans disappeared, I thought we could finally play together, without my having to worry. But Spots and Dots were anxious to know where their humans had gone. That's why they went to the wall."

"So something happened to Dots at the wall, then," Rocky said.

Stripes twitched her tail. "Like I said, it's not for me to tell." She quickly glanced around. "Oh! I got so lost in my story I almost forgot where we were going. We're here."

The skunk pointed a paw past the train tracks. Just beyond an overgrown lawn was a wide white structure topped by a rust-red roof. In the center was a two-story building with a sign over the front door that read DEQUINCY RAILROAD MUSEUM. Two wings connected to the central building, and attached to the west wing was a train platform. A flag hung limply on a pole just outside the main entrance.

Max didn't see any trains, but he could smell the smoky scent of coal, and beyond it the musk of animals.

"This way to Spots!" Stripes announced as she crawled over the train tracks.

Max, Rocky, and Gizmo followed her across the lawn and onto a concrete path, past the main entrance to the back of the museum—and all three dogs stopped to gape.

"Would you look at that!" Rocky wagged his tail excitedly. "It's just like in the movies my pack leader watched on TV!"

Max blinked. Behind the main building sat a big black steam engine under a metal awning.

It was a massive machine, like no other vehicle Max had ever seen, and definitely not like the sleek monorail train he'd ridden in several weeks before. No, this locomotive—as Stripes described it—seemed heavy and ancient, its black finish dulled and aged.

The entire front was a long pipe, with smaller pipes on top to let out steam. It was connected to a cabin, behind which was a trough filled with coal. The whole contraption sat on slender, grooved wheels. There were glass lights and narrow platforms attached to its front end, and all sorts of tubes running along its length. The number 124 was painted in white on its side.

Rocky and Gizmo bounded forward to investigate,

but before they reached the platform, Gizmo stopped to gawk at the car behind the locomotive. Her ears perked up, her tail wagged, and she cried, "I know what that is! It's a caboose!"

She ran toward the bright red car and leaped inside through its sliding door. Rocky followed her, and the two small dogs sniffed at every last part of the interior, wriggling with excitement.

Max wagged his tail, then looked down at Stripes. "Sorry, we've never seen a real, live train before."

Stripes sat down and rubbed her front paws together. "It's no problem. Spots will appreciate your enthusiasm. Plus, it seems like you three have gone through a lot to get here, braving that storm and all. You could use a little playtime."

Max padded across the gravel under the big metal awning. He leaped up into the caboose, landing on an old wooden floor. Inside, it smelled of hay and dust.

There was an open door on the other side of the car, so he stuck his head out to investigate—and saw the tiny town.

Past the big trains, next to another set of tracks in a field behind the museum, was a line of buildings just big enough for human children to play in.

The corner building, the biggest of them all, had a swinging door under a sign that read SONNY'S SARSA-PARILLA SALOON. Next to it was a smaller building with GENERAL STORE painted on its side. There was a white building with a pointed roof and a steeple on top, and a sheriff's station with WANTED posters in the windows.

But what was most interesting about this town of half-sized buildings was the miniature train sitting on real tracks that circled the town in a big loop. It was a replica of the big locomotive, painted a polished-apple red. Behind it was a jet-black coal car, connected to a boxcar with its top half cut off, and at the very back a caboose with its doors open to reveal an empty interior.

Max could almost see the train filled with happy, cheering kids, the steam engine tooting its horn as it rode all around the small town. He bet Charlie and Emma would have loved to visit this place. Suddenly he ached for them, wishing they were here and not beyond some electrified wall, lost in a city of tents.

The wall. He'd let himself get distracted. They weren't here to explore. They had to find Spots.

"Rocky," Max barked over his shoulder into the caboose. "Gizmo. We need to get moving."

"Okay, big guy," Rocky said, alert and focused as he came to stand at Max's side. "Boy, that was fun, though!"

"Yeah," Gizmo said softly as she joined them, her tail drooping. "It was nice to play for just a little bit."

"We'll have plenty of time to play once we find our families," Max said. "Let's see if Stripes has located Spots."

Max leaped down from the caboose onto the gravel, Rocky and Gizmo behind him. Stripes was already making her way across the back lawn toward the tiny town.

"Hello in there!" Stripes called out as she waddled toward the mock saloon. "Has anyone seen Spots?"

As Max and his friends followed Stripes into the miniature town, a small dog emerged from the swinging doors of the saloon.

He had a pert muzzle and especially long ears that dangled below his snout. His long, sleek fur was white with orange splotches, with darker fur on his ears and around his eyes, and a white stripe running from his forehead to his nose. Though he was little more than a foot tall—the same height as Gizmo—the dog was as big as he was going to get.

The dog was a breed with the impressive name of Cavalier King Charles Spaniel. Max had met several at the kennel. This one had a bright blue handkerchief tied around his neck.

The Cavalier Spaniel cocked his head, his long, fluffy tail wagging slowly and warily. "What can I do you for, Stripes? I trust these newcomers are friendly?"

"Howdy, Chuck." The skunk nodded her small head at the dog, then sat at the foot of the small saloon's narrow steps. "And yup, these three are all right. We're looking for Spots. You seen him around?"

Chuck sniffed. "I smell him, but I haven't seen him since this morning." Raising his snout, the Cavalier Spaniel howled, "Attention, citizens! Anyone seen Spots? No need to keep hiding; Stripes says the new folk are safe."

At this, Max, Rocky, and Gizmo looked around. Slowly, the doors on the other buildings opened and the heads of several small animals peeked out. A fleecy white kitten emerged from the grocery, shaking her head. Two puppies, mixed breeds with shaggy brown-and-black fur, crawled out of the sheriff's office. "Haven't seen him," they yipped.

"Aw!" Gizmo whispered. "Look at the puppies. So cute!"

A thump sounded behind them, and everyone turned to see the small raccoon crouched on the building with the steeple, examining her tiny fingers.

"Oh, great," Rocky muttered. "She's back."

Ignoring Rocky, the Silver Bandit drawled, *"I've* seen the Train Dog. I can't believe you missed him. He's supereasy to find."

"Hi, Tiffany!" the kitten mewed from the grocery store. "Do you want any vegetables? I have lots and lots and lots."

"Not now, Snow," Tiffany said with a scornful hiss. "I don't have time to play."

"We don't want to play with her, anyway," one of the mutt puppies—a girl—said with a growl.

"But Regina, you said you hoped she'd come play thieves and hunters," her brother said with a cocked head.

Regina nipped at him. "No, I did not, *Rufus.*"

"But—"

Regina leaped at him and wrestled him down on the

porch. "Stop lying. We don't play with rude animals like Tiffany!"

Chuck, the Cavalier Spaniel, barked loudly. "Citizens! We've got newcomers in town. Behave!"

The two puppies untangled themselves, their ears drooping. "Yes, Chuck," they said in unison.

Tiffany examined her small hands. "Baby animals can be *so* embarrassing. Not like me. I'm wonderful."

Chuck groaned. "Good luck with her!" he said, turning to go back into his saloon.

"Have you really seen Spots?" Max asked the little raccoon.

"Sure!" Tiffany said. "He's in the museum. *Obviously.*"

Stripes fluffed out her tail. "I suppose it can't hurt to take a look."

Leaving the miniature town behind, Max, Rocky, and Gizmo followed Stripes to the back of the main building. Max heard a rustling and looked to see Tiffany darting toward the giant locomotive. Trailing her were the kitten and the two puppies.

Turning away, Max followed Stripes onto the concrete path. The midday sunlight streamed through the dusty windows in the back of the museum. Inside, Max saw a large open space filled with model train sets, conductors' uniforms, and framed black-and-white photos of men posing in front of steam engines.

"Hello?" Stripes called out. "Spots? It's me. Are you in there?"

"Noooo!" a voice howled from inside, so loud the windows rattled. "Leave me alone! I don't want to see anyone!"

Stripes waddled forward, then jumped up to press her paws against the windowpane. "But Spots, I have dogs here who have questions about the wall. They need—"

"They need a swift ride out of town on one of my trains!" the dog howled. "If any of you mutts tries to come in here, I swear I'll send you full steam ahead right off a cliff!"

"Yeesh," Rocky muttered. "You weren't kidding about the Train Dog being unfriendly."

"He doesn't mean it," Stripes said softly as she lowered herself to the ground, leaving tiny paw prints on the window. "Like I said, he just hasn't been the same since his visit to the wall. It . . . changed him."

"Maybe if we just talk to him, he'll want to help," Gizmo said. "It can't hurt to try, right?"

"Maybe," Stripes said with a frown. "But whenever Spots goes to the museum, he locks himself in. We have no way to get inside."

Someone cleared her throat, and Max looked up to find Tiffany draped atop the red tile roof, swishing her ringed tail.

"Oh, that's not true," said the devious little raccoon. "You just need someone nimble and clever to get inside. Someone like *me*."

CHAPTER 12

SNEAKING IN

The three dogs heard meowing and yipping, and they turned to see the kitten and the two puppies peeking up over the edge of the concrete path.

"Tiffany's not allowed in there, is she?" Rufus asked Stripes.

"Like she cares," Regina said with a growl. "She's a bad, bad animal."

Snow snapped her tail. "Can I go in with you, Tiffany?"

Tiffany sighed. "No, you can't. Stop following me."

Max wagged his tail, looking up at Tiffany. "Would you really go inside for us?" he asked the little raccoon.

Tiffany gripped the edge of the roof with her front paws and swished her head back and forth. "Nope!" she said. "You dumb dogs never believed me when I warned you about Stripes. So why should I help you now?"

For a moment, Max felt defeated, but then he saw a spark in Gizmo's eyes—she had a plan, Max could tell.

Gizmo sat next to Max and lowered her head. "You know, you're right," she said sweetly. "We should never have doubted you, Silver Bandit. It's a wonder it was only Stripes and Spots we heard stories about and not you."

Rocky looked at Max as if to say, *What is Gizmo doing?* Max motioned for Rocky to keep quiet.

Leaping to her feet, Gizmo wagged her tail into a blur. "I know!" she barked.

Startled by Gizmo's sudden motion, the raccoon let go of the roof's edge. "You know *what?*"

Gizmo spun in an excited circle. "We can be the ones to tell the world how wonderful and amazing you are! I bet animals would come from miles around to see you outrun wild cats and leap between trees."

"Oh, brother," Rocky muttered.

Lashing out with her hind leg, Gizmo nudged Rocky on his snout.

Clearing his throat, Rocky jumped up and down. "I mean, oh, brother! Gizmo sure is right! Except..." He dropped to all fours, tail tucked between his legs. "We can't move on until we know where the wall is, and Spots is the only one who can help us."

Gizmo sighed. "It is quite the problem."

Stripes waddled away from the museum windows to stand next to Max. Whispering to him, she asked, "What are these two going on about?"

Max said quietly, "Just wait and see."

Up above, Tiffany flopped onto her belly and slapped her tiny hands against the tile. "So," she said, "what exactly would you tell folks about me?"

Gizmo gazed dreamily off into the distance. "Oh, what *wouldn't* we say? The Silver Bandit may look adorable, but don't you dare cross her. She's swift and silent, moving through the night like...like a streak of molten moonlight!"

The young raccoon's ears perked up. "Ooh, I like that."

Rufus the puppy barked wildly, "The Silver Bandit sounds great!" The puppies yipped and ran in excited circles while the kitten rolled onto her back and swatted at the air.

"Who knew you had someone so famous in your small town?" Gizmo said to the baby animals.

"I'd love to tell the whole world that the Silver Bandit is a master at breaking human locks to boldly go where no other animal has gone before, but—" Rocky pointed his snout at the glass double doors to the museum. "Well, we haven't seen her do that yet."

Tiffany swished her tail. "You don't think I can?"

"Of course we do!" Gizmo barked up at her. "It's just,

if we could see it for ourselves, it would give us another story to share."

Rocky wagged his tail. "It's all in the details."

Max watched in awe as Tiffany scratched the underside of her muzzle, then slowly nodded her head. "True, true."

"Do it, Silver Bandit!" Rufus howled.

Dropping to all fours on the roof, Tiffany said, "All right, I'll do it! But only if you three dogs *promise* to tell *everyone* you meet about me."

"We promise," Gizmo said.

"Most definitely," Rocky said.

Tiffany pointed a finger at Max. "What about you? You're awfully quiet."

Max wagged his tail. "I'm just amazed by your talent, Silver Bandit. I would be proud to spread word of your accomplishments all over the world."

"Excellent!" the raccoon squealed. "Now watch as a master thief goes to work!"

With a running start, Tiffany jumped from the museum's roof to the open second-story window on the main building. She landed lightly on the sill, looked to make sure the dogs were watching, and then leaped into the darkness. The two puppies and the kitten cheered.

"You all laid it on pretty thick," Stripes said as she padded to the glass doors.

"Yeah," Rocky said, "sometimes you gotta slather them up good and gooey, even if you'd really rather chase them up a tree. Usually that's my job, but it seems our friend Gizmo picked up some new tricks."

Gizmo licked Rocky affectionately. "I learned from the best!"

Max, Rocky, Gizmo, and Stripes sat in front of the glass double doors, waiting, the puppies and kitten behind them. Beyond the dusty glass, they could see the museum interior with its iron-and-wood benches, displays, and a rack of postcards on a cashier's desk.

What they couldn't see was Tiffany.

But they could hear her.

The sound of her claws scrabbling over the wooden floors echoed through the museum, followed by a thump, a squeal, then a series of loud thuds.

"Who put those boxes there?" Tiffany's voice said from inside.

Baring his teeth, Rocky asked, "What is she doing?"

Stripes sighed. "She's just being Tiffany."

Little Rufus nipped at Stripes's side. "It's the *Silver Bandit* now," he said indignantly.

Gizmo pressed her face up against the glass. When she couldn't see anything, she stepped back, leaving a wet nose print and feathery wisps where her bushy fur had brushed away the dust.

"Can anyone see her yet?" Gizmo wagged her tail at the baby animals. "How about you? You must have sharp eyes."

Inside the walls, a pipe groaned, and Max could just

make out Tiffany's shadow as she landed on a drinking fountain, one paw on the button as the other lifted handfuls of water up to her snout.

"There!" the kitten yowled. "I see her!"

Max raised a paw and slapped it twice against the door. The shadowy figure that was Tiffany jerked up her head in surprise.

"Can you open the door yet, Silver Bandit?" Max barked.

Tiffany waved a paw at him, then returned to drinking from the fountain.

Max turned to Stripes. "She sure is making a lot of noise in there. Why isn't Spots after her?"

"He's gone back to sleep, I suppose," Stripes said. "That's all he does these days—goes to the museum and sleeps. I think that's how he avoids thinking about Dots and his missing human family."

Gizmo nudged Max's leg. "Hey! She's on the move again."

All seven animals peered through the murky glass doors, watching as the tiny shadow that was Tiffany scrabbled up a big metal pipe that ran up the front wall and connected with a yellow box. There were multicolored bulbs attached to the box and levers and buttons built into the face.

"What is she doing?" Max asked Stripes.

Stripes swished her bushy tail. "I have no idea."

Tiffany jumped onto the box, landing with a metallic clang. Then she examined a stack of square items that looked to be made of cloth. Standing on tiptoes, she reached as high as she could, squeezing the topmost item in her hand—and sent the entire stack tumbling off the yellow box.

"Whoa!" Tiffany cried.

As the dogs watched, she pinwheeled her arms while the items rained down to the floor below. Unable to keep her balance, the raccoon fell backward through the air, squealing.

The cloth items and Tiffany landed hard on a stack of red-and-gold boxes that contained replicas of train cars. The shiny boxes cascaded to the floor, carrying Tiffany with them and burying her underneath. The noise was tremendous, echoing through the two-story room like blasts from a cannon.

The commotion kicked up a cloud of dust, shrouding the room in shadow.

"She fell!" Regina cried.

Gizmo looked at Max, worried. "Do you think she's all right?"

Max didn't have to answer. A moment later, a gray face with masked eyes popped up from the rubble. Tiffany scrunched her snout and sneezed, then wriggled her shoulders and backside until she was free.

Next, as everyone watched in bewilderment, she dove headfirst into the pile of boxes, and for a moment all they could see was her ringed tail and back paws.

When she emerged once more, she had one of the cloth items from the yellow box propped squarely on her head. It was a pale blue striped hat, just like those the conductors wore in the photographs on the museum's walls.

Her hat in place, Tiffany bounded off the mountain of train boxes and waddled confidently toward the glass double doors.

Rocky scratched at the glass. "What was that all about?" he barked.

A few feet from the door, Tiffany sat back on her haunches and pointed at the hat with both hands.

"I got the hat!" she squeaked, her voice muffled by the walls.

"I see that," Gizmo said, barking loudly enough for Tiffany to hear. "You look very nice."

Tiffany waved a dismissive paw. "It's not about looking *nice*. It's a disguise! This way, if Spots sees me opening the door, he'll just assume I'm a human and leave me alone." She clapped her hands together. "Brilliant, right?"

Rocky's whole body trembled and his jaw hung open. "A disguise?" he sputtered. "After you made all that noise?"

Max leaned down and nudged Rocky. "Don't scare her off now," he whispered.

Gizmo offered Tiffany a wag of her tail. "Um, very... *smart* of you. So, do you think you can open the door?"

"Of course!" Tiffany said. "Now, watch carefully; you don't want to get the details wrong when—"

"What in tarnation is going on in here?" a voice bellowed.

Max jerked in surprise, then looked over Tiffany's head to see a big, shadowy figure looming behind her in the dark museum.

The animal padded forward into the beams of light streaming down from the high windows. He was a big dog, slightly larger than Max, with a broad, muscular chest; a long, wide snout; and two black, drooping ears. His coat was sleek and shiny, a mix of mottled white and black that seemed almost blue in the afternoon light.

It was Spots, the Train Dog.

Tiffany slowly turned from the door to face Spots. She offered a wave of her small paw.

Spots went wide-eyed at the sight of her, backing away in horror. "No!" he howled. "How dare you!"

"How dare I what?" Tiffany asked.

The coonhound reared back on his hind legs, then landed with a hard thud. "You are not an official rail-system employee! Take off that hat this instant!"

Tiffany clutched the hat and pulled it down between her ears. "Never! I need it for my disguise!"

Spots stamped a front paw. "Those hats are for conductors only. All *you've* ever conducted is trouble."

"Lies!" Tiffany squealed, clearly outraged. "I once

conducted a whole herd of trains across the woods. I'm a master conductor!"

Growling, Spots lunged at the raccoon, but she was too quick, and his jaws clamped onto empty air as Tiffany scrambled away from the doors.

Barking madly, Spots gave chase, nearly slipping on the wooden floor, chasing Tiffany behind the display cases.

"Aah!" Rufus yelped, backing away from the door.

"He's gonna be so mad," Snow yowled.

"Gotta hide!" Regina barked, already bounding off on the path toward the town.

In a flash, the three frightened baby animals were gone.

Rocky backed away from the doors, tail tucked. "This is getting crazier by the minute. Maybe we should just try to find the wall on our own."

"Don't give up on Spots," Stripes said. "He's a good dog, I promise. He's just a little rough on the outside."

From inside the museum came a great crash, then a tinkling of glass shards across the floor. Max could see Tiffany's shadow as she leaped onto the cashier's desk, knocking the postcard holder into Spots's path.

"Maybe you can talk to him?" Gizmo asked Stripes. "We met a dog named Belle who was just as mad at everyone as Spots. But we spoke to her and calmed her down, and it turned out she was just lonely."

Stripes swished her bushy tail. "I can try."

142

Waddling over to the door, Stripes jumped up to press her paws against the glass. "Spots!" she cried. "It's me, your old friend Stripes! Please stop chasing Tiffany. Come speak to us!"

Over the sound of another pile of boxes collapsing to the ground, Tiffany's muffled voice screeched, "I told you, the name is Silver Bandit now!"

Spots howled.

Tiffany darted at full speed into the center of the room, the hat still on her head, as Spots lumbered out from behind a display.

Max and his friends backed away from the doors just as Tiffany leaped up. She landed on a narrow push bar and fidgeted with a lock on the inside.

A *thunk* sounded as the lock turned, and Tiffany forced open the door. Then she leaped over Max's head and landed on the concrete walkway behind him.

"He's your problem now!" the raccoon squealed.

And as Max, Rocky, Gizmo, and Stripes watched in surprise, the large, very angry Train Dog came howling toward the door, seconds away from barreling right into them.

CHAPTER 13

THE TRAIN DOG'S LAMENT

"Watch out!" Max barked at Rocky, Gizmo, and Stripes.

They leaped out of the way just in time.

Spots lowered his head as he ran toward the door, butting it open so hard that it slammed against the white brick wall. The wooden doorframe cracked, and one of the glass panes fell out, shattering on the pavement.

Huffing, the big Train Dog came to a stop among the animals, his giant head darting back and forth. "Where is she? Where is that little impostor?"

Tiffany sauntered out from behind Max on the concrete walkway, holding the conductor's hat in her hands.

"Fine, here, have it!" she squealed, looking up at Spots. "I don't need a disguise, anyway."

She tossed the hat into the air, and it landed squarely on Spots's snout.

Spots tossed his head to free it from the hat, then growled down at Tiffany. "That's not good enough, you varmint."

The big dog lunged at the little raccoon, his teeth bared. Max was about to leap forward to protect her, when Stripes let out a high-pitched, angry squeal.

"I have had enough!" the skunk shouted.

She waddled forward and shoved Tiffany aside with her wide body. Then she turned so that her backside was aimed at Spots's face. Hefting up her bushy, striped tail, she took aim.

"You calm down this minute, Spots," Stripes said, "or I will let loose right in your face. You'll never get the smell out without a human to help."

Spots's eyes went wide. Slowly, he backed away from the skunk. "You wouldn't," he said, his voice trembling. "Not to an old friend like me."

Stripes pressed her chest against the concrete, hefting her wide bottom up even higher. "You haven't been acting like a friend to anyone lately," she said. "But if you promise to behave like a nice dog, I won't make it so you smell for the rest of your days. Deal?"

Letting out a soft whine, Spots said, "Deal."

Slowly, Stripes lowered her tail, then turned to look up at her friend. Spots nuzzled his big snout against

Stripes's tiny black-and-white head. She leaned in, purring like a cat.

Tiffany flung herself on her back and scrabbled at the air with her little hands and feet. "Boring," she said. "I was really hoping *someone* would get squirted today."

"I think it's nice," Gizmo said. "I knew if Spots just listened to Stripes, then he would be willing to talk to us."

Spots jerked his head up and growled at Gizmo. "Who are these mutts?" he asked. "I didn't give them tickets to ride on my train."

Rocky darted forward to stand between Gizmo and the big coonhound. "Hey! Don't growl at her. And we're not mutts. We are pe-di-gree."

Slapping his tail angrily against the concrete path, Spots said, "Could have fooled me."

"Spots..." Stripes said, a warning in her voice.

The big dog lowered his head, but he did not stop glaring at Rocky.

Max padded forward, careful to avoid the broken glass from the door. Wagging his tail, he said, "I'm Max. These are my friends, Rocky and Gizmo. We didn't mean to bother you, sir. We just need some help."

Spots sniffed warily at Max. "What kind of help?"

Max sat down next to him. "We've been traveling west for days and days, following a path left for us. But that big storm washed away our trail, and we were chased by wolves. We'd heard that you might know of the place

146

where we're headed, so we were hoping you could tell us how to get there before the wolves find us again."

"And where exactly are you aiming to go?" Spots asked.

"To the big city of tents where all the humans have gone," Rocky chimed in.

"Yes," Gizmo barked. "The one behind the silver wall."

Spots's jaw went slack as he stared at Max and the others. Then, rearing back his head, he howled, long and loud and sad.

"No!" he cried. "I can't talk about that place. The memories are too awful!"

Stripes nuzzled the old dog's front leg. "Spots, they came all this way. To see *you*."

"You're the only one who can help us," Max said to Spots. "Help us find our people."

"I don't care," he barked. "Why did you all have to bother me? Why couldn't you have just stayed away?"

Shoving past Max, Spots leaped off the concrete walkway and bounded toward the big, old train cars on display behind the museum. He slipped past the gate, then jumped into the cab of the great iron locomotive.

Tiffany rolled onto all fours. "What a *whiner*," she said. "I almost fell asleep listening to him. I'm going to see what Chuck and those annoying babies are doing."

Retrieving the conductor's hat she'd tossed at Spots, Tiffany plopped it back on her head, then raced off toward the miniature town. "Don't forget you promised to tell everyone my adventures!" she squealed as she disappeared.

"I'm gonna guess that isn't the last we see of her," Rocky grumbled.

Gizmo looked up at Max, ears drooping. "Spots seems so upset. Should we talk to him?"

Max looked over at the big, ancient locomotive. Spots was still inside, pacing back and forth. "We don't really have a choice," he said. "We had a head start on Dolph, but between sleeping last night and spending all day here in town, he could catch up if we don't hurry."

Stripes paced in a circle. "I did spray the outskirts of town, you know. That should keep the wolves out."

"Maybe *other* wolves, lady," Rocky said. "But *this* pack of wolves is determined to track us down. If that smell didn't stop us, it sure won't stop them."

"Let's just hope the spray masked your scent, then," Stripes said.

"Come on," Max said. "Maybe Spots has cooled off."

It was late in the afternoon, and the golden twilight reflected off the glass lights and polished silver at the front of the train. The three dogs and the skunk walked single file toward the locomotive, with Max in the lead and Stripes taking up the rear. Inside the cabin, Spots pressed buttons with his snout and pushed levers with his paws. The evening light shimmered off his mottled fur.

"All aboard for DeQuincy," the old dog said softly. "Next stop, DeQuincy, where you can meet Spots the Train Dog, mascot of our world-famous train museum."

Memories came back to Max of Charlie and Emma. When they were younger and he was just a puppy, the kids both loved to wear overalls, tie kerchiefs around their necks, and put on caps like the one Tiffany wore. They played with toy train cars that ran on a wooden track, only those cars were brightly colored, with painted faces.

Gravel crunched beneath his paws as Max carefully approached the locomotive's cabin.

"I bet my pack leaders would have enjoyed seeing you at work," Max barked up at Spots.

Spots glared down at Max. He didn't say anything.

"They've always loved trains," Max went on, wagging his tail. "In fact, I think Emma wanted to be a conductor when she grew up."

The old coonhound's tail thumped against the metal floor. "Your human family loved trains, too?"

"Yup!" Max said. "I think a lot of kids do. I don't blame them. These machines are so neat." He cocked his head. "Do you mind if I jump up there with you?"

Spots bowed his head. "Come on aboard, partner."

Max glanced back at Gizmo, Rocky, and Stripes, then leaped up into the cabin of the big locomotive. The metal floor was cold beneath his paws, and there wasn't much room with the two big dogs inside. He looked around at the old iron machinery.

"Do you know how all this works?" Max asked.

"Of course!" Spots said. "I watched my pack leader show off the controls all the time." He aimed his snout at different parts of the panel. "Those things that look like little clocks show the water level in the boiler and the steam pressure. This lever here controls the brakes that make the train stop, and this one here tells it to go." Dropping down to the floor, he tapped on a little door. "That's where the coal goes to heat up the water and create steam. The steam makes the train run."

Max glanced outside to see Rocky, Gizmo, and Stripes watching silently from below, sitting on the gravel next to the locomotive's towering wheels.

"That's really neat," Max said again. "Is Dots a train dog, too?"

"Naw," Spots said, sniffing at the firebox door. "He was always a homebody, though he came to visit from time to time. He got along best with our lady pack leader, while me and the man were always best buddies."

Then Spots turned to glare at Max. "But like I told you, I *don't* want to talk about Dots and my pack leaders."

Max ducked his head. "I understand. I miss my family a whole lot, too. It's hard not knowing where they are."

Stamping his front paws, Spots barked, "But I *know* where they are! Behind that big, dumb wall. That's why Dots and I went there in the first place." Something changed in Spots's expression—his ears drooped and

150

he no longer looked angry, just sad. "And that's where I lost my brother."

From outside, Gizmo asked, "Can you tell us what happened?"

Spots glanced out the dirty front window, then met Max's eyes. "Your pack leaders really loved trains, like mine?"

"They did," Max said. "They *do*. And I really wish I could find them."

Sighing, Spots lay on his belly with his great head hanging out of the cabin. "Fine," he said. "I'll tell you what happened. But I ain't talking about it again, so listen close."

Max lay down next to Spots while Rocky, Gizmo, and Stripes huddled together on the gravel below the cabin.

"We were desperate after our pack leaders disappeared," Spots said. "For a while, we waited, hoping they'd come home. Dots kept the homestead tidy, and I made sure to keep the other animals from coming in and wrecking the museum." He growled. "Or at least I did—until Tiffany broke in today."

"Yeah, she's the worst," Rocky grumbled.

Spots went on. "I came here every day, keeping the place running, making it fun for the littler pets. But after a while, Dots and I just couldn't wait anymore. We knew our family had headed west, and we wanted to find them."

From below, Stripes sighed. "I tried to make you stay," she said. "I had a bad feeling."

"I know you did, darlin'," Spots said. "And I shoulda listened. But Dots and me, we were always stubborn fellows. No one could stop us. So one morning we set off in the direction of the setting sun, following the train tracks.

"The trip took days and days, and we were tired and thirsty. And then we saw the wall."

At the mention of the wall, Max craned his neck forward.

"It was big and metal," Spots continued. "An ominous thing if ever there was. But that didn't matter, because as we got close, we could smell 'em: humans, thousands and thousands of them, their scents strong and angry. We could hear 'em, too, their voices mingling in a muddled stew. We just knew our pack leaders were on the other side, trapped and waiting for us to rescue them. So we dug."

Groaning, Spots rose to his feet. He stretched and began to pace in the cramped cab.

"We tore at the dirt with our paws day and night, scarcely stopping to eat or drink, let alone sleep."

"You didn't *eat*?" Rocky whispered to himself. "That's crazy!"

"Then, one evening," Spots said, "we broke through. Between the two of us we'd moved aside all the earth in our way and made a tunnel underneath that stupid wall."

Spots rested his big head on his paws, despondent. "It should have been *me* that went through first, since it was my idea to go after our family. But Dots was so excited that he climbed under before I could even get a word out. I started to follow, and even saw a bit of the other side. And then—"

The old dog went silent.

"What happened?" Gizmo asked softly.

Spots sniffed. "I don't rightly know. A flash of white light flared up through the hole, then darkness, as a rush of something came to fill it in. I was so shocked I didn't know what to do except back out as quick as I could. Then, I heard my brother's muffled bark from the other side, telling me to run as far away from the wall as possible—and that he'd come after me when he could." Spots let out a long, low grumble. "I never saw him again. And I never will. He's gone."

"You think he died?" Rocky asked from outside. "You can't be sure of that, pal. He could be just fine."

Spots shook his head, sending his long ears flapping. "No, a brother knows when his brother is gone. There's an emptiness inside me, gnawing at my chest something fierce. There's a dog-shaped hole in my heart that only Dots could fill."

Max nuzzled Spots's neck. "That's a very sad story. But I don't believe the humans would kill your brother. Maybe you can take us to the wall and show us where you dug the tunnel, and—"

The old coonhound leaped up to all fours, landing with a heavy clang against the metal floor.

"No!" Spots howled, his voice echoing in the locomotive's cabin. "I'm never going back there. Never! You dogs can just get. The location of that deadly hole is going to the grave with me." Then Spots leaped up against the control panels once more, angrily nosing the levers.

Tiny clangs sounded behind Max; he turned to see Stripes climbing awkwardly up the narrow steps into the cabin. She waddled up to Spots and wrapped herself around his hind leg.

"I know it hurts, old friend," Stripes said. "But don't take it out on these nice dogs."

Spots let his front legs slide off the panel, and he landed on all fours. Sitting down, he looked at Max and Stripes in the cabin with him, and Rocky and Gizmo still sitting patiently outside.

"We want to be reunited with our families," Max said softly. "Just like you do with yours."

Spots's eyes went distant, watery. "Emma, you said her name was?" he asked. "She wanted to be a conductor, eh? Just like my pack leader."

"That's right." Max gave his head a gentle scratch. "She also wants to go to the moon, I think."

Spots barked a laugh. "Maybe she can grow up to do both." He fell silent, and the others sat still, waiting. All Max could hear was everyone's soft breathing, and the distant chirping of crickets.

Finally, Spots said, "I suppose it wouldn't be right to keep two little train enthusiasts from their dog friend."

Outside, Rocky jumped up, excited. "Does that mean you're gonna help us, pal?"

"I mean to say that I could be persuaded to help all of you." The old coonhound met Max's eyes, and it seemed like there was a new spark within him. "But first I'll need *you* to do something for *me*."

Max didn't hesitate. Wagging his tail, he gave his answer.

"Anything."

CHAPTER 14

ALL ABOARD

"I'm telling you, Tiffany, all I have to serve is water."

"I'm an international egg thief, and I drink only the finest of aged milks, sir. And the name is Silver Bandit!"

The barks and squeals of Chuck and the feisty little raccoon echoed over the tracks as Spots led Max, Rocky, Gizmo, and Stripes behind the old train cars to the miniature town.

Dusk had fallen, bringing a navy sky and shadows in the distant trees. The town was aglow with lamps in front of the doors and twinkling white lights strung up under the eaves.

"Look, I have lukewarm water, and I have cold water," Chuck told Tiffany as he backed toward the swinging doors of the saloon. "My final offer."

Tiffany flung her arms in the air, then flopped down on the porch. "After a long, hard day riding trains to herd up all the local bobcats, I don't want to drink *water*. I want milk!" She tugged at the brim of her striped conductor's cap. "I'll just stay here until you find me the good stuff."

Growling, Chuck nudged Tiffany with his snout. The raccoon went limp and refused to move.

"This varmint giving you trouble, Chuck?" Spots asked.

Chuck's tail immediately set to wagging. "Spots! Good to see you! Want to come in for a drink?"

"Naw," Spots said with a shake of his head. "I've just brought my new friends to town so they can help me get the train ready."

Max noticed Tiffany peeking at them from underneath her conductor's hat. As Chuck descended the saloon steps, she reached out and tugged his tail.

"Psst," she said. "Don't tell Spots I'm here. I think he's mad at me."

Chuck ignored her. Yanking his tail out of her hand, he circled Max, Rocky, and Gizmo, sniffing them.

Gizmo nudged Rocky with her head, then gestured to the fields beyond the tiny town. "Look, Rocky!" she said. "They're chasing fireflies."

Max looked over and saw the two mutt puppies and the snow-white kitten out in the dark grass, leaping up at the buzzing, glowing insects. They tumbled over one another, barking and meowing as they hunted their iridescent prey.

Stripes climbed up the steps of the building with the steeple and curled into a ball. "The kits love chasing the fire bugs. Even though they never like the taste when they actually catch one."

Gizmo gazed at them. "Aww. Puppies can be so cute," she said dreamily.

"Let's get to business," Spots said to Max. "You probably want to know why I brought you here."

"Of course," Max said.

"I'd like to know that, too," Chuck said in agreement.

"It's this little train." Spots pointed his snout at the red locomotive in front of the buildings. It was a quarter the size of the big one they'd just left behind. "See how the tracks loop in a big circle around the town? My pack leader used to put kids in it and let them ride around the loop, and sometimes I'd ride with them."

Spots turned toward the set of tracks that ran past the town, cutting through the museum's back lawn to eventually connect to the main rail line. "These tracks are for when we bring the miniature train into storage during the winter," he said. "Notice that even though the train is small, the tracks are the same size as the tracks here in town."

Max glanced at the loop of track that circled the

little town. Spots was right—even though the apple-red locomotive looked like a toy train, it was built to run on full-sized rails.

"What do you want to do?" Max asked.

Spots turned back to face Max. "It seems to me," he said, "that if we can find a way to connect these two tracks together, we could ride the small train on the *real* railroad track and take it all the way to the wall. Instead of walking for another week, you could get there in just a couple of days and save your paws the trouble."

Rocky's tail became a blur. "A leisurely train ride instead of more hiking in the hot sun? Sign us up!"

"That's wonderful!" Max said.

Spots ducked his head. "I'm glad you think so, 'cause that's my condition to assist you. You help me figure out how to make a real, live train trip, and I'll show you the hole we dug under the wall."

"You don't know how to make the train go?" Gizmo asked.

Lying down, Spots said, "The controls on the red locomotive are different from the real steam engine. I know there's a little lever to make it go, but it doesn't do anything when I push it now. And I was never able to figure out how to connect the circle of tracks here with the main line, even though I've seen my pack leader do it."

From the steps beneath the steeple, Stripes asked softly, "Are you sure this is what you want, Spots? If these dogs can get the train running and it goes right to that wall, they don't need you to come along. You said you never wanted to go back."

His brown eyes watery, the mottled old dog gazed forlornly down the main tracks. "This here is a train, Stripes," he said. "And a train needs a conductor. Dots always liked watching me ride the rails. This would be one last ride, in his honor."

Everyone fell silent, save for the distant barks and meows of the small animals, still playing in the field.

"We'll figure out how to make it run," Max said softly. "For your brother."

Spots's tail thumped against the ground. "Thank you."

Rising to his feet, Max looked down at his friends. "Rocky and Gizmo," he said, "we need to figure out how the little train gets power and how to turn it on. You two go investigate the locomotive, and I'll see how we can get it onto the main track."

"I'm on it, buddy!" Rocky said.

"Me, too!" Gizmo added.

The two small dogs darted off and jumped into the shiny red locomotive.

Max lowered his snout to sniff at the small train's tracks, then turned and ran toward the main line. As Spots and Stripes watched, he paced back and forth along the tracks, looking for clues.

He found what he was looking for in front of the

sheriff's station: a long piece of track with hinges so that it could swing like a door to connect to the main line.

"You find something?" Spots barked.

"I think so," Max said. "It looks like this part of the track can move."

An orange-and-white head popped up from the coal car behind the small locomotive—Chuck.

"Hey, that's right," the Cavalier Spaniel said. "I remember seeing that piece move. The people would go behind the sheriff's office and fiddle with something; then it would happen."

Max rounded the sheriff's station, and sure enough, there was a rusting metal lever beside the track, pointing up at the sky. Max figured it worked like a light switch: If he could make the lever point down, it would change the track's position.

Max jumped up and pressed down against the lever—but it didn't budge. His paws stinging, he tried again, but the thing felt stuck.

"Hey, Max!" Rocky barked.

Dropping back to the ground, Max saw Rocky and Gizmo racing around the jailhouse.

"We think we figured it out," Gizmo said as the two dogs skidded to a stop in the grass. "There's this little window next to the lever in the locomotive, and inside it are three colors: red, yellow, and green. There's an arrow pointed at the red area now, but if we can make it point to the green I bet we can make it go!"

Rocky spun in an excited circle. "On days like today, being smart sure comes in handy."

"Definitely," Max said. "Do we need coal to make it run, like the big locomotive?"

Rocky wagged his tail. "Nope! It runs on electricity."

The Dachshund darted around the other side of the sheriff's office. "Look here!" Rocky said.

Max found his friend jumping up and down in front of a yellow box attached to the back of the building. Two pipes were connected to the box, one that disappeared into the ground and another that snaked through the grass to a second box next to the track.

Max nosed open the door on the bigger box, its hinges squeaking in protest. Inside were lights, levers, and buttons.

"This looks familiar," Max said.

"Oh!" Gizmo said. "It's just like the one inside the museum, where Tiffany found all those striped caps."

Rocky jumped back onto his hind legs and rested his front paws on the bottom of the yellow box. His tail wagged slowly as he studied the labels.

"The light is on next to the button that says 'Automatic Lights,' so that must be why all the buildings are lit up," Rocky said. "This one here says 'Locomotive Charge.'" He pushed the button with his nose. "But nothing is happening."

"That's 'cause you have to turn it on inside first," squeaked a voice from above.

Max looked up to see Tiffany lounging atop the grocery store's roof.

"You know how to get the power on?" Max asked her. "Why are you only just now telling us?"

The raccoon straightened the conductor's cap between her ears. "I was hiding on the saloon porch, silly," she said. "I had to remain perfectly still so Spots didn't try to go after me again. But then I got bored, so I came to see what you dogs were yapping about."

Max looked over at the museum, then turned to peer at the smaller box next to the track. His mind raced.

"You getting any ideas, big guy?" Rocky asked.

"I think so," Max said, turning to Tiffany. "Silver Bandit, can we ask one more favor of you? Can you go inside the museum and flip every lever in that box where you found the hats?"

Waving her ringed tail, Tiffany asked, "What's in it for me?"

"You can come on the train ride with us," Gizmo said. "I know you climb aboard trains all the time, but this will be even more fun, because the train will be moving."

That got Tiffany's attention. Ears perked, she said, "I'm on it. Silver Bandit, away!" The small raccoon darted off the roof and disappeared toward the museum.

"All right," Max said, "Rocky, Gizmo, we need to pull down the lever that makes the track move. I couldn't do it by myself, but I bet if you found some rope, looped it

164

over the lever, and then had a bunch of dogs tug on it, we could do it."

"What if we got those puppies and the kitten to play tug-of-war with the rope?" Rocky said. "They'd just think it was a game."

"Oh, good idea!" Gizmo said, wiggling with excitement. "I'll go get them!"

She darted toward the little animals, who were still leaping in the overgrown field. Rocky started after her, then looked back at Max. "What'll you do, big guy?"

Max padded to the small yellow box next to the tracks and looked inside. As he'd suspected, there was a socket where something could be plugged in. "Looks like we need to get the train here before we can charge it up," he said. "That's a job for me and Spots."

Barking with glee, Gizmo leaped at the fireflies in the distance, tumbling with the puppies while the kitten watched. "Come on, Rocky!" she called.

"Gotta go," Rocky said as he bounded after her. "Good luck!"

Max ran back to the red locomotive. Chuck had disappeared inside his saloon, clattering away at something. Max carefully stepped over the tracks to stand behind the small train's caboose, then shoved it with his head.

It took all his strength, but ever so slowly the four train cars squeaked forward on the rails.

"What are you doing over there?" Spots barked from the grass.

Panting, Max stepped away from the caboose. "We need to move this train around the back of the tracks. Can you help?"

Grunting, the old dog got to his feet and joined Max behind the caboose. "I remember now," he said. "The engine needs to charge back there. How did you figure that out so fast? You work with trains like this before?"

Max considered telling the dog about Praxis. Instead, he wagged his tail and said, "Nope. My friends and I just learn things quickly. Ready to push?"

"Ready," Spots said.

Together, the two big dogs braced their legs against the ground and shoved the engine forward with their foreheads and shoulders. The wheels on the four train cars rolled a bit, squealing in protest. Slowly but surely, Max and Spots pushed the train along the bend in the tracks.

As they shoved, Max heard a chorus of barking as Gizmo, Rocky, the puppies, and the white kitten all raced back into town.

"We're going on a trip!" Regina barked.

"We'll be train dogs, just like Spots!" Rufus yipped.

Softly, the kitten meowed, "There's rope in my store, Gizmo. The dogs like to tug on it."

"Very good, Snow," Gizmo said. "That'll be a big help."

Still shoving the train, Max glanced over at the

miniature grocery store. All the smaller dogs huddled around the entrance while Snow went inside her little shop. Rocky sniffed at a plastic apple, licked it, and then scrunched his snout in disgust.

As they pushed the train past the saloon, a click echoed across the museum's back lawn, and suddenly, festive music blared overhead. Startled, Stripes jumped off the white building's steps. Chuck stuck his head out of the saloon, his long ears flopping.

"What's going on?" the Cavalier Spaniel bellowed.

Panting, Max and Spots stared back at the museum, just as all the lights in the building came on. Bright floodlights glinted off the windows of the big train cars.

"It's Tiffany," Max said. "She's getting the power on for us." Noticing Chuck, he asked, "What are you doing in there?"

"Wait just a sec and I'll show you." The Cavalier Spaniel darted back inside the saloon and reappeared a moment later dragging a small sack of kibble. Letting it plop against the porch, he wagged his tail. "Supplies for the trip!"

"Great idea," Max said.

Hearing a commotion, he looked around the saloon to see Rocky, Gizmo, and their young charges running to the back of the sheriff's office. "Maybe you can help them tug that lever," Max said to Chuck. "The more of you yanking on the rope, the easier it will be to pull down."

"Will do!"

Chuck raced after the other dogs, as Max and Spots turned back to the little train. It took all their strength, but Max and Spots finally got the red locomotive into position next to the small yellow box.

"What now?" Spots asked, panting from the effort of moving the train. He let his tongue hang out and shook his head back and forth.

Max sniffed at the side of the red locomotive and saw a little door. He nosed it open and found a two-pronged plug, just like those on the appliances in his farmhouse's kitchen. Usually, those plugs were on cords so that they could reach the electrical sockets—Max carefully took up the plug in his jaws and pulled. Sure enough, a black cord emerged.

"How did you know to do that?" Spots asked, bewildered. "I never would have figured that out."

Max carefully plugged the pronged cord into the sockets on the small yellow box. It fit perfectly. "Just a lucky guess."

"Huh," Spots said. "Sure was."

The bigger box at the back of the grocery store hummed with electricity now. As Max approached, he heard the loud screech of metal against metal.

"Tug!" Gizmo called out. "Pull the rope as hard as you can! Almost there!"

A loud thunk sounded, and the cat and dogs cheered—

the hinged piece of track must have connected to the main line.

Spots padded over to Max's side. "We're doing it," he said. "I can't believe it, but we're doing it."

Max wagged his tail. "Believe it, Spots. You're going to ride the rails again."

Yipping and meowing, Rocky, Gizmo, Chuck, the puppies, and the kitten practically tripped over one another as they raced to join Max and Spots. Stripes waddled toward them, too, and with a thud, Tiffany landed heavily on the grocery store's roof.

"What are you waiting for?" the little raccoon squealed. "I got the power on, didn't I?"

"You sure did," Max said. "Great job, Silver Bandit. Now let's get this train running."

As all the animals watched, Max pressed his nose against the button labeled LOCOMOTIVE CHARGE. The front lights on the locomotive lit up, and the console inside glowed red and green.

"We did it!" Rocky said as he ran in an excited circle. "No more walking for me!"

"No, sir, no walking necessary," Spots said with a slobbery grin. "On my train, everyone gets to relax in the lap of luxury."

Max, Rocky, and Gizmo watched the controls inside the small red locomotive as the arrow slowly moved from red to green. Yipping and squealing with glee, the other animals helped Chuck drag his bag of kibble to the train and shove it into the coal car. The Cavalier Spaniel, the puppies, and the kitten climbed into the caboose, while Tiffany leaped onto the kibble bag.

Sighing, Stripes climbed up to sit next to the raccoon. "I suppose I should come along to help look after the little ones," said the skunk as she settled in for the ride, wrapping her striped tail around herself.

Spots sat next to Max, watching the power meter. When the arrow finally clicked all the way into the green zone, he sniffed and called, "All aboard!"

"You got it, Conductor," Max said.

Max carefully pulled the plug from the box, and its cord zipped back inside the locomotive. That done, he leaped up into the boxcar between the coal car and the caboose. Rocky and Gizmo climbed in as well, tucking themselves in on either side of him.

Awkwardly, Spots climbed inside the locomotive car, just barely managing to fit. Before he could press the lever to start the train moving forward, though, Tiffany jumped to her feet. "Wait!"

Spots growled and looked back at her. "What is it?"

Removing the striped cap from her head, she climbed through the locomotive's back window, plopped the cap on Spots's head, and then returned to her seat next to Stripes.

"There," she said. "Now we're ready."

Spots wagged his tail and looked ahead once more. "Here we go!"

With his snout, Spots shoved the lever on the control panel into the on position.

And the train began to chug forward.

It went at a crawl at first, then quickly gained speed as the locomotive pulled the cars along the tracks that looped between the grocery store and the sheriff's station. Instead of continuing on in a big circle, though, the small train followed the long length of movable track, which, thanks to Rocky, Gizmo, and the other small animals, was now connected to the main line. Someone yelled, "Wahoo!"

Music blared as they zipped behind the museum, past the big locomotive and caboose. Then, the melody faded away as the little train raced through the darkness. A breeze rose, and all the dogs hung their heads out of the cars, letting the cool wind brush through their fur and blow back their ears. The town rushed by in a blur as they chugged westward, toward the mysterious wall and their human families.

Spots bit onto a loop of rope that hung from the locomotive's ceiling, and the pipes on top tooted long and loud.

Barking in happiness, the old dog called out into the night, "This is for you, Dots!"

CHAPTER 15

OASIS

Max lay on his side in the bottom of the boxcar. Rocky and Gizmo were curled up together next to his belly. The wooden floor bumped and vibrated as the train rushed along the track, passing empty factories and thick woodland.

It was nighttime now, and the sky was free of clouds. The moon was full and round, glowing like a beacon, and the dark expanse was dotted with thousands of twinkling stars. Images of Madame Curie's black, white-flecked coat floated through Max's mind.

Up front, in the locomotive, Spots hummed a melancholy tune, barely audible over the rumble of the wheels. Every now and then Tiffany would try to join in, but her words were nonsense, and Stripes would shush her so that they could listen to Spots's sad melody.

In the caboose, Max could hear the puppies and kitten pacing back and forth.

"We're gonna get in so much trouble when Mama finds out," Rufus whimpered.

"Naw, Rufus," Regina said. "You ain't gonna tell, are you, Chuck?"

"This ride will be our secret," the Cavalier Spaniel assured her.

Snow said, "I keep seeing eyes glowing in the trees. What do you suppose is out there?"

From the coal car, Tiffany called, "Bears, mostly. But no need to worry about them. They're too busy trying to dam the rivers to create pools where they can lay their eggs."

From Max's side, Rocky groaned. Peeking up over the edge of the boxcar, he sniffed at Tiffany.

"Bears don't swim," he told her. "And they sure don't lay eggs."

Tiffany waved a paw at him. "Naw, they definitely do," she insisted. "The lakes around here are positively over-flowing with bear eggs. They're as big as boulders, and the baby bears pop out full-grown and ready to swim!"

Furious at Tiffany's outright lies, Rocky bared his teeth and prepared to bark at her. Gizmo nipped him on the heel first.

"Be nice," she said.

"Yeah, yeah," Rocky said as he dropped back into the boxcar and cuddled up next to Max and Gizmo.

"You should pay attention to my stories, Rocky," Tiffany taunted. "You have to remember all the details so you can tell everyone—just like you promised."

"Oh, we will," Gizmo assured her with a wag of her tail. "We're just going to be very, very quiet now, so we can think about everything you've said."

"Good," the raccoon said, curling up on the bag of kibble.

As the moon rose higher into the sky, the nervous barks and idle chatter of the animals gave way to soft snores as, one by one, they drifted off to sleep. Max's own eyes were heavy, leaden things that he could no longer keep open, and his view of the vast night sky slowly turned into a sliver.

"Hey, Max?" Gizmo asked.

Max forced his eyes open. Lifting his head from the dusty floor, he looked at the fluffy terrier. Rocky was asleep next to her, his chest rising and falling slowly as he wheezed through his snout.

"Yeah?" Max asked her.

Lifting up a back paw, Gizmo scratched at the green collar around her neck. "Do you suppose Dr. Lynn has found a cure yet?"

Max tilted his head. "I don't know," he said. "She said she'd come for us when she did, so I think she must still be working on it."

Gizmo's ears fell. "Oh."

"Are you all right?" Max asked her.

"I don't know," Gizmo said. "I'm a little afraid of what we'll find at the wall. Those horses and the mice, they all said the humans may not want us around anymore." She ducked her head. "Now we're heading toward a big metal wall that shocks animals, and when one dog got past it he disappeared."

"You don't need to worry," Max said. "You're the most courageous dog I know. If anyone can handle what's at the end of the line, it's you."

"I suppose so," Gizmo said. "I don't usually get this scared."

Max licked her between the ears. "As long as you, me, and Rocky are together, we'll be just fine."

At that, Gizmo whispered, "You and me and Rocky. Family."

"That's right," Max said, and after a few moments, the two of them drifted off to sleep.

Max was atop the silver wall.

He was so high that clouds swirled around him, enveloping him in cool, foggy mist. Above, the sun seemed to fill the entire sky. The steel beneath his paws was as cold as ice, and the pads of his feet tingled with each step. Electricity hummed within the wall, but it did not sting him.

Max paced back and forth uncertainly. On one side

of the wall was an endless expanse of desert, with tents of all shapes and sizes as far as he could see—just as had been shown on the mall television. There were small green pup tents that were little more than tarps and string, and big gray domes with shiny barbecue grills out front. There were cars and trailers and RVs.

Canvas tent flaps fluttered in the dry breeze. Tangled, dead weeds rolled through the dusty aisles between the makeshift shelters. Hot dogs left out on a grill had burned to ash. A lone radio played a tinny, cheerful tune that filled the empty streets.

The endless dark cloud that had chased Max for so long was on the other side of the wall. It flowed around storm-damaged houses and overgrown trees, spilling into trash-filled gorges. From the darkness, animal voices brayed and barked, howled and mewed.

This is our world now, the animal voices growled. *Join us in the wild. Let us run free.*

But other animals howled, *We miss our human families. Bring them home.*

The voices rose louder and louder in a din of angry shouts, pleading cries, and howls of fear.

Max dropped to his belly. "Be quiet," he barked, his eyes shut tight. "Please, be quiet!"

Everything went silent.

And Max awoke.

Max's eyes felt dry and itchy. His throat was parched; his fur and skin were baking beneath the hot sun.

He was alone in the boxcar.

And the train stood still.

Panic snapped him awake, and Max sat up, looking for his friends. A bright sun glared—night had come and gone while Max slept. In the daylight, he saw that they weren't in the fields and forests of Louisiana anymore.

All around him were vast, dusty yellow plains, dotted with small, blackened bushes. The train track cut through the empty expanse, disappearing into the horizon. A fence made of small scraps of wood and barbed wire lined either side of the track, held crudely in place by rocks.

A few wispy, feathery clouds floated in the pale blue sky, but they did nothing to shield Max from the sun. This landscape was different from the desert in his dreams. Here, he could see distant towers of rock, but not a single glimpse of silver. Still, somehow it felt like the same place.

Dr. Lynn's beacons might have blown away in the hurricane, but his dreams had taken Max here all the same.

The end of his journey was near.

Laughing, happy barks came from Max's right, and he turned to see all the animals from the train. They had settled just past a trampled-down fence post, lounging in the shade beneath two slender trees that grew on the banks of a pond. Grass and buttery-yellow weeds sprouted on the shores of the shallow pool.

Max jumped out of the boxcar, landing heavily on the hard-packed earth. He made his way past the fence to join the others.

"All right, citizens," Chuck said. On the opposite side of the pond, the Cavalier Spaniel paced back and forth in front of the white kitten and the two mutt puppies, who sat in a straight row. "Since there are no humans around to teach you, I think it's high time you learned how to fetch."

"We *know* how to fetch," Regina said.

Chuck stopped pacing and touched his nose to the puppy's. "You know how to do it on dry land," he said. "But how about in the water?"

"Ooh!" she yipped, her whole body squiggling with glee.

"I don't know if Mama wants us to get wet," Rufus said.

"I *know* mine doesn't," Snow yowled.

Max saw Rocky and Gizmo cuddled together on a patch of grass at the base of one tree, next to the open bag of kibble. Under the other tree, Spots and Stripes lay side by side, watching Chuck's training session.

Gizmo noticed Max first. She leaped up and raced to him. "Good morning!"

"Morning," Max replied. "Why did we stop? Is everything all right?"

"Oh, yes," Gizmo said, wagging her tail. "It was so hot, and we were all so thirsty. When we saw this little pond we decided to stop and relax in the shade. We tried to wake you, but you were deep asleep."

"I must have been," Max said as he padded to the edge of the pond. "Are you feeling better than last night?"

"What's that?" Rocky asked as he left the shade to join them. "You didn't feel good, Gizmo?"

"Oh," Gizmo said. "No, I'm fine. You should drink and eat, Max. I bet you're starving."

Max ducked his whole head into the shallow pool, then pulled up with a splash. The cool water was refreshing against his dry fur. "Nice!" He lapped at the water dripping around his jaws, then lowered his head to drink his fill.

On the other side of the pond, Chuck picked up a branch with his jaws, spun in a wild circle, and then let the branch fly loose. It flew through the air and landed with a small splash in the center of the pond, sending out ripples.

"Go get it!" Chuck howled.

Regina bounded into the water without hesitation, her head high as she paddled her tiny legs. Her brother made it to the water's edge, then looked warily over at Spots and Stripes.

"What are you waiting for, son?" Spots asked.

"My mama..." he said.

Stripes swished her tail. "It'll be all right, Rufus. If she finds out, I'll take full responsibility."

Above the old dog and the skunk, nestled in the

crook of the tree, was Tiffany. "You already left town and came this far," she told the puppy. "Dive in! That's what the Silver Bandit would do!"

From the pond, the girl mutt panted, "Almost got it!"

That was all the convincing Rufus needed. He dove in, yipped once, and then swam after his sister.

Tiffany tossed a bundle of leaves down at the kitten. "What about you? You afraid, too?"

The kitten glared at Tiffany, then slowly stalked to the water's edge. She pawed once, twice at the ripples, hissed, and then backed away.

"They're so funny, those pups," Rocky said.

Gizmo wagged her tail. "When I was that little, swimming seemed like the bravest, most dangerous thing you could do. I couldn't wait!"

"Not me," Rocky said. "If you'd have told me that I'd be diving into pools, rivers, sewers, and oceans, I never would've left my crate at Vet's house."

Max wagged his tail at his two friends. "I'd say we're all expert water dogs by now."

While the puppies, kitten, and Chuck continued to play, Max went to the bag of kibble beneath the tree and ate his fill. With his belly content and his body rested, Max felt renewed with purpose. He needed to reach that wall and find his pack leaders and Dr. Lynn—before Dolph caught up with them once more. He'd almost forgotten about the wolves, but they were as much of a threat as ever.

"How do, Max?" Stripes asked as Max came to lie next to her and Spots.

"I'm thankful," he said. "I'm glad we got to ride the train and rest, instead of walking through the night."

Spots gazed up at the apple-red train, which gleamed in the bright morning light. "For a toy, it's proved a sturdy locomotive," the old coonhound said. "I prefer the smells and sounds of the steam engine my pack leader drove, but I suppose electricity works just as well."

"Speaking of electricity," Max said, "I wanted to ask you more about the wall."

"Like what?" Spots asked.

"Is it just a wall in the middle of the desert?" Max asked. "Are there buildings around it? Or other obstacles?"

Spots rested his head on his paws. "Well, there are three sections you have to look out for. First thing is one of those chain-link fences topped with sharp wire, like the wire on the fence by the track here. That's easy enough to get under.

"After that is a stretch of road leading up to the real barricade, the metal one. The wall is as high as three humans standing on each other's shoulders, and it disappears under the ground, too. It took Dots and me days to dig under it—often we'd have to stop and hide when the gate on the chain fence opened to allow trucks to roll through."

"There were humans there, then?" Max asked. "Were they friendly?"

182

Spots looked away from Max for a moment before responding. "I was excited to see them, I admit," he said. "But Dots said those trucks reminded him of when the men in green uniforms came through town and made all the people leave. He didn't trust them, so we hid behind some trees until they went away.

"Those trucks came back regular, though," he continued, "sure as the sun rises and sets."

Max hadn't seen the trucks that had come to take away the humans, but he'd heard stories from other animals. Some of the people in the trucks had worn uniforms and black masks; others, baggy white suits with hoods. He shivered, hoping none of those people had forced his own pack leaders out of their beds and into the back of vehicles headed toward this wall.

Softly, Spots went on. "When the trucks came to drive on the stretch of land between the fence and the wall, we hid. After the wall parted and they went inside, or when the fence opened so they could ride into the desert, we were safe to dig. Dots was so excited when we made it all the way under the wall that he dove right in and out the other side. I barely got a glimpse of those tents on the far side before that light glared, and the hole caved in. Now..." He whimpered. "Now Dots is gone forever."

Stripes scooted in close to the old dog's side. "Whether Dots is gone forever or if he's just gone for now," she said, "you still have me, Spots."

"I know I do," he replied, then licked her small head. "You're family just as much as he was."

Max wanted to ask more, but he could tell Spots was too worn out with sadness to say anything else. That they'd convinced the old Train Dog to bring them this far was a miracle.

Max let the small animals play for a bit longer before he announced that they needed to continue on. Max, Chuck, and Spots helped drag the bag of kibble back to the train while the others climbed into the cars. At Tiffany's suggestion, the puppies shook themselves free of water next to Snow—who yowled and zipped ahead.

With everyone situated, Spots took his place in the locomotive and barked, "All aboard!"

"Yes, Conductor!" Stripes answered.

Satisfied, Spots nosed the lever. The train jolted, and squeals rose as the wheels began to move them forward. The wooden boxcar rumbled as the train gained speed.

Closing his eyes, Max let the breeze from the moving train pick up his ears and ease the heat from the desert sun. But the wind lasted for only a few moments before his floppy ears fell down on either side of his head. The rumbling lessened to a jostle, and the locomotive's engine wheezed. Then the train came to a slow, gentle stop not far from where they'd started.

"What's going on up there?" Rocky barked. "Give us some more juice!"

"I keep pressing the throttle, but nothing is happening," Spots said. "If this happened on the big locomotive, we'd shove in some more coal."

"What does that mean?" Gizmo asked.

"I think," Spots said, "it means we're out of electricity. We're stranded."

CHAPTER 16

DESERT TOWN

Yelps and mews of distress rose from the boxcar behind Max.

"I want my mom!" the kitten yowled.

The little raccoon appeared out of nowhere, like the masked bandit she claimed to be. Climbing through the locomotive's back window, she leaped up to the lever that made the train run, shoved it forward, and then squealed with anger when nothing happened. Meanwhile, Max jumped out of the boxcar, landing beside the tracks. Rocky and Gizmo plopped out behind him, and the three dogs peered into the locomotive.

Max saw right away that Spots was correct: The arrow on the control panel had dropped all the way out of the green part of the gauge and back into the red.

The train no longer had any power.

"What are we gonna do?" Rocky said.

"We have to walk the rest of the way," Max said, lowering his head. "There's no other option. We can't stay here, in the middle of nowhere."

Tiffany climbed atop the roof of the red locomotive and splayed onto her back, letting the sun warm her gray belly. "You can't expect me to walk all the way to some wall," she said. "I'm the Silver Bandit! I have to save my strength."

Stripes peeked her black-and-white head over the edge of the coal cart. "She's right," the skunk said. "It was one thing when we had a train to carry us, but these kits' mothers are going to worry if we don't get back soon."

Gizmo spun in a circle next to Max. "Maybe there's some way we can charge it up again," she said. "Another little power box, like back at the tiny town."

Max glanced around. Save for the pond shaded by the two trees, there was nothing for miles but endless, tan desert. A dry breeze rose, kicking up dust, and Max sneezed.

Sighing, Spots dropped down out of the locomotive. "I'm afraid this is as far as the train can take us," he said. "If it were a proper steam engine, we could just load up more coal and get her running again. But it's not."

"Could you come with us?" Max asked. "To show us where to go?"

Spots sat on the gravel next to the track, then raised a back leg to scratch behind his ear. "Afraid I can't," he said. "I'm too old to go hiking all the way there again, then all the way back to DeQuincy. I think it's best I lead these young'uns home."

Gizmo padded toward the old coonhound and nuzzled his side. "We understand. Thanks for coming as far as you did."

Tail thumping, Spots said, "It was my pleasure, little terrier. Since I lost Dots, I'd forgotten what it was like to enjoy myself. It was a fitting final ride."

Gravel crunched, and Max watched as the puppies and kitten trotted obediently into a line behind Chuck.

"What's going on, Conductor?" Chuck asked as he and his three tiny followers joined the group. "Are we going back home?"

"That we are," Spots said. "But not on the train. We have a bit of a walk ahead of us."

"Oh, no," Rufus yipped. "What about the bears in the woods? And the bobcats!"

"What will we eat?" his sister asked. "What will we drink?"

Whimpering, the small animals huddled together. "Buck up, citizens," Chuck barked. "I'm sure Spots has a plan. Right, Spots?"

Spots licked his jaws. "To be honest, not really. I was just planning on following the tracks."

"Oh, no!" Rufus howled. "We're doomed!"

In a flash of silver, Tiffany leaped off the top of the locomotive and landed with a crunch atop the remaining kibble in the coal car. She glared down at the frightened little animals.

"What a bunch of whiny babies," she scolded, pinching her nose in disgust. "I'm barely older than any of you, and you don't see me being all afraid, do you?"

"But what about the things in the woods?" Snow asked, her white fur standing on end.

"You have me with you," Stripes said. "All any of those scary animals need to see is *this*"—she hopped in a circle and hefted up her backside and tail—"and they'll run away if they know what's good for them."

"You sure?" Regina asked.

Chuck licked her forehead. "We're positive, little lady. And me and Spots will bark and growl at anyone that tries to hurt you."

"You three are lucky," Rocky said to the puppies and kitten. "You have two guard dogs traveling with you, and a skunk and a Silver Bandit, too!"

Gizmo wagged her tail. "It'll be fun," she said. "Just imagine how jealous the other puppies and kittens will be when you tell them about your train ride."

"Yeah!" Regina barked, leaping onto her brother. "When do we start?"

Groaning, Spots climbed onto all fours, towering above everyone except Max. "In just a few moments, pup," he said. "Everyone gather behind the caboose and wait for me. I need to speak to Max, Rocky, and Gizmo before they head off."

Chuck jumped up, his kerchief fluttering in the breeze. "You got it, Conductor. Citizens, follow me!"

Taking the lead, the long-eared Cavalier Spaniel led the kitten and puppies toward the back of the train.

"Bye, Gizmo!" Regina barked. "Bye, Rocky!"

Gizmo wagged her tail. "Bye! Be good!"

Stripes plopped out of the coal car and waddled up to Max, Rocky, and Gizmo. "Thank you for getting Spots out of his funk," she said with a nod of her small black-and-white head. "I feared my old friend was gone for good."

Spots whimpered and looked away.

Rocky licked the skunk, then stepped back with his nose twitching. "It was our pleasure." Turning so that she couldn't see, he hung out his tongue and forced a sneeze to get rid of her odor.

"We would never have found Spots if it weren't for you," Max told Stripes. "Be careful on the way home."

"You don't need to worry about us," the skunk said. "Good luck finding your people, even if humans aren't always kind to animals like me."

"Thank you," Max said. "We appreciate it."

Tiffany leaped down to join them, landing right next to Stripes. "Hey, don't let her take all the credit," the raccoon bandit said. "I helped a lot, too!" Pointing a finger at Max, she added, "And don't you forget, you promised to tell everyone you meet about me!"

"We won't forget, Silver Bandit," Gizmo said.

"Trust me," Rocky added, "it'd be hard to forget you."

Tiffany rubbed her hands together. "Of course. See you later!"

With her striped tail held high, the little raccoon raced away, disappearing behind the red caboose. Stripes offered the four dogs a friendly purr before joining the rest of the DeQuincy animals to wait for Spots.

"If good-byes are done," Spots said, already walking away, "kindly follow me."

Spots led Max, Rocky, and Gizmo to the front of the locomotive. He stood in the center of the tracks, on a wooden tie half buried beneath rocks and weeds.

His snout aimed at the horizon, the old spotted dog said, "I'd say you have a day or so left to walk before you reach the chain-link fence that runs across the track. That is, assuming you take the time to rest at night."

Max followed Spots's gaze. The tracks seemed to go on forever through the desert, disappearing in a haze of heat on the horizon. Even though they'd just had their fill of water, Max felt parched under the boiling sun.

Sensing Max's concern, Spots said, "Don't worry. It may not seem like it now, but there will be more places to drink along the way."

"That's good," Rocky said. "I'm thirsty already."

"When we reach the chain-link fence, is that where we should dig?" Max asked, squinting into the sun.

"No," Spots said. "Once you reach that fence, you'll

head south until you find two big boulders next to a road. On the southern side of the boulders, behind some bushes, is where we dug under the chain-link fence.

"After that, it's a straight shot to where we dug the tunnel under the metal wall. Just remember to keep an ear out for trucks. When you hear them, you should run south along the wall to an old, withered tree and hide. Once the trucks have gone by, it'll be safe to dig some more."

"Thank you," Max said. "We appreciate everything you've done for us."

"And even though you think he's gone," Gizmo said to the coonhound, "we'll look for Dots once we're there. Won't we, Max?"

"Absolutely," Max said.

Spots gazed longingly one last time at the shiny red locomotive. "I don't think you'll find anything," he said softly. "But...I appreciate that you'll look anyway."

"Stay safe, Train Dog!" Rocky said.

"You be safe, too," Spots said.

And then the old dog ran off behind the caboose to join the ragtag group from DeQuincy and lead them home.

Hours later, Max walked slowly down the center of the abandoned tracks, Rocky and Gizmo at either side. His head ached, and his tongue hung free from his jaws as he panted, desperate to ease the dryness in his throat. His skin felt as if it was roasting to a crisp.

The desert heat was relentless. It wouldn't have been so bad if there had been some shade, but the landscape was empty of trees or buildings.

Rocky and Gizmo weren't faring much better. Neither of them spoke as they slogged along, not even when they saw a scorpion clatter out from beneath the tracks, its sharp tail raised as it darted away.

By midafternoon, Max felt ready to collapse. Even thoughts of Dr. Lynn and his family—and Dolph—were barely enough to keep him going. But just as he was about to sink down beside the tracks, he saw a mobile home off to the south.

Like all the trailer homes he'd seen, it was long and narrow, with corrugated metal roofing. It had once been white, but time had tinged its corners yellow, and dust coated its windows. Red rust had eaten through the roof's overhang, leaving a jagged hole.

Behind the trailer, cordoned off by fencing, were mounds of junk, mostly sheets of metal but also stacks of tires and steel tire rims. Out front, on either side of a potted cactus, were two armchairs. They were faded brown, the torn upholstery revealing springs and foam inside. Nearby, a tall windmill creaked back and forth in the gentle breeze.

There was clearly no one home, but that wasn't important. It was a sign of civilization.

Lifting his head, Max stared down the tracks. Through the hazy veil of heat he could see buildings not too far ahead. A town!

"Guys," Max said, his voice rough from lack of water. "Look."

Raising her head, Gizmo saw the town, too. "Do you think we can rest, Max?" she said. "I know Dolph is still out there, and you're eager to reach the wall, but…"

Rocky groaned. "I hope there's food, buddy. It's so hot that I don't want to eat, but my stomach is telling me I need to."

Max licked his exhausted friends one at a time. "Let's see what we can find."

The town was built on the southern side of the tracks. Past the station platform was a main street made of packed dirt. The buildings there were almost like a modern, bigger version of the small town back at the train museum. The largest building was a grocery store the size of a single-story house. Above its porch, a wooden sign read WALTER CHANG'S MARKET. Next to the market was a tower made up of metal beams supporting a large barrel. Painted on the barrel were the words CITY OF PERFECTION.

It wasn't much of a city, Max thought as he led his friends to the market. There were a few other wooden buildings, and some more trailer homes, but everything was in a state of disrepair. Holes in walls were patched with metal sheets, and rusty trucks without wheels or seats were parked outside ramshackle shacks.

Max padded up the dirty steps of the market, the dry wood creaking beneath his paws. The shaded porch was a welcome escape from the sun, though it was still achingly hot. On one side of the market's front door, a rocking chair sat beneath a horned skull that was mounted on the wall. On the other side of the door was a big white box with a sign that read ICE.

"Ohhh," Rocky moaned. "Ice. Let's open it and see if there's any inside."

Max remembered being in the kitchen of his old farm home, watching his pack leaders licking red and orange Popsicles from the freezer. Beads of colored water would drip down their hands as they gave Max a taste. He thought of the times the farmhands had given him an ice cube to play with. Suddenly, frozen water became all he could think of.

With his snout, Max hefted up the big white icebox's metal lid, which slammed back against the wooden wall with a heavy clang. Max stuck his head over the box's edge.

And found it to be full to the brim with water, plastic bags floating on the surface.

Max figured that whatever power had kept the machine full of ice had probably failed only recently.

Not that it mattered. He stuck his head into the icebox, shuffled aside some of the plastic bags with his snout, and began to lap up great mouthfuls of water. It was lukewarm and tasted strange, but he didn't care.

"What's inside?" Gizmo asked.

Max finally pulled his head free, panting. "Water," he said, wagging his tail. "A whole big tub full of water."

Max shoved the rocking chair across the porch to the ice chest, and Rocky and Gizmo hopped up so that they, too, could reach the giant water dish. Their thirst slaked, they turned their attention to the market.

The door swung open on hinges, so they didn't have to fuss with doorknobs or locks. Inside, the three dogs sniffed at the dusty wooden floor, trying to pick up the scent of food.

The store was dark. Most of the windows had been boarded up, and barely any light streamed in. But it was enough to see by.

Three tall shelves formed aisles between the checkout counter and the back wall. Cans of food and bags of flour lined some shelves, while others held tools like hammers and screwdrivers. The market was stocked with all sorts of strange things, from postcards showing the water tower to bows and arrows displayed on the wall.

What it *didn't* have was kibble.

"Hey," Rocky said, huffing at some people snacks hanging from pegs. "These smell like meat."

Max joined Rocky at the end of the aisle. The packages were filled with brown strips that looked like tree bark but smelled of smoked meat. Printed on them were the words BEEF JERKY.

"Did you find something?" Gizmo asked.

"Let's see," Max said.

He yanked down several of the packages with his teeth, then wrenched one open with his incisors. Carefully he picked up one of the dried strips and started to chew. And chew.

The flavor was tremendous—sweet and smoky and beefy. Though it was the texture of leather, he quite liked having something to bite into, and he found himself gobbling up one strip, then another, and another.

Rocky moaned in ecstasy as he rolled onto his belly, a piece of jerky in his jaws. "This is the best thing I've ever eaten!" he said. "And I've eaten…a lot of things!" Gizmo lay next to him and nodded in agreement, gnawing on her own piece, practically purring with delight.

It was still daylight outside, but Max was so exhausted from the heat, and so thrilled to have found this market with its water and jerky, that he decided they'd traveled enough for the day. The wall wasn't going anywhere. And the wolves—

Outside, the front porch creaked.

Max had been so busy chewing that for a moment he wondered if he'd just imagined the noise.

But the wooden boards on the porch groaned once more. Something was outside.

Rocky and Gizmo heard it, too. Jerky still clenched in their jaws, they went still, their ears alert. Max swallowed his last bite, his eyes at the bottom of the swinging door. A shadowy, four-legged creature paced in front, huffing. Max sniffed, his heart pounding, wondering if somehow Dolph had caught up with them.

The musk he smelled was wild and furry. It was similar to wolf but different, smoky and not as sour.

"What is that?" Rocky whispered. "It doesn't smell like wolves."

Max shushed him as he carefully backed behind the checkout counter. Leaving the scraps of their meal, Rocky and Gizmo followed him into the shadows.

Slowly, the swinging door creaked open, letting in harsh, yellow daylight. The huffing creature stood in the doorway, its shadow doglike.

No, Max realized, the animal was definitely not a wolf.

It was worse.

CHAPTER 17

COYOTE COUNTRY

Light from the grimy window illuminated the creature. Its head was shaped like a wolf's, with large ears that rose to a point. They would have looked funny if not for the animal's bared fangs and the devious glare in its yellow eyes.

The animal stepped all the way into the store, letting the door swing shut behind it. It moved slowly and carefully toward the checkout counter, following Max, Rocky, and Gizmo's scent.

Its coat was tawny brown, shaggy and wild, with ruddier fur on its ankles and the sides of its snout. Its bushy, black-tipped tail was alert, and its body was slender and taut with muscle.

A coyote.

Max had heard stories of wild coyotes. They had no qualms about sneaking into yards to steal away livestock and even small dogs and cats. They were clever, brazen creatures, and their high-pitched howls struck fear into anyone that heard them.

And now a coyote was right here, feet away from Max and his two snack-sized friends.

"Hello?" Gizmo asked tentatively, leaving Max's side and stepping out from behind the counter.

Max nipped at her tail, trying to force her back into hiding, but she spun around and swatted at his snout.

"It's just one animal," she whispered to Max. "Maybe we can convince her we're friendly."

"Gizmo, wait, she's a—"

But the terrier darted away.

The coyote had frozen at the sound of Gizmo's barks, hovering over the torn jerky wrappers. Her big ears were aimed forward.

Gizmo crept into the dingy daylight, offering a slow wag of her tail.

"Hello," she said again. "I'm Gizmo. Is this your territory?"

The coyote bared her sharp teeth.

Hesitating, Gizmo stopped with one paw raised, midstep. "Um, my friends and I, including my very large, very strong friend Max, were just resting," she said, her fur standing on end. "We'll be moving on soon."

Drool dripped from the coyote's jaws, plopping on

the shredded jerky wrappers. The coyote tensed, preparing to make her move.

Rocky raced out from behind the counter, barking loudly as he ran in circles around Gizmo.

"Get out of here!" he yelped. *"Get!"*

Max stalked out of hiding to join his friends, his hackles raised, his own teeth bared as he growled deep in his throat.

Then the coyote did something he did not expect.

She raised her head all the way back, opened her snout, and let out a high-pitched "yi-yi-yi!" that echoed through the dusty market.

Outside, another coyote called back. Then another, and another.

The coyote's gleaming eyes met Max's, and she took a purposeful step forward. "You are in our territory," she said. "And you are surrounded. Come with me."

Panting, Rocky stopped running and growled at the beast, who towered above him. "And what if we don't?"

The coyote slowly lowered her head until she was snout-to-snout with Rocky. The smell of decay wafted on her breath. "Then my pack mates will storm in here," she said, "and shred you all to bits."

Tucking his tail, Rocky took a step back. "All right, that's a convincing argument."

Standing, the coyote looked at Max once more and said simply, "Come."

Max hesitated, his eyes darting from side to side. The

coyotes had them cornered. Going outside would bring them face-to-face with the rest of the pack, but at least they'd be in the open, with a better chance to escape.

Lowering his tail in a show of concession, Max padded toward the swinging door. The coyote growled at him as he passed, but she did not move; she just watched as Max held the door open for Rocky and Gizmo to dart through.

A dry late-afternoon breeze rose as Max, Rocky, and Gizmo came to stand side by side at the top of the steps. Down below, on the hard-packed dirt road, were five more wild coyotes. They were similar to the female coyote in shape and coloring, though one had a torn ear, and another had a thick scar running through an eye that he kept closed.

The door squealed as the female coyote exited the market, then pushed past Max and leaped down the stairs. She stood next to the one-eyed coyote.

"Your smell sense was strong and true, Sharpshard," she barked to him. "These were the intruders I found: three domesticated dogs."

The coyote with the notched ear snapped her jaws. "The two small ones are perfect for an evening snack. The large one will provide us a feast."

The other coyotes, save for one-eyed Sharpshard and the female who'd found them, howled and yipped in response.

"Quiet!" Sharpshard barked, his eyes on Max. "You know the rules, Moonrise."

The coyote with the notched ear—Moonrise—bared her teeth and pawed angrily at the dirt, but she did not respond.

Max raised his head high and stepped forward. "What do you want with us?" he asked. "We mean you no harm, and we don't want to fight."

Sharpshard barked a vicious laugh. Turning to the first coyote, he said, "Prickle, surely these starving dogs do not think we fear them."

Prickle snarled. "They think themselves mighty," she said. "The smallest of them approached me as though we were equals. And the long one thought to chase me off. They are peculiar."

"The rules say that only Bonecrush and Shadow can decide what to do with any significant intruder," Sharpshard barked. "They must come with us."

Rocky sat down and cleared his throat. "You know, I don't know them *personally*, but I'm sure Bonecrush and Shadow are busy, being bosses of your pack. So why don't you just let us go and resume hunting whatever it is you hunt?"

"The rabbits are few these days," Prickle said, her hackles raised. "Which is why we are glad you are here to possibly become our next meal. Now come!"

All the coyotes stepped forward, growling, closing in on the dogs.

"Let's do what they say for now," Max whispered. "We'll get out of this."

Rocky and Gizmo huddled close to Max as the three dogs came down the porch steps. The six coyotes formed a circle around them, with Prickle and Sharp-shard in the lead.

As the coyotes in the rear nipped threateningly at Max's heels, the dogs and their captors trotted silently around the ramshackle buildings and headed farther south into the desert. Rusted shacks and abandoned junk gave way to tall, spiny cacti and scrubby, leafless brush. The distant bluffs grew closer as the three friends were led farther away from the tracks that could bring them to the wall.

"Should we make a run for it?" Rocky whispered.

"Not yet," Max said. "We'll need someplace to hide."

Gizmo's ears and tail drooped. "I'm sorry for saying hi to that Prickle," she said. "I thought being friendly might help."

"You couldn't have known," Max reassured her. "And she smelled us hiding there anyway."

"Still," she said. "I should have been cautious."

In front of them, Prickle spun around, kicking up dust. "No talking!" she howled.

All three dogs clamped their jaws shut and fell in line.

Max had no idea how long they'd walked when night fell. The blazing sun was finally, mercifully gone, and a surprising chill overtook the desert. Just like the night before, when he'd ridden comfortably in a train, the sky was free of clouds, letting the full, silvery moon illuminate the rocks and sparse plants.

The coyotes slowed their pace as they neared a pair of large, flat boulders. Two shadowy figures lay atop them, their heads and big ears raised and alert. Down below, at the base of the giant boulders, were the bones of some animal, mostly picked clean. The creature had been large—larger than Max by far—but he couldn't tell what it was.

Prickle and Sharpshard stood in front of Max, Rocky, and Gizmo while the other four coyotes stood in a line behind them. Max could smell their hunger. He could feel their anticipation deep in his own limbs.

"Bonecrush!" Sharpshard yipped. "Shadow! We found intruders on our land. And as you have commanded, we have brought them to you."

One of the dark figures rose to all fours, stretched, and opened its lethal-looking snout in a yawn. He leaped down from the boulder, landing heavily next to the animal carcass. The coyote wrenched one of the bones free and stalked forward.

"Bonecrush," Prickle and Sharpshard said in unison, ducking their heads.

Bonecrush brushed past them without a word, his glowing eyes focused on Max. He was larger and thicker than the other coyotes, and, like Dolph, scarred from many battles. One old, flesh-colored wound ran almost perfectly straight through the center of his forehead and halfway down his snout.

Gnawing on his bone, the lead coyote slowly circled

Max, Rocky, and Gizmo, huffing and sniffing. He nosed Rocky so hard that the little Dachshund almost fell over onto his side.

Max held himself straight, refusing to show fear. He had to wait for the right time before they could escape. He had to make sure that Gizmo and Rocky would be safe—he would not let these coyotes hurt them.

Finished with his examination, Bonecrush came to stand before Max, then spat his partially chewed bone into the dirt. "You wear the bands of human dominance," Bonecrush said, his voice low and gruff.

It took Max a moment to realize the large coyote meant their collars. "Yes," he said, "these were given to us by a human."

"So you are *pets*." Bonecrush spat the last word with disgust. "Captives of the two-legged fiends. Yet those humans in the town where we found you know better than to keep pets, for we have eaten many of their dogs and cats. The humans who lived there know that our hunger is not always sated by rabbits and voles and insects, not in these lean times."

"We're not from that town," Rocky said.

Bonecrush snapped his head to look down at Rocky, and growled. "You allow your pack to speak for you?" Bonecrush asked Max, incredulous. "And one so small?"

"Hey!" Rocky called.

Max stepped forward. "We speak equally," he said. "And like my friend said, we are not from around here.

We're just passing through, on our way to the wall out west."

Bonecrush's eyes went wide. "The wall?" he asked. Turning, he called to Shadow. "You hear that, my mate? These dogs want to go to that wall!"

"Ha!" Shadow barked from her boulder. "Dogs. So predictable."

The entire pack broke into howling laughter, their snouts aimed at the moon, their calls rising in a chorus of mocking *yi-yi-yi*s that echoed through the desert. In the distance, another pack of coyotes joined in.

Shadow leaped down from the boulder and came to stand near Bonecrush, between Prickle and Sharpshard. She took one sniff at the dogs, then scrunched her snout.

"What do we do with you?" Bonecrush said as he paced in front of the dogs, his tail twitching. "Shadow, my dear mate, tell me what you would want."

Shadow stalked forward to Gizmo. Lowering her head, she licked between the small terrier's bushy brows. "I say we let them go."

Gizmo shuddered and bunched herself as small as possible.

Rocky's whole body practically heaved with relief. "You're going to let us go?"

Shadow turned to Rocky and wagged her tail. "Sure thing, small pet. I will let you *go*...straight to my belly."

All eight coyotes formed a tight circle around the

three dogs, their eyes glimmering an unearthly yellow. They closed in, teeth bared, relishing the scent of fear, and let out an eerie round of laughter that chilled Max to the bone. He glanced at Rocky, who was trembling, and then at Gizmo—who seemed surprisingly fearless, as if she was formulating a plan at that very moment.

And then she spoke.

"Oh, well, I suppose that's more rabbits for everyone else, then," Gizmo barked loudly.

She was so calm and assured that the pack of coyotes stopped in place. Shadow's large ears perked up, and she looked down at Gizmo with renewed interest.

"Rabbits?" Shadow said. "There is a scarcity of rabbits in these parts. We have been looking for such delicacies for a long time. Where did you see rabbits?"

Gizmo plopped to her belly and let out an exaggerated sigh. "Never you mind," she said, her voice muffled by the dirt. "At least the other dogs will be able to eat the rabbits in peace."

Leaning into Max, Rocky asked quietly, "Uh, did I miss something, big guy?"

Max answered, "Remember what Gizmo said at the train museum—she learned from the best."

None of the coyotes paid Max and Rocky any attention. All eyes were on Gizmo.

"I demand you tell us," Bonecrush barked, curling up his lips in an evil snarl. "Where are these rabbits now? We long ago sensed they were driven away."

"I can't eat another lizard," Moonrise moaned with a feral, wild expression. *"I want rabbit."*

Gizmo lifted up her head. "I thought *everyone* had heard about how on the other side of the wall, the humans—I mean, of course, the two-legged fiends—have rounded up all the rabbits in the entire desert. They've been breeding them to be fatter and juicier, a carnivore's feast!" She let her tail droop. "That's the whole reason we were going to the wall. It's sad that I'll leave this life not having tasted a nice, meaty bunny ear."

The coyotes scrunched their snouts, confused.

"Ear?" Prickle asked.

"I mean thigh," Gizmo said. "Thighs, right? Yeah, that's what I meant."

Sharpshard snarled and walked in an agitated circle. "What good are rabbits on the other side of the wall?" he yipped. "We can't get past it."

"If you only..." Gizmo said, looking up at the night sky. "Never mind."

Shadow lowered her front half to meet Gizmo snout-to-snout, her backside raised. "You know something, don't you, pet? Tell us."

"Well," Gizmo said again, her small nose brushing against the coyote's. "We were sent this way by a dog named Spots. He'd already dug a hole under the wall, one that leads directly to the rabbit hutch. It's as big as that whole town back there and just overflowing with bunnies. So many bunnies they're stacked three high!"

Excitement coursed through the coyote pack, and they broke ranks, leaping and nipping at one another in a hungry frenzy.

"We shall feast forever and ever!" Moonrise howled up at the stars.

Bonecrush loomed over Gizmo, drooling, his eyes wide and frantic. Max restrained himself from jumping between the small dog and the coyote. He had to trust that Gizmo was still in control.

"Tell us where this place is," Moonrise demanded. "You and your friends are scrawny, and your meat will be tough and chewy. We prefer the rabbits."

Gizmo climbed to all fours and turned her back on the coyote pack leader. "You want us to tell you so that you can kill us and eat all those plump, scrumptious rabbits by yourself? No, thanks."

"We will eat only our fill," Bonecrush said.

"And we can make your deaths quick," Shadow offered.

Rocky scooted closer to Max. "Great," he muttered.

"I don't think so," Gizmo said. "Though, if you promise to let us go after we arrive, we could lead you to the secret hole."

"Hmm," Bonecrush said.

The coyote leader backed away from Gizmo. He yipped, and the rest of his pack joined him in a huddle. They barked and growled at one another, deciding what to do.

Gizmo trembled next to Max, and took in slow, shallow breaths. "I think it's working," she said.

"I couldn't have done it better myself," Rocky said, nuzzling her neck. He eyed the coyotes, whose barks rose in pitch as they leaped up and down, arguing. "Should we make a break for it while they're distracted?" he asked.

"Not yet," Max said. "We're too out in the open. We need to wait until we have somewhere to hide."

"Enough!" Bonecrush bellowed over the yelps of his pack. "I have decided. Come."

With Shadow by his side, Bonecrush approached the three dogs once more. "We will let you lead us to this hole and to the rabbits," he said, his bushy tail held high.

Gizmo let her tongue hang free as she wagged her tail happily. "And then you'll let us go, right?"

Bonecrush hesitated. Instead, it was Shadow who barked, "Oh, yes, of course."

A lie. Just like Gizmo's lie about the rabbits.

But with nowhere to run, the three dogs had no choice but to agree to the deal. With Bonecrush and Shadow nudging them into the lead, Max, Rocky, and Gizmo walked side by side, leading the pack of salivating, bloodthirsty coyotes to the west.

Gizmo had bought the dogs some time—and now Max had to figure out how to outsmart these deadly coyotes for good. Because rabbits or not, once they reached that wall, the coyotes would make the dogs their feast.

CHAPTER 18

CANYON RUN

As the pack of coyotes followed Max, Rocky, and Gizmo through the desert night, the wild animals sang of hunger and death, and of the joys of hunting with their pack.

The coyotes didn't sing with words, but in howls and cries aimed up at the vast, starry sky. The song was a celebration. It warned other packs away, while declaring how brave, smart, and ruthless Bonecrush and his fellows were. Max found himself swallowed by the wild verses, some part of him deep inside wishing he could join in.

But of course he couldn't. Wildness had been bred out of him and the other domestic dogs long ago. Coyotes— and wolves—feared and distrusted humans, while Max felt lost without humans by his side. It was a difference that would forever keep the species apart.

The caravan of dogs and coyotes headed west past endless boulders, cacti, and bushes. Sensing their presence, small creatures—lizards and snakes, hairy spiders and scorpions—darted away to hide. One of the coyotes yipped as it snatched up a fleeing vole; the others growled, jealous of his snack. Max kept his eyes open for a place where they could lose the coyotes, but everywhere he looked was wide, open space—the desert held few opportunities for escape.

Soon, walls of rock rose around them, a shallow canyon cut into the earth. It was a craggy maze of stone, its pathways bathed in black.

And Max knew: This was where they could make their getaway.

Lowering his head, he whispered softly to Rocky and Gizmo, so the howling coyotes could not hear him.

"Keep your eyes open for a passage off the main path," he said. "One just big enough for us to fit through. When one of us makes a run for it, the other two will follow—then we'll lose the pack in the maze."

"Got it," Gizmo whispered back.

"Will do, big guy," Rocky said.

They didn't have to walk much farther before Max spotted an opening.

Turning to face the pack of coyotes, Max leaped

up and down, wagging his tail in a show of excitement. "Look!" he barked. "Up there! A deer!"

"Where?" Shadow asked, spinning around.

"We will devour it!" Bonecrush howled.

With the coyotes distracted, Max spun back to his friends. "Go!" he said, and made a break for the passage.

They shot through one by one, Rocky in the lead, followed by Gizmo. Max brought up the rear, slipping behind a bend in the passage just as the coyotes realized they'd been tricked.

Bonecrush roared in rage. "After them!"

The three dogs bounded blindly down the dark, narrow path between the rock walls. The fit was so tight that the craggy stone scraped Max's sides. He didn't care—if the coyotes caught them, the pain would be much worse.

Panting for breath, they veered down side passages in the mazelike canyon, trying to lose their pursuers. Coyote yips echoed off the walls and into the sky, surrounding them with the predators' rage.

At last, they shoved through a dried bush and stopped short, finding themselves face-to-face with a towering wall of black rock.

A dead end.

"We're okay," Max said, even as the coyotes' cries grew louder. "We'll just turn around. Come on."

"What if the coyotes are right behind us?" Rocky asked, trembling.

"We'll outsmart them again," Max answered. "They still don't know that Gizmo was lying about the rabbits."

"Let's hurry," Gizmo said, shoving past Max and climbing over the bush once more. "Come on!"

Just then, something shifted in the shadows, and Max froze in place. Several round stones rolled free from an alcove up ahead. It could have been an avalanche of rocks loosened by the commotion, except these stones—one large as a basketball and four the size of tennis balls, all dark in color—rolled together to block Gizmo's path.

"The stones," Rocky said with a gasp. "They're alive!"

It was impossible. Stones couldn't move by themselves. Had the coyote's howls somehow summoned them?

Gizmo flattened her ears and bared her teeth as she slowly backed away from the round balls.

And one by one, the stones unfurled themselves into strange-looking creatures.

The largest one was as big as Rocky and Gizmo combined. It appeared to have the long, narrow head and ears of a hairless rat, with a thick, tapered tail. It walked on four short legs, its feet tipped with sharp claws.

But the most unusual part was its body. The creature's back looked like the rounded shell of a beetle or other insect, with colors and textures that mimicked the rocks around them. Somehow it had managed to roll its head, legs, and tail up inside this hardened, bony shell, forming a ball.

Next to the creature were four tiny versions of itself. They huddled beside the big one, unrolled just enough to see what was going on.

"What are you?" Max asked, astounded. "Where did you come from?"

"There's no time to explain," the large armored creature said, huffing with her long snout. Her voice was urgent but kind. "The coyotes are after you, yes?"

"Yes, ma'am," Gizmo said, letting her hackles down.

"Quick, then." She shuffled toward the hidden alcove. "Get into my burrow. There will be just enough room for all of us."

Max couldn't help but notice the animal's sharp, shredding claws, and he wondered if he should trust her. But coyote howls rose from very close by, and he realized he had to take her on faith.

He stepped past Gizmo and dropped to his belly. There was a hole dug beneath the wall of rock, leading into a wide, dark underground burrow. He crawled in, dirt and stone scraping his sides, then shuffled over to the burrow's back wall.

Rocky and Gizmo came next—he couldn't see them, but their smells were reassuring as the two small dogs nestled into his flank. Curled into balls, the four tiny animals rolled in, followed by the big one. Once again, from the inside, the wall of rock looked complete and impenetrable.

As the eight animals waited silently in the burrow,

Max's ears twitched at the sound of footsteps just outside. He could hear coyotes sniffing the dirt, picking up Max's, Rocky's, and Gizmo's scents but surely confused as to how they had disappeared. The coyotes' own stench swirled into the burrow, smelling of anger and urgency and decay.

"They were here," one coyote said, her voice muffled by the dirt and rock.

"They must have looped back into the canyon," another coyote growled, scratching angrily at the ground. Bits of soil were flung into the alcove, landing on the hidden animals.

Rocky took in a sharp breath—Max could see he needed to sneeze. The Dachshund held it in as best he could—then snorted, a tiny, forceful sound.

"What was that?" one of the coyotes asked.

Max's heart pounded so fast that his chest hurt. He could see the shadows of coyote paws just outside the armored creatures' burrow. They were so close. Any second he expected one of the wild beasts to shove its snout into the hole, teeth bared and ready to rip into Max and his friends.

But just then, a loud "yi-yi-yi!" echoed through the canyon: Bonecrush calling for his pack.

The coyotes outside the burrow growled ferociously, then bounded away, their paw steps fading as they left the narrow alley.

Max, Rocky, Gizmo, and the five other animals lay

still, silent—for how long Max couldn't tell. He heard the snorts of his friends, and as his vision grew accustomed to the scant moonlight that leaked into the burrow, he saw the round balls of tan armor relax and unfold.

"They gone, Mama?" one of the tiny creatures asked.

"They're gone, sweet baby," the big armored animal cooed, holding her little ones against her soft belly.

Max shifted, and his head scraped the stone ceiling above. The burrow these animals had dug was deep, tall, and wide, with a ditch around the outer edge to catch whatever rainfall might pour through. Warm water filled the ditch. It was dark inside the space, but some light from the outside filtered through cracks in the rock wall.

"Thank you," Max said. "We would have been trapped if it weren't for you."

"It wasn't a problem," the large creature said. "My name is Edwina, by the by. And these are my babies, Abel, Hilty, Shuck, and Urial. We've made our home in this canyon until they're big enough to travel someplace with more water."

"Hello, hello, helloooo," one of the babies said, waving his paws as he rocked back and forth in his strange shell. He looked like a hairless mouse or mole mimicking a human sitting in a rocking chair.

"Hi!" Gizmo stood up and shook herself free of dirt. "What a cutie! How old are you?"

"Two months!" one of the little creatures cried. "This many!" He held up his two front paws.

Rocky stood up and stretched. "I'm Rocky," he said. "And these are Gizmo and Max."

"You are dogs?" Edwina asked, her ridged tail curling protectively around her babies. "Pets for the humans?"

"That we are," Max said. "I don't think we've ever met an animal like you before."

Edwina shifted her weight to sit more comfortably, and the plates that made up her shell clinked against one another. Though her back, forehead, and tail looked leathery, from the sound the protective armor must have been harder.

"We are armadillos," Edwina said, sounding amused. "You must not be from around here if you haven't met one of us."

The smallest of the baby armadillos—Shuck—crawled to sit in front of Gizmo. The terrier positively towered above her.

"Hi," the tiny animal whispered.

"Hi!" Gizmo said back.

"Hi," Shuck said again, her paws holding her soft belly protectively.

Max tried to wag his tail, but there wasn't enough room in the burrow for it to move. "We're actually from very far north of here," he said to Edwina. "We've been traveling for months now, ever since the humans disappeared. We were heading west to the wall when the coyotes found us."

Edwina nodded slowly as her sharp claws dug a

deeper, softer trench in which to rest. "Oh, I've heard about that wall," she said. "Ever since it appeared, all the desert creatures have been spreading word of its danger. You need to be careful if you choose to go there."

"Hi hi hi!" Shuck suddenly squealed, scooting toward Gizmo with each word.

Gizmo wagged her tail and licked the little armadillo's rough, hard shell. "I see you; don't worry."

One of the other babies—Abel, Max thought—scratched at his mother's side.

"Mama, can't they just roll up?" he asked. "Roll up and be safe, like us?"

Edwina pressed her snout to his. "Dogs can't roll up like armadillos. We're special that way. But they have other means to escape danger."

Rocky scratched behind his ears with a hind leg. "Yeah, don't sweat it, kid. We've faced off with giant alligators. This wall isn't any trouble for us."

Urial rolled through the dirt and opened up his shell in front of Rocky. "What's an alligator?" he asked. "Is it scary?"

"You know those lizards you see running around?" Rocky said.

"Uh-huh," Urial said, rapt with attention.

"Imagine one a hundred thousand times larger, bigger than your mama—bigger even than my friend Max here!" Rocky spun in a circle. "They chased us through a swamp!"

The babies all gasped, clutching their front claws together under their snouts, listening intently.

"What happened?" Shuck whispered.

Rocky looked between the four babies. "One night," he started, "it was raining so hard we could barely see. And the alligators showed up, cornering us against a big hole in the ground."

Abel leaned in. "Did you fall?"

"Almost," Rocky said. "But we managed to make it inside a building. We thought we were safe...but then we met the Mudlurker." Leaping back, Rocky aimed his snout up at the craggy roof of the burrow and said, "He howled like this." Then he let loose his own version of the Mudlurker's haunting cry.

The four baby armadillos squealed. Then they curled into balls, and rolled over to their mother.

"Don't worry," Gizmo said, glaring at Rocky. "The Mudlurker turned out to be a perfectly nice dog, and we were safe from the alligators with him. What Rocky *means* is that even though we don't have armor like you, we have our own ways of avoiding danger."

Edwina stretched, extending her long, sharp claws. "It's all right, babies. There's nothing to worry about. Alligators could never live where we do. There's not near enough water."

Max ducked his head. "Sorry," he said. "We didn't mean to scare them."

Her ears twitching, Edwina said, "It's no worry. They need to learn to fear most other animals, anyway. Our armor is good protection, but if predators ever got to our soft bellies, well..."

The baby armadillos shivered and curled into leathery spheres, cuddling against their mother. Still, they seemed to calm down quickly; it wasn't long before Max could hear their soft, muffled snores.

"All the excitement has tuckered them out," Edwina said, laughter in her voice. "And let me tell you, I'm glad for it. Often they have far more energy than I do, and they keep me up half the night!"

Gizmo walked to Edwina's side and dropped down next to her, as Edwina turned her attention to Max. "That wall you're going to is a topic of controversy," she said. "I don't care much either way if the humans come back, but I do know many of the desert animals are happier without them. Even those who liked the humans felt differently after being shocked when they touched the wall."

"We understand," Rocky said, resting his head on his paws. "But we're not giving up on finding our human families. Right, buddy?"

Max licked Rocky and said, "That's right." He turned to Edwina. "Are we very far from the wall?"

"Quite the contrary," Edwina said. "You're very, very close. Why, I'd say you could be there tomorrow morning.

But you have to be careful. And not just because of the wall itself."

"What, then?" Max asked, his furry brows raised.

Edwina curled in on herself, pulling her slumbering children close to her belly. "The humans abandoned the roads leading to the wall, and now they're overrun by all sorts of wildlife. Not the least of which are coyotes like the ones that chased you into the canyon here."

"We know," Max said. "Like Rocky said about the gators, we've faced a lot of obstacles. We can't give up now, no matter how dangerous the road ahead may be."

"I respect that," Edwina said. "Really, I do. But for tonight, I insist the three of you stay here and rest where it's safe."

"We don't want to put you out," Max said. "We can always climb out of your burrow and sleep somewhere in the canyon."

Waving a paw, Edwina said, "Nonsense. Tonight you rest here. Then tomorrow, if you still insist on heading to that wall, I'll lead you out of the canyon and send you on your way."

Gizmo licked the underside of Edwina's hairless snout. "Thank you, Miss Edwina. We really appreciate it."

"Sleep sure does sound good," Rocky said, then opened his jaws wide in a yawn. "Just yesterday we were figuring out how to make a train work and going for a ride. Then today, we hiked through a desert and tangled with coyotes. I sure hope tomorrow is easier."

"Me, too, buddy," Max said. "Me, too."

One by one the dogs and the armadillos closed their eyes and drifted off into dreams. Max waited until they were all asleep before he let his own eyelids close.

The wall—and the humans on the other side—were only a morning's walk away. But something told him that reaching Charlie, Emma, Dr. Lynn, and all the other people wouldn't be as simple as digging a tunnel and running into their arms.

CHAPTER 19

THE PROMISE

Max was on the other side of the wall.

The field of empty, fluttering tents lay before him, and the shimmering metal barricade was at his heels.

Max didn't know how he'd made it over, but he was glad that, at least for now, the dark storm and its inky tendrils were kept at bay on the side he'd come from, its roars and screams muffled.

He padded forward, sniffing the air, ears alert. Human smells were everywhere, but he saw no one. The tents and motor homes were abandoned. One RV had a square of fake grass lying beneath its side door, an awning spread over its top, providing shade to two white plastic chairs. Crystal wind chimes dangled from the awning, tinkling as they shifted in the breeze. The sound was almost like children's laughter.

No, the laughter wasn't coming from the chimes. It was real.

Max stopped in place, and the tents and vehicles in front of him shifted aside, revealing a path. At the end of the path, shadowed by the sun, were Charlie and Emma.

He'd found his family!

The children sat next to each other, building castles in the desert sand. They didn't seem to see him.

Tail wagging and tongue hanging free, Max bounded forward, running as hard and as fast as he could.

And then Madame appeared in front of him, blocking his way.

She sat down and cocked her head curiously at Max as he skidded to a stop in front of her.

Have you forgotten something? she asked, her voice echoing in Max's head, though her jaws did not move.

Max leaped up and down. "Of course I haven't," he barked to his old mentor. "Charlie and Emma are right there! I found them. I finally found them!"

He rushed past her, kicking up dust and dirt as he flew toward his human family's waiting arms.

And again, Madame appeared to block his way.

Look around you, she said.

Max heard panting, and he turned to see Rocky and Gizmo sitting perfectly still, watching him.

A circle of glowing white appeared around Gizmo, then another around Rocky. A tingling sensation ran up Max's legs, and he looked down to find himself in a ring of his own.

Though none of the dogs moved, the circles carried them to stand in a row, connecting the edges of each glowing ring.

Madame paced in front of Max, Rocky, and Gizmo. *What do the rings mean?* she asked.

"They are a sign of what happened to us," Max said, even though he didn't fully understand.

That's right, Madame said. *What's more, the rings will be linked forever, if you let them. They were forged by all that you've been through. Do not let them break.*

A great tremor rose under Max's feet, and he felt the earth shuddering and shifting. A boom came from behind them, and Max looked over just in time to see the silver wall buckle and fall to the ground.

The great storm surged into the tent city, thundering toward Max and his friends. *Hold on!* Madame barked over the raging black tempest. *Remember everything I've said. It's almost time.*

Max awoke.

Pale morning light spilled into the cool earthen den, prying open Max's eyes.

He yawned, then looked around. As usual, he was the

last to wake—the burrow was empty, though he could hear the baby armadillos' squeals of delight from outside.

Crawling on his belly, Max made his way to the ditch at the burrow's end and lapped up some of the warm, murky water that had pooled there from the last rain. Then, he squeezed himself out of the burrow, the stones scraping his back.

It was very early. The sun was only just rising over the eastern horizon, but already the air was uncomfortably warm. Max rose to his full height, stretching his sore muscles and hoping Edwina would prove right about how close they were to the wall.

"Can't catch me, Urial!" one of the baby armadillos— Shuck—squeaked as she half ran, half waddled around the nearby bush.

"Yes, I can!" her brother squealed back. He curled himself into a ball and rolled after her, and Hilty did the same.

Max peered over the bush and found Gizmo and Rocky playing with the other baby, Abel, wagging their tails and rolling the little animal back and forth like a toy ball. Abel seemed to love it, and Edwina lay nearby, watching with amusement.

"Good morning," Max said. "And thank you again, Edwina, for letting us stay the night."

Rocky swatted Abel gently with his paws and sent the tiny armadillo in Gizmo's direction.

"You ready to go, big guy?" Rocky asked.

"I'm more than ready," Max said.

Hilty, Urial, and Shuck stopped chasing one another and stared up at the dogs.

"You have to leave?" Shuck asked.

"But we're playing!" Abel said, unfurling and clinging to Gizmo's side with his claws.

Gizmo's ears drooped even as she licked Abel on the patch of hard armor that covered his forehead.

With a grunt, Edwina rose on all fours and nosed each of her babies with her long snout. "Now, now," she said, "it's not polite to keep guests longer than they'd like. Go back in the burrow, my babies. I will show them out of the canyon, since they do not know its tunnels and turns, and then I'll be back for you."

"Aw!" Urial said. "I wanna go, too!"

Edwina nosed him harder, forcing the small armadillo to scoot toward their hidden home.

"Our new friends need to be on their way," she said. "And I'm afraid your tiny legs will be too slow to keep up. Say good-bye to Gizmo, Rocky, and Max, and stay inside while I'm gone."

"Bye-bye," the four baby armadillos said sadly. Then they ducked their heads as they crawled one by one back inside their home.

Gizmo whimpered as she watched them go, and Max walked over to nuzzle her side. "Are you all right?" he asked.

"Yeah," Gizmo said softly. "I'm a little worried about what will happen to us after we reach the wall."

"No need to worry," Rocky said, his tail wagging. "I have a good feeling about today."

Gizmo offered him a weak wag of her tail in return, but she said nothing else.

Edwina led them single file through the mazelike passages etched into the canyon and back to the main path. The smell of coyote was everywhere, wild and angry. The animals were no longer in the cavern, that much Max could tell, but they'd clearly searched through every last nook and cranny before they'd left.

Not long after the dogs and Edwina reached the main path, the ground rose, leading them back out into the wide, open desert.

"This is as far as I can take you," Edwina said, stopping at the base of the incline leading out of the canyon. "I don't dare leave the shadows—not with the wild beasts out there."

"We understand," Max said. "Thank you again for your help!"

"Bye, Edwina!" Gizmo said.

The armadillo mother nodded at the dogs, then turned to waddle away, back toward her children.

Though it had been warm down in the canyon, the walls had at least provided some shelter from the sun. As the dogs climbed out of the canyon, heat overwhelmed them. A few feathery clouds drifted in the sky, not nearly enough to shade the desert from the unrelenting sun.

But the sun didn't matter anymore when, on the horizon, Max saw the barest glint of silver.

The wall.

It was real this time, not just part of a confusing dream. The wall that signified the end of their long journey was finally within sight.

"Come on!" Max barked, already racing past cacti and skinny trees toward their destination.

Tall utility poles ran in the direction of the wall, power lines strung between them. Next to the poles was an asphalt road coated with desert dust. Max bounded toward the road, his heart leaping at something he hadn't seen since Dr. Lynn had driven off in a van many towns back.

Fresh tire tracks.

He ran down the center of the road, no longer caring that his fur was burning, that his throat was scratchy and dry, that he hadn't eaten since yesterday's meal of beef jerky. Rocky and Gizmo followed as fast as they could, but Max quickly left them behind, his long legs carrying him toward his people. His people!

Noticing how far back his friends had fallen, Max stopped to let them catch up, leaping up and down, his whole body quivering with excitement.

"Hurry," he barked happily. "My family is so close."

Rocky leaped up, licking Max's side and batting at

his fur. "We did it, buddy! We had to walk a billion miles to get here, but we made it!"

Max's gleeful, wagging tail slowed when he noticed that Gizmo had stopped a little ways back on the road. Her tail was tucked and her head hung down.

"What's wrong?" Max asked as he walked over to her side. "Do you need to rest? Is it too hot?"

"No," Gizmo whispered, not meeting Max's eyes. "It's just what you said. We're almost to your family. Not mine."

Rocky sat next to her. "What do you mean? Max's family is going to love you. Everyone loves you!"

Gizmo let out a soft, sad whine as she looked between Rocky and Max.

"That's the thing, though," she said. "They're Max's pack leaders. Unlike you two, my humans didn't put a tracking chip in me, so Dr. Lynn couldn't find out my name or where my family lived. What if we find your families and neither one wants to take me in? What if... what if I never get to see you again?"

Growling at the thought, Rocky leaped up to his feet. "Don't you think that for a second. You're never going to leave our side. Right, Max?"

Max lowered his head, his excitement evaporating. Because Gizmo was right. There was no guarantee that they wouldn't be split up once they were reunited with their people. He had never thought about what would happen to the three of them after their journey was over.

Even if Rocky's owner took him back in, they still lived close enough to visit. But where would Gizmo go?

Gizmo rested her fluffy head on her paws. "I'm just like a lot of the animals we met on the way here," she said. "I don't have a family, not the way I used to. I've been a stray for a very long time. Maybe my place isn't with the humans anymore."

"Of course it is, Gizmo," Max said.

"I don't know," Gizmo said, her ears drooping. "I've been thinking a lot about what I should do when we finally reach the wall. My pack leaders lost me long before all the humans had to leave. I don't think they'll be looking for me anymore. So maybe now that you'll have Charlie and Emma and Vet again, I should go find somewhere new to live. I could always head back to DeQuincy; that seemed like a nice enough town. Maybe—"

"No," Rocky said, spinning in a frantic circle. Rearing back his head, he howled a defiant "No!"

Gizmo flinched. "Rocky," she said.

The Dachshund paced on the dusty road, leaving a trail of paw prints.

"You can't leave," he said. "You just can't, Gizmo. I don't know what I'd do without you." He gazed up at Max. "Either of you."

Rocky stopped pacing. "I remember when all this started," he said. "I was fat and lazy and selfish. But then I met Max, who was locked in that cage, and he saved me from Dolph and his wolves. And then I met you, Gizmo, and—" He ducked his head. "You made me want to be a better dog. To be brave and kind, just like you. Because you and Max are two of the best animals I've ever met. If my human family tries to take me away from you, I...I don't know what I'd do."

"Aw, Rocky," Gizmo said softly, her eyes shimmering. She stood up and nuzzled his side. "I've learned so much from you, too. How to be cautious when needed, and how to use words rather than growls when faced with bad animals. You always stayed loyal and friendly, even when times were hard. I would miss you—both of you—a lot."

Max's dream from the night before came back to him. He remembered the images of his friends linked together in their three rings, protecting one another from the dark, uncertain future.

"So that's what's been bothering you," Max said. "You're afraid we're going to be kept apart. You've seemed so sad sometimes, and I didn't know why. I would never abandon you, Gizmo."

Gizmo leaned against Max's leg, inhaling his scent. "Max, your pack leaders are on the other side of that wall. If it comes down to being with them or me, you have to choose them. You've been with your family your whole life. Me, I'm just some lost dog you met in the woods a few months ago."

"Listen to me," Max said, looking her in the eye. "After all we've been through, you, me, and Rocky aren't just friends. We're more than that. I meant what I said to those mice back at the mall, Gizmo: We're a family. I will do everything I can to make sure we stay together for the rest of our lives."

Quivering, Gizmo whispered, "You promise?"

"I do," Max said.

Rocky raced in a circle. "Together forever!" he barked. "Friends till the end!"

Gizmo barked as, tail wagging, she leaped on top of Rocky, and the two of them rolled in the center of the road, nipping each other playfully.

After a minute, Gizmo rolled off Rocky and shook herself free of dust. "Well, let's get to that wall, then!" she said. "Oh, I hope they have a big pool or a pond or a lake to swim in."

"Better yet, some fresh bowls of kibble," Rocky said.

Max galloped ahead. "Let's go find out!"

With renewed excitement, the three dogs bounded down the road, the shimmering silver wall growing larger on the horizon. The stench of coyote was stronger as they neared the wall—Bonecrush's pack had come this way, too.

A hill rose off the southern side of the road, and Max left the asphalt to climb it and get a good look at what lay ahead. Rocky and Gizmo leaped over the tumbling weeds as they chased after him.

Panting, Max came to a stop at the top of the hill. Just as Spots had described, the road they'd been following led to a chain-link fence topped with barbed wire that seemed to spread forever in either direction. The gate through the fence was next to two boulders and some bushes.

Beyond the fence, the road and the electricity poles ran right up to the big, silvery wall—a sheet of metal that stretched as far as Max could see. Like Spots had said, it was tall, not as tall as the giant wall of Max's dreams, but at least as high as a three-story building. If there was a gate or door where the road reached the wall, Max couldn't see it, though the power lines extended over the top.

Max was about to bark to his friends that they'd made it at last, when he saw the figures of a dozen or more animals converging on the road, just past the chain-link fence. A dry breeze rose from the west, carrying their smells to Max's nose.

Coyotes.

And wolves.

Dread flooded Max, and he backed away down the hill, trembling and shaking his head.

"Is it...?" Rocky asked, incredulous.

"Oh, no," Gizmo said.

"It is," Max said as the fences and animals fell out of view. "Bonecrush and his pack made it to the wall.

"And somehow," he added in a growl, "Dolph made it here first."

CHAPTER 20

A DANGEROUS PLAN

Max stood, halfway down the hill, bewildered. It didn't make sense. How was Dolph here? How had the wolf managed to catch up to Max at every stage of the journey?

Of course Dolph would have found a way to lead his pack out of the gorge they'd fallen into during the hurricane. And unlike Max, Rocky, and Gizmo, Dolph wouldn't have let his followers take long breaks by desert pools, or be herded off the path by a bunch of coyotes, or sleep all night in a comfortable burrow. Somehow, the wolves must have known where Max and his friends were heading, that their ultimate destination lay here, at the big metal wall.

This journey was long and hard enough without

having to worry about the wild canines who thirsted for Max's blood. If only there was some way to talk sense into Dolph. But there was no way Max would ever get the wolves to show him mercy. Like the coyotes, the wolves knew no love for the humans, not like Max. They never would.

Gizmo nudged Max. "What do we do?" she asked him.

"Any ideas, big guy?" Rocky asked.

Max looked down at his two friends—his family—and saw them gazing back up at him with confidence. Even now, they trusted him to get them out of this.

He hadn't failed them, Max realized. Not yet.

He refused to give up, not now that they were so close.

"Keep very quiet," Max said as he padded back up the hill. "And stay low. We need to see what we're dealing with, and then we can figure out how we're going to get past."

Rocky and Gizmo followed Max to the highest point on the hill, and then all three dropped to their bellies on the hot dirt, keeping their heads low so that no one would spot them.

As Max had seen earlier, the wolves and coyotes were gathered on the main road between the chain-link gate and the metal wall. They circled one another. The largest figures—Bonecrush and Dolph—growled at each other, their hackles raised as they sized up the other one's pack. Both must have found the hole that Spots and Dots had dug under the fence.

240

There were only six wolves now, Max realized. Last he'd seen the pack, there had been eight, including Dolph. Two must have run away since then—or been left behind, badly injured after the fall into the gorge. Still, six wolves were much stronger and more dangerous than a Labrador, a Dachshund, and a Yorkshire Terrier.

The boulders and bushes next to the gate was where Spots said he and his brother had crawled beneath the fence.

The road where the wolves and coyotes faced off was slightly elevated. A low ditch ran along the road's edge, from the boulders to the metal wall. Meaning that if they were quiet enough, Max, Rocky, and Gizmo would have a place to hide, out of sight, on the other side of the fence.

"What do you think those boxes are for?" Gizmo asked, gesturing with her snout.

Farther south inside the fence, past the bush and the gate, a red box was attached to a support pole. There were more poles and boxes farther down at even intervals. Wires snaked out of the boxes, winding up the poles to a box with mesh covering the end, like the speakers Max had seen at the mice's mall.

"They remind me of those yellow boxes back at the train museum," Max said to Gizmo. "They may have buttons, too."

"I wonder what they do," Gizmo said.

Rocky growled and scratched at the dirt with his

hind legs, frustrated. "Why does it matter? There's nowhere to hide once you get past that fence. We'd be out in the open."

"There's a ditch," Max reminded him. "It's not much, but it's something."

Gizmo sighed, her attention back on the snarling beasts. "So what do we do now? Wait for them to leave?"

"Sure," Rocky yipped. "Let those wolves and coyotes fight it out. Whoever is left standing will be way too tired to try and attack us."

"I'm not sure that will work," Max said. "I get the feeling Dolph would win, and we all know he's not going to let some battle wounds keep him from confronting me."

"Oh, I guess you're right," Rocky grumbled.

As Max studied the fence again, his eyes kept coming back to the boxes and the little speakers atop the fence posts. The speakers reminded him of how Samson had used the sound system to frighten off other animals. Surely the red boxes wouldn't connect to the speakers unless they could trigger some sort of noise.

Max's tail thumped in the dirt. "I have an idea," he said. "I think we can get rid of Dolph, Bonecrush, and everyone else using those boxes." He licked his friends. "You ready to give it a try?"

"We trust you, Max," Gizmo said.

"We'll follow you anywhere, big guy," Rocky said.

Tail still wagging, Max said, "We're not home free yet. Stick close, and stay quiet. Ready?"

"Ready," Rocky and Gizmo whispered back.

Still on his belly, Max crawled down the other side of the hill, his eyes on their destination, the boulders next to the gate. Stones and scrubby plants scraped his underside, but Max clamped his jaws shut and snorted in and out, ignoring the pain.

When he reached the bottom of the hill, Max climbed back onto all fours. Checking that Rocky and Gizmo were with him, he ducked his head low and ran across the desert toward the big rocks.

The stench of coyotes and wolves overwhelmed Max as he ran closer. The air was noxious with their scents of dominance and anger, fear and anxiety. Their barks and howls echoed as the two pack leaders squared off.

"I will not tell you again," Dolph was growling. "Leave here. I have unfinished business with the mutts. And they are on their way."

"And I say again," Bonecrush snarled back, "so do we. You forest dwellers are as much strangers to these lands as those three pets. They promised us a feast of rabbits. They will deliver on this promise, or we will devour them."

"There are rabbits?" one of the wolves asked.

"None for you!" the coyote Max recognized as Moonrise yipped. "They are our rabbits. You are strangers!"

"We care nothing for rabbits," Dolph roared. "I must have Max. I will destroy that mutt and his two companions!"

Max came to a stop behind one of the boulders, waiting for his friends to catch up. He tried to ignore Dolph's rage-filled words, tried not to think about what the wolf intended to do with him.

Get past the wall, Max reassured himself. *Then you'll never have to deal with Dolph again.*

The wolves and coyotes howled, the tension between them threatening to break at any moment. Rocky and Gizmo crept into the shade of the boulder next to Max, panting quietly.

So far, the dogs hadn't been spotted. And the dry breeze must have been carrying their scents to the east, away from the beasts' strong, wild noses.

"This way," Max whispered.

Once more he dropped to his belly, crawling along the ground to the bushes.

Tufts of gray and red-brown fur were caught in the spiky leaves, and the scent of the wolves and coyotes was strong here. Fresh-turned earth formed mounds next to the bushes, where the other animals had enlarged the hidden passage.

Max let Rocky go first, then Gizmo. The small Dachshund and terrier made it through easily. Max crawled under last, careful not to get his own fur tangled up in the metal links.

Then they were all on the other side, between the fence and the wall.

Max saw the old, withered tree that grew next to the

wall, near where Spots said he and Dots had dug their tunnel. Sunlight reflected off the metal, glaring into Max's eyes. But he didn't care. He would get to the other side, where the humans were. He just had to.

As he'd guessed, the ground here was lower than the asphalt road, forming a ditch. It was enough space for the dogs to huddle together and hide, at least for now.

"Stay here," Max whispered.

Rocky and Gizmo curled up in the ditch, trembling. Keeping low, Max padded forward to peek onto the road. There, he saw that the coyotes and wolves had formed a rough circle, and in the center of that circle, Dolph and Bonecrush were pacing.

They were similar in size, though Dolph's bushier fur made him seem slightly larger than the desert coyote. Even so, it was clear that chasing Max across the country had taken a toll on the wolf. He still moved with a slight limp, and Max could see his ribs poking beneath the exposed skin where some of his fur had been burned away in the riverboat fire.

Bonecrush was better fed and had the larger pack. But Max knew the wolf's single goal was to take him down. He would never bet against his old enemy.

Dolph had nothing to lose. If a fight broke out with the coyotes, he would go dangerously feral. Max was certain he'd be the last beast left standing.

And then he'd be free to attack Max without any opposition.

Max carefully backed away from the growling packs. Turning his head, he looked down the chain fence at the nearest red box. There was a black button set in its center, and above it was a sign: ALARM.

Crawling back to his friends, he barked softly to get them to come in close. They lay huddled in the ditch, snout-to-snout.

"They're going to fight any minute," Max whispered. "But I think if we can press the button on that red box, it will make a noise that might send them scattering. The sign says it's an alarm, so even if they don't run away, I bet humans will come and scare them off."

Gizmo's tufted ears drooped. "That's if we can even get to the button before the wolves and coyotes see us. It's right out in the open."

Rocky let out a whine. "And we can't just make a run for the tree next to the wall. There's nothing but wide, open desert between here and there." Tucking his spiky tail, Rocky muttered, "I still trust you, buddy, but I'm beginning to get nervous."

Max scanned the distance between the hole in the fence and the silvery wall. Everything Rocky and Gizmo had said was true. As soon as they stepped out into the open, the wolves and coyotes would be on them.

Then an idea flitted through Max's mind. A dangerous, deadly idea.

From the road, the growls rose even louder.

"Last chance," Bonecrush howled. "Leave here or die."

"I say the same to you, desert rat!" Dolph bellowed back.

The fight between the leaders of the wolf and coyote packs was about to begin. And even though the ditch provided some cover, Max and his friends weren't exactly hidden. At any moment, a shift in the wind could alert the wolves and coyotes to their presence.

Max had no time to think about what he was about to do, no time to reconsider.

He looked down at his two best friends in the whole world. Gizmo with her fluffy face, bushy brows, and happy, trusting eyes. Long, slender Rocky, his black fur shining under the bright sun, his gaze fearful but steadfast.

Max would not let them down. Not now.

"I have a plan," Max said softly, his words almost lost under the noise from the road. "You're not going to like it, but you have to trust me, one last time."

Rocky sat up, alert. "What do you mean, one last time?" he yipped.

Gizmo trembled. "What is it?" she asked.

Forcing his tail to wag, Max said, "The only way to sound that alarm is if we have a distraction. You two press the button, then make a mad dash for that tree by the wall, where Spots said he dug a tunnel. The coyotes and wolves will try to escape here, by the boulders. And since you'll be hiding, any humans that come in the big trucks won't see you. They'll be busy chasing off the other animals, anyway." He let his jaw hang open and his tongue dangle. "See? Easy."

"Where are we going to get a distraction, buddy?" Rocky asked.

Gizmo raised her bushy brows in stunned realization. "It's Max," she said. "Max is going to distract them."

Rocky spun in a frantic circle. "No," he yipped. "No way."

"Rocky..." Max said.

Growling, Gizmo turned her back on Max and looked through the chain-link fence, back the way they'd come.

"You said we would be together forever," she sniffed. "You said you would never abandon us."

Max crawled forward and nuzzled her side, then leaned over to lick Rocky's forehead.

"I'm not abandoning you," he said. "I have every intention of meeting you at that tree, alive and well."

Gizmo turned back to face him, her tail tucked. "It's fourteen of them against one of you."

"I've faced worse," Max said.

"Not alone," Rocky said.

Max wagged his tail, for real this time. "Well, I'm not alone, am I? I won't let them catch me. Because I made a promise to you that we'd be family forever, and I keep my promises."

Ducking his head, he added, "But if the worst does happen, get under that wall. Find Dr. Lynn. See if you can find Dots. And never leave each other's side."

Roars and snarls echoed from the road. The fight had started.

Not letting Rocky or Gizmo say anything further, Max jumped up on all fours, spun around, and raced toward the road.

"Press the alarm!" he barked over his shoulder.

Suppressing every instinct that told him this was an awful idea, Max barreled through the dusty ditch next to the road, trusting that his small friends had listened.

Taking a deep breath, Max bunched his hind legs, then launched himself into the air. He leaped onto the scalding asphalt between two coyotes, who reared up, startled by the sudden appearance of a dirty, panting, yellow Labrador Retriever. Across from them, the skinny wolf Rudd snarled in surprise.

Dolph and Bonecrush leaped at each other, connecting chest to chest. Their eyes were wild and their ears flattened, their heads darting side to side as they lunged for each other's throats.

"Hey!" Max barked loudly.

Panting, the two pack leaders dropped to all fours. Fourteen pairs of beastly eyes glared at Max.

"*You*," Dolph snarled.

"Yup," Max said. "I'm here. Now come and get me."

And without waiting another second, Max turned on his heels and raced away from the angry, vicious wolves and coyotes, as fast as his legs could carry him.

CHAPTER 21

THE FINAL CHASE

Max ran south, away from the road, away from the tunnel he knew lay beneath the towering metal wall, the tunnel he was meant to dig through to find his people.

The wolves and coyotes did not hesitate to follow him.

The wolves howled, an unearthly, vicious sound that spoke of months of repressed rage, of the long miles they'd traveled to fulfill Dolph's quest for revenge.

The coyotes' calls were higher-pitched, full of righteous indignation, fury at being tricked by Max, and demands for the rabbits they were owed.

Dolph was the only one who did not howl.

He roared.

The wolf leader's cries rose over the mingled voices

of both packs. He had claimed Max for his own kill, and his roars were a warning: If anyone intervened, they risked their own deaths.

Max looked for his friends as he tore over the hot, rocky ground. He got a quick, blurry glimpse of Gizmo climbing onto Rocky's back by the fence, reaching for the button on the red box, the button that would set off the alarm.

It seemed slightly too high. What if they couldn't reach it?

But Max couldn't think about that.

The noise of the galloping wolves and coyotes behind him were like nothing he'd heard since the stampede of horses. Their paws dug into the dirt, kicking up a great cloud of dust that swirled into Max's nostrils and throat. Their cries were overwhelming, hammering his ears.

His head pounding, Max darted past a lone cactus. The stretch of desert between the chain-link fence and the massive wall seemed to go on forever, with nowhere to hide.

He could sense his pursuers at his heels, one wolf so close that Max could smell the decay on his breath.

He couldn't run forever. But he had to.

"I will catch you," Dolph snarled from directly behind him.

"You cannot get away, meat!" another wolf barked. Rudd.

The coyotes joined in, yipping insults.

"You are a pet. You were not made for this desert, not like us."

"The desert will claim you, pup! Then we will devour your remains!"

"Bring us the rabbits that we were promised!" Bone-crush barked.

Max did not waste his energy on a reply.

The wall was a shimmering blur beside him. Every muscle in his body screamed in pain, demanding that he rest. His lungs ached, and his heart leaped in his ribs, pumping as fast as it could.

The alarm was the only thing that could save Max now.

But it still hadn't sounded.

Daring another glance back, he saw the gleaming eyes of his pursuers. The dust cloud they'd raised was like a storm of sand behind them. Their teeth were bared, their ears flattened. Saliva streamed from their fangs.

And Dolph, the biggest of all the beasts, had pulled ahead of both packs. He was so close that with one lunge he could have snatched the tip of Max's tail in his jaws. In the quick glimpse of the wolf leader's eyes, Max saw a manic rage.

A crack sounded as Max's right front paw smashed against a rock.

Yelping in pain, he pitched forward, losing his footing and landing on his side against the hard-packed earth.

Adrenaline flooded his veins as, frantic, Max tried to jump to all fours and continue running.

But when he put pressure on his paw, it felt as if a bolt of lightning had zapped it. The agony was unlike anything he'd ever felt, and he dropped to the ground once more.

The wolves and the coyotes weren't prepared for this. Dolph barreled right past Max, the other creatures leaping over Max's trembling figure to continue the chase before realizing they hadn't just jumped over some rock that was in the way.

"He has fallen!" Prickle barked in glee.

Notch-eared Moonrise leaped up and down. "Let us at him. Let him lead us to our rabbit feast."

The pack of coyotes made to lunge at Max, but Dolph's wolves snarled and leaped at their throats, forcing them back. Rudd stalked in front of the desert canines.

"Max is ours," Rudd growled. "You have not earned the right to his flesh."

"We do not wish to eat his gamy meat," one-eyed Sharpshard yipped. "We demand our rabbits!"

Dolph flattened his ears and glared at the restless, panting coyotes. "You are fools. Living in the heat of this desert has burned away all your sense. Do you truly believe this domesticated mutt would eat wild meat like rabbits—or even know where to find it?"

"He promised," Shadow said, her tone uncertain.

"You were tricked," Dolph bellowed. "That is what this evil mutt does. He lies and tricks!"

Max watched the two vicious packs face off again, his jaw clenched tight against the pain. He climbed up on his three good legs, his front paw raised, throbbing in a constant rhythm that sent jolts of fire up his leg.

His tail tucked, Max hopped backward, away from the two packs of animals who agreed only on wanting to finish off Max and his friends.

Dolph turned his scarred snout away from the others. His black lips pulled back to reveal deadly, yellow fangs. The wolf leader approached Max slowly and purposefully, limping slightly.

"You are done," Dolph said, his voice low, menacing. "You are injured and cannot run."

Max forced himself to meet Dolph's stare. "You don't need to do this," Max said. "We made peace back in the town where we fed you and your pack, and when you helped us with Belle. Can't you let go of this idea that you need to hunt me? You are hurt, too. Don't you want to rest?"

"Rip his throat out, Dolph!" a gray-furred wolf barked.

Shadow lunged at her. "Killing the pet will be the honor of *my* mate, not yours!"

The she-wolf and Shadow leaped at each other as the rest of the packs watched. Only Dolph ignored them.

"I cannot rest," Dolph said as he paced in a circle around Max. "Every time I close my eyes, I have dreams

of you defying me in front of my pack. Of you and that sausage dog trying to light me on fire."

Max hopped, following Dolph's path, keeping his eyes locked on the wolf's.

"We didn't start that fire at the veterinary clinic," Max said. "You did."

"Lies!" Dolph roared up at the cloudless desert sky. Looking back at Max, he snarled, "You caused this when you refused us the food promised by your tiny mutt follower. Instead, you decided to fight, harming a member of my pack. You set this in motion." Standing once more in front of the wolves and coyotes, Dolph said, "You must die."

Max's ears twitched. He strained to hear some noise, some indication that even though the alarm hadn't sounded, the humans on the other side of the wall had heard the wolves and coyotes and had sent someone to investigate.

There was nothing.

This was it. He'd taken a chance to lead these vile, vicious beasts away from his friends, and his risk hadn't paid off. Any minute, Dolph would end their feud, as he'd promised long ago.

At least Rocky and Gizmo would be safe. Somehow, they'd get through the tunnel. They'd find Dr. Lynn and Rocky's pack leader, and after following Max through so much danger, they'd have a chance to rest.

Still, he wished he could have seen Charlie and Emma one last time.

Fighting a whimper, Max raised his tail and lifted his head up high. He lowered his injured paw as much as he could without pressing it against the ground.

If he was going to die, he was going to do it standing tall and proud.

The coyotes and wolves fell silent. They stared at Dolph and Max, watching and waiting.

Dolph stalked forward, his teeth bared, ready to lunge, to bite, to kill.

"You still think you can stand against me," Dolph said, moving nearer.

Max stood firm. "Do what you must," he said. Anger and despair rushed through him, and he barked each word louder and louder. "Try and finish me, Dolph. But be warned—I will *not go quietly*!"

And as though he had commanded it to happen, the alarms all along the fence rose into a ferocious din, their shrill noise piercing the desert.

Panic swept over the wolves and coyotes. They yelped in surprise, leaping back and colliding with one another, flattening themselves against the ground, their eyes wide and frantic as they looked for the source of the noise.

Even Dolph was startled. He shrank back from Max, fear flashing in his eyes. Max could smell the uncertainty wafting off him.

Bonecrush trembled as he glared at Max. "How have you done this?" he snarled, his voice barely audible over the screeching alarms. "How have you brought this noise? Make it stop!"

Max's own ears throbbed, but he refused to show fear. Hopping on three legs toward the confused, huddled beasts, he barked, "You have no idea what I'm capable of. I'm NOT just some house pet who got lost." He jumped forward again, hackles raised and teeth bared. Louder, he barked, "I have summoned blazing fires to destroy my enemies! I have made giant mountains come alive to trample those who dared to attack my friends! A cloud of bats came at my friend's call, swarming Dolph's pack and tossing them into a chasm. Dolph knows what I can do. When he asked for my help when he was starving, I gave it. But every time he attacks, I strike back even harder. You came after me—and now I make this noise to drive you crazy!"

"It's true!" howled the other gray wolf—one of the last members of Dolph's original pack. "I was there for all of it. Max is not just a normal dog. He is not!"

Max knew he was bending the truth, attempting to trick the beasts, as Rocky or Gizmo would have done if they'd been here. But it was all true enough that Max saw the fear in the eyes of the small wolf pack, who were clearly remembering what they'd been through in their leader's single-minded pursuit of Max.

Rearing back on his hind legs, Max bellowed, "You have underestimated me. Now you will find out what I'm truly capable of!"

The alarms squealed, undulating in pitch. With their sensitive hearing, no canine could withstand the noise for long. Max himself could only bear it knowing the noise would be his salvation and not his doom. Now the coyotes and even some of the other wolves were backing away.

"Come," Bonecrush yipped. "We must leave this place!"

None of his pack questioned him, not even notch-eared Moonrise, still salivating over rabbits that did not exist. Flattening their large ears in an attempt to stifle the noise, the eight coyotes raced past Max and the wolves, back toward the road and the hole that led under the chain-link fence, back to their home in the open desert.

The female gray wolf hesitated, then darted after the coyotes. The other gray wolf tucked his tail and chased after her.

"You cannot leave!" Dolph howled after them. "You will regret this betrayal!"

Over the blaring alarms, the female wolf barked in reply, "I do not fear you. I fear *him*."

Dolph growled in frustration and turned his attention to the remaining members of his pack: Rudd and two other red wolves. They whimpered and lay in the dirt, their front paws over their ears, afraid of the alarm but also of their pack leader.

"We stand fast," Rudd said through clenched jaws.

Max stood there, his paw raised, wishing desperately for the alarms to shut off but also hoping the remaining wolves would run away first.

But Dolph turned back to Max, quaking with rage.

"I do not need those traitors," he spat, stalking forward. "I wanted them to witness my triumph, but if they are too dim to see through your trickery, they do not deserve the honor."

Max felt as if the desert floor had dropped out beneath him. His energy was sapped, and his body throbbed with pain. He bared his teeth in a show of defiance, but if Dolph attacked, he knew he could not defend himself.

Then, from behind him, yipping louder than the alarms, came a defiant "Hiiii-YAH!"

A tiny black blur soared past Max and leaped into the air.

Rocky!

The Dachshund, once so fearful, now flung himself at Dolph. He was all claws as he landed with his front paws on Dolph's shoulders, his hind legs scrabbling at the exposed skin on the beast's side.

"Leave my friend *alone*!" Rocky barked as he bit down on a hunk of skin.

Dolph howled up at the desert sky. He leaped onto his hind legs, then dropped back down with such force that Rocky's paws slipped. But the Dachshund's jaws held firm, refusing to let go of the skin on Dolph's neck.

Dolph flung his head from side to side. As he spun in a circle, faster and faster, Rocky couldn't hold on.

With a yelp, Max's small friend flew off and landed hard on the rough desert dirt. He tumbled over scrubby brush until he landed against the nearby chain-link fence with a clang.

"Rocky!" Max barked, limping to his friend's side. "What are you doing? Why aren't you at the wall?"

Rocky raised his head, swaying back and forth, woozy.

"You didn't really think we'd leave you behind, did you?" he asked.

Dolph stormed at his remaining wolf pack, blood staining his light coat. "Stop cowering," he roared over the screeching sirens. "Get to your feet. Help me destroy these mutts!"

Rudd obeyed immediately, climbing to all fours with his tail tucked between his legs. The other two wolves were slower to oblige.

Before Max could ask Rocky if Gizmo was all right, before he could figure out how to get away with only three working legs, the alarms stilled.

The absence of sound was disorienting. Max's ears still rang with the memory of the piercing noise, but it was as if the entire world had gone silent.

Then came a new noise.

It was a quick, horrifically loud blast that reminded Max of the sound the elephant named Mortimer had made back at the Praxis laboratories. It was like the roar of some giant beast, echoing between the great wall and the fence.

They all looked north to the distant road. Large, boxy shadows on wheels veered off toward where the animals stood, kicking up a dust cloud ten times larger than the one the coyotes and wolves had created.

The shadows were trucks, Max realized.

The alarms had worked.

The people were coming.

CHAPTER 22

NOWHERE TO RUN

"Humans," Rudd said.

"They are back," said one of the other red wolves. "They will hurt us!"

The final three members of Dolph's pack turned tail and fled. Max could see the wolves and coyotes crowded around the ditch, barking and scratching at one another as they tried to squeeze under the fence.

One of the approaching trucks pulled away from the rest and parked next to the boulders where the desperate beasts were trying to escape. Human voices shouted, though they were so far away Max couldn't hear what they were saying.

A passenger in the truck raised a slender can with a horn attached to it, pressed a button, and let loose another blast of noise directly at the fleeing animals. A woman leaped from the vehicle, waving her arms and shouting, trying to shoo the beasts away from the small trench and toward the open gate. Some of the coyotes got the hint. They left their pack and tore through the gate, back out into the desert.

A flash of tan fur caught Max's eye, and he saw Gizmo racing as fast as her short legs could carry her along the fence. Seeing her friends, she stopped short, then looked up at Max, panting wildly.

"You're all right! I ran toward the tree by the wall after the alarm went off, and next thing I knew, Rocky was gone. I figured he'd come after you."

Max started to answer, then winced as a sharp pain lanced through his injured paw. He dropped to his side, near Rocky, keeping the paw raised.

He expected Dolph to take the opportunity to lunge at him or to run away after his pack.

Instead, the scarred, battered wolf leader stood, midway between the fence and the giant, gleaming wall, his body tense as he watched the trucks come closer.

Rocky groaned as he sat up. "Max, buddy, what happened to your foot?"

He and Gizmo huddled around Max, gently licking the fur near his injury. Max didn't respond. His throat was too dry to make a sound, scratched by his desperate barking. Instead, he kept his eyes on the vehicles.

There were three trucks coming toward them. The one in the lead was painted dark green. The roof, sides, and windshield were missing, though black poles outlined where they should be. The driver was a man in a tan uniform. Sitting next to him was a woman wearing a sleeveless white shirt and shorts, a baseball cap shading her eyes.

Behind this vehicle were two big trucks with dark canvas over their beds. Max could see more uniformed figures inside.

Animals from all over the country had warned Max about these trucks. These weren't the good people. They were the ones who had worn frightening black masks over their faces as they'd torn humans from their homes, forcing them away from their beloved pets. They had spirited all the people away, packing them in tent cities like the ones Max had dreamed about, past the wall.

When they'd met Dr. Lynn, she had told the three dogs to follow her but to steer clear of humans—many of them distrusted animals now. Spots's brother had gotten caught, and now he was gone. What they'd done to Dots, Max didn't know, though he hoped for Spots's sake that his brother was still alive.

The green truck came to a stop a short distance away from Dolph, as the two other trucks pulled up next to it.

Dolph stood his ground. When the smallest truck

kicked on bright, glaring headlights, the wolf leader did not move. He didn't even flinch when the woman in the baseball cap blasted her horn.

"What is he doing?" Gizmo asked.

Max raised his head, wincing at the effort. His whole body throbbed with pain now. Though it hurt him to speak, Max barked, "Don't be a fool, Dolph! Run! This is over now."

Trembling, Dolph turned his head to face Max. "It is over," he said, "when I say it's over."

And then Dolph darted forward.

Not toward Max, or Rocky, or Gizmo.

Instead, he raced toward the nearest truck, the one without windows or a roof.

The woman with the horn shouted and dropped back down in her seat. The man quickly turned and reached behind him.

"Max is mine to destroy!" Dolph howled.

The wolf leader leaped onto the hood of the car, landing with a heavy, metallic thunk. He reared back his head and bellowed.

"You humans cannot deprive me of this! You are supposed to be gone! This is our world now. You do not belong! Leave here!"

The man turned to the front with something in his hand. He aimed it at Dolph, and *pop!* A new noise stung Max's ears, and a feathered dart embedded itself in Dolph's neck.

Dolph's snarl turned into a surprised yelp, and his entire body went slack. He fell against the hood of the vehicle with another heavy thud, then slowly slid down toward the front bumper, his eyes closed.

Max, Rocky, and Gizmo huddled together next to the fence, watching slack-jawed.

"Is he..." Gizmo whispered.

Dolph's chest rose and fell, ever so slightly.

"He's not," Max said, feeling an odd sense of relief. "He's asleep."

The man and woman hopped out of the truck to investigate the fallen wolf. Another man in tan pants and a white shirt, with dark glasses propped on his nose, ran to join them from one of the other trucks.

"Mask on, Les!" the sunglasses man said as he neared them. "You haven't been inoculated like Cassie and I have."

"Yes, sir, Ben," the man in the uniform said. He reached into the car, producing a little white mask that he put over his mouth and nose. The man with glasses— Ben—and the woman in the baseball cap—Cassie— didn't seem concerned about doing the same.

"That was a clean shot, Les," Cassie said, adjusting her cap. "I thought the wolf was going to jump into the truck."

Les laughed, his voice muffled by the mask. "No problem, Cassie. Sometimes you need a good old-fashioned tranquilizer to knock out those wild ones."

Cassie rolled her eyes. "Please, you weren't doing it to help me. You just wanted to protect that pretty face of yours from the big, bad wolf."

"I dunno," Les said. "I'd probably look pretty cool with a scar."

While they talked, Ben pushed his sunglasses onto his head and examined Dolph. He lifted up Dolph's black lips and shone a penlight in his eye, then gingerly touched the scars, burns, and fresh wounds on the wolf's gray-furred body.

"This guy," Ben said as he stood up, "is not from around here."

Turning toward him, Cassie said, "No kidding. We're in the middle of the desert. And that is definitely not a coyote."

Ben shook his head, bewildered. "I don't mean this wolf just hopped the border. This species is exclusive to the north. He had to have traveled hundreds of miles to get here. And judging by his scars, he went through a lot."

"What do we do with him?" Les asked.

Ben stroked his chin and looked Dolph up and down.

"Put him in the back," he said finally. "We'll figure out something."

Wearing gloves, Cassie took Dolph's hind legs while Les hefted up the great beast's head and shoulders. Together, they gently placed Dolph's sagging, limp form in the back of the small truck.

"What are they going to do with him?" Gizmo asked.

"I don't know," Max said.

Again, Max recalled the sad, harrowing tale of Dots digging through to the other side of the wall. There'd been a flash of light—headlight beams from a truck like this one?—and then Dots was gone. Could he have been shot with a tranquilizer, too? Max wasn't entirely sure what that was, except that it seemed to have put Dolph to sleep.

Side by side, Ben, Les, and Cassie strode purposefully past the trucks, directly to where Max, Rocky, and Gizmo lay huddled together.

Les still held the thing that had sent a dart to put Dolph to sleep.

This was it. Max had been warned many times about these people. He had met so many animals who claimed they preferred a world without the two-legged humans.

And Max himself had reassured so many abandoned pets that the people still loved the dogs and cats they'd had to leave behind.

But the world had changed.

Maybe only a few humans, like Dr. Lynn, still cared for their lost animals.

Maybe the rest of them wanted to shoot dogs with darts and throw them into the back of trucks to be carted away.

As the humans approached, Max whimpered. Sensing his pain and fear, Rocky and Gizmo stood tall between him and the people.

If this was the end, Max thought, at least Rocky and Gizmo were here. At least he was surrounded by those he cared about, when Dolph, Bonecrush, and their packs would have forced him to die alone.

But he did not want this to be the end, not when Charlie and Emma were so close. With the chase over and the wall looming just beyond the parked trucks, he could hear the murmur of thousands and thousands of voices on the other side. Two of those voices belonged to his pack leaders. He knew it deep in his aching bones.

As the humans drew near, Rocky growled and Gizmo flattened her ears.

"Whoa," Cassie said, adjusting the brim of her cap. "Looks like we've got some feisty ones here."

Ben put his hands on his hips. "They'd have to be to have come this far."

Les raised the thing that had shot the dart at Dolph. "Should I tranq 'em?"

Cassie said, "That thing has way too big a dose for dogs this size. We'd need one with a dosage like we used on the coonhound that dug under the wall."

"That the dog you're keeping in quarantine by the mobile lab?" Les asked.

Cassie nodded. "The old man and woman who own him have been sitting vigil outside his kennel for weeks now. They don't seem to care if Dots gets them sick."

Max's ears perked up at the name. Dots wasn't dead after all—and he was with his people!

Ben knelt down in front of the dogs, his lips pursed. "These aren't just any dogs. They've got collars with trackers on them. Looks like the big dog is favoring his paw."

"Are they the ones Dr. Sadler is looking for?" Cassie asked.

"Could be," Ben said. He stood up. "You remember the breeds?"

Cassie shrugged. "I thought one was a yellow Labrador, like this guy."

Rocky and Gizmo relaxed, ceasing their shows of aggression.

"They don't seem like they want to hurt us, big guy," Rocky said.

Gizmo licked between Max's ears. "Yeah! They seem nice. The lady even said Dots is safe on the other side of the wall!"

Max closed his eyes, shutting out the bright, blazing sunlight. He inhaled, taking in the scents of the humans: their sweat, their crisp clothing, the mixture of soap and deodorant.

They were people. Real, live people, just like Dr. Lynn. People who wanted to help them.

Rocky and Gizmo rose up in frantic barks as Max felt someone loom above him. He opened his eyes just in time to find Ben clipping a leash to his collar. He flinched, wanting to recoil—he didn't know this man or where he intended to take him. But he didn't have the energy to resist.

"Shh, shh," Cassie said, her hands held out for Rocky and Gizmo to sniff. "I smell like a nice lady, right?"

The two small dogs huffed at her hand, but Max could tell they were anxious.

"Up we go," Ben said as he helped Max roll over onto his good feet. "We need to get a look at that paw of yours."

"What should we do with the other two?" Cassie asked.

Ben turned to her and said, "Put them in the back of truck two. We'll scan them for the virus and decide if they need to join Dots in quarantine. I'll put this injured guy in the back of my truck."

Gizmo's ears snapped up, alert. "What?" she yelped. "No! Max, don't go with them. They're going to separate us!"

Rocky recoiled from Cassie's fingers and spun in a frantic circle, howling, "We need to find Dr. Lynn, big guy!"

Les shifted uncomfortably, holding his white mask close to his face. "Why are they doing that?"

Cassie backed away slowly. "Something's agitating them. Could be coyotes coming by on the other side of the fence, maybe?"

Ben started back toward his truck, tugging on Max's

leash. "Come on, boy," he said. "It'll be all right. I'll make the hurt go away."

Gizmo leaped up and down. "Please let us go with him. We're a family now."

Max sat down and yanked back with his neck, resisting the urgent tugging that he knew was meant to make him follow, a tugging he hadn't felt in many long months.

"It's all right, boy," Ben said.

"Don't freak out," Cassie told the dogs. "Remember, it's been a long time since they've seen humans," she said to the two men.

"They can't understand us," Rocky said, tucking his tail. "They don't know who we are."

Gizmo dropped to her belly in despair. "What do we do?"

Tires squealed and an engine roared. The three confused humans and the three dogs all looked up to see another small truck—the one that had veered off to scare away the wolves and coyotes. It came to a screeching halt, and a figure jumped down from the passenger side. The woman waved her arms to brush away the dust that had enveloped her.

And as the dust cleared, Max saw who it was.

Dr. Lynn.

She was just as he remembered her: flower-print shirt, white hair tied back, and a giant straw hat to keep the sun off her kindly, wrinkled face.

Happiness flooded Max's body. Despite his exhaustion and the pain in his paw, he leaped back onto his hind legs and barked, "Dr. Lynn! It's me, Max!"

All three dogs' tails went into overdrive as they quivered with unbridled glee. Their tongues lolled free, and they barked their greetings.

"We missed you!" Gizmo yipped happily.

"Come tell these bozos who we are," Rocky barked.

Cassie laughed. "So I think you know these guys."

Ben nodded respectfully as Dr. Lynn ran past him, straight toward Max. "Dr. Sadler," he said to her.

And then she was on her knees in front of Max, ruffling the fur on his sides, graciously taking all the licks he had to offer.

"Come here, Rocky," she said, spreading one arm wide to welcome him into her embrace. "You, too, Jane," she added, using the name she'd given Gizmo when she couldn't retrieve any information about her, back in the little town.

The three dogs huddled together, letting Dr. Lynn take them into a great big hug. The other humans watched, amused.

"I take it these are the ones you told us about," Ben said, handing Dr. Lynn the leash he'd attached to Max's collar.

Dr. Lynn stood and straightened her straw hat. "That they are," she said, detaching the leash from Max's collar and tossing it aside. "These three dogs are the ones who helped save us. I want them with me at all times."

She turned to the dogs. "I think we found each other just in time, my friends," Dr. Lynn said. She smiled wide. "I have located your families."

CHAPTER 23

REUNION

Les was the one who carried Max to the truck.

The white mask he'd worn now dangled below his chin, since Dr. Lynn had said Max and his friends posed no threat of infecting him with Praxis. The soldier shoved his sleeves up to his elbows, crouched down, and carefully took Max in his arms.

Max leaned into the man as he walked around the backside of one of the large, canvas-covered trucks. Les smelled of the ocean, briny and fresh. He whispered softly to Max.

"That's a good boy," he said. "You're doing great."

Max narrowed his eyes in contentment, then gave the man a long, appreciative lick on his face. His cheeks were rough against Max's tongue from the stubble growing on his jaw.

Les laughed. "I think he likes me!" he said.

Someone held the green cloth flap aside so that Les could climb into the back of the truck. It was dark in there and warm, with a sweaty, damp heat. Another uniformed man sat on a bench. Gently, Les laid Max on a low metal table, cool beneath his matted fur.

Max moved his paw, then immediately whimpered.

"Poor guy," Les said, scratching between his ears.

The other man wiped the back of his hand across his sweaty forehead. "Never thought I'd see the day again," he said. "But here we are, petting dogs like nothing ever happened. I still can't believe Dr. Sadler found a cure."

Max leaned his head into Les's scratching fingers, lingering on the simple joy of a human's touch while idly listening to the two men.

"We're not out of the woods yet," Les said as he moved his hand to rub Max's belly. "The doctor says these three are safe, but she's still got to do her science stuff before we can all go home. Cassie—you know, the girl with the baseball cap, one of Dr. Sadler's assistants?"

"I know her."

"Well," Les went on, "she told me they need to manufacture a cure for everyone who's gotten infected before they can mass-produce vaccines for the rest of us, and they need to release some airborne component to get rid of Praxis in all the wild animals. Then there's all that damage to clean up before it's safe to go back to the cities...." He shook his head. "I try not to think about it. You don't think about much, do you, Max?"

Max barked, "I actually think about a lot," but of course Les couldn't understand him. The man just laughed at the dog trying to answer him.

Crossing his legs, the other soldier leaned back, put his hands behind his head, and asked, "You a dog man, Les?"

"I always had cats, actually," Les said. "I grew up in the city."

"Naw, I don't do cats," the other soldier said. "It's all about dogs. Big ones like Max here. Best friends you'll ever have."

More people approached the back of the truck, and Max held up his head to watch as Ben climbed in holding Rocky, followed by Cassie with Gizmo.

"Hi, buddy!" Rocky barked.

Max wagged his tail. "Hey, guys."

Carefully, Ben and Cassie placed Rocky and Gizmo in a black plastic crate next to the machinery. They immediately jumped up with their paws atop the crate's edge, their tails wagging.

"Thank you!" Gizmo barked. "That was fun!"

Rocky turned to Gizmo. "What's a dog gotta do to get some kibble around here?"

Max's own tail wagged even harder, thumping against the tabletop.

And suddenly, Ben and Cassie had attention only for him. They offered him comforting shushes as they stroked his fur. Max was so consumed with pleasure that he barely noticed when they pricked him with a syringe.

Panic flooded him at this new, small hurt, and he tried to sit up. His injured paw smacked against the table, and he howled.

Footsteps sounded as one more person climbed into the truck. Max smelled her before he saw her: Dr. Lynn.

She shoved past her assistants and took Max's head in her hands. Stroking his cheeks, she stared deep into his eyes.

"It's okay, Max," she said. "This is just to help with the pain while we fix you up. You're fine."

"I'm fine," Max barked softly, even though he knew she couldn't understand him.

Muscles relaxed in Max's body, one by one, until he found himself lying back on the table. It felt as though he'd melted into a fizzy liquid, becoming a weightless puddle. His tail wagged once, twice, and his eyes fell into slits. The human faces hovering over him turned hazy and indistinct.

Distantly, he heard the truck's engine roar to life, felt the vibrations beneath his belly as it started to move over rough terrain.

He drifted in and out of dreams.

One moment, he was in the truck, feeling someone moving his paw. The next, he was hundreds of miles away, back in his kennel. The cages were full of dogs, barking madly, but one by one they faded away until it was just Max and Madame.

Choose the right path, Maxie, Madame said.

Max felt the truck bumping and jostling as it climbed back onto the main road. He heard sounds like metallic wheels straining to turn—the enormous wall opening to let them through.

But in his dream, Max was in an abandoned city. Dogs marched side by side through streets and alleys, following the Chairman, who somehow led them from high above the skyscrapers.

Rocky was next to Max, and Gizmo, too. *We're always with you,* they told Max.

Then Max was on a boat. A giant elephant sat on the deck, his trunk raised to trumpet at the sky. A large, rotund pig trotted in a circle around him, oinking at the other animals.

The boat spilled into an ocean, and Max was alone in the waves. He paddled to shore, where he heard playful laughter.

Fully healed, he walked down a long road, alone. A dark, inky cloud flowed up toward the sky behind him, growing larger with each step.

He crossed a bridge over a murky swamp to a perfect small town. A mansion, once grand but now decaying, was on his left. And on his right was an old-fashioned train pulled by a steam engine.

Then he reached a fork in the road.

At the end of the left path, he saw Rocky and Gizmo, sitting happily inside their golden circles. The third linked ring was empty, waiting for him.

Standing on the right path were Charlie and Emma. They knelt down, smiling, their arms held out to embrace him.

The darkness swelled, as though unsure which path to take.

There was a center road. But it stretched out forever on the horizon, and Max couldn't tell where it led.

Madame's voice echoed once more. *Make your choice, Maxie.*

Max awoke.

Before Max could open his eyes, smells overwhelmed him.

Smoky fires melded with the scent of seared meat and charred vegetables. Intense body odors swirled through the air: the musk of humans, some of it blended with flowery perfumes. There was the rancid smell of overflowing trash cans, and the heady pungency of gasoline and rubber.

Then there were the voices. He heard thousands upon thousands of people talking, some laughing, a few shouting, all mingling in a constant hum. Somewhere, someone was playing music on a guitar, while others sang along. There were electronic pings and beeps, the noises of human games.

It was the sound of city streets and rural markets. Of families crowded around a dinner table, of farmhands calling to one another in the fields.

It was *human*.

Max jerked awake, accidentally hitting his paw against the tabletop. He winced, expecting a flood of pain.

Nothing came.

His paw was wrapped tightly in white gauze that smelled of medicine. A throbbing numbness ran up his leg, but it was a dull ache compared to the pain he'd felt before.

Barks rang out, and he angled his head to look down at Rocky and Gizmo, who were still in their plastic crate. They were hopping and wiggling with excitement.

"He's awake, Dr. Lynn!" Rocky yowled. "The big guy is back from dreamland!"

Gizmo said, "They fixed you up just in time, Max. Dr. Lynn is outside right now. She says your people are here!"

"My people," Max said. Then, realizing what that meant, he sat up, his floppy ears jerking to attention. "My people!"

Strong hands massaged his side, ruffling his fur, and he looked back to find Les petting him once more.

"Look who's feeling better," Les said.

The canvas flap opened, letting bright afternoon sunlight into the truck. A familiar face peeked through: Dr. Lynn.

"I hear Max is awake," she said with a wide grin. "I think it's time he is reunited with the family he traveled so far to find."

"Yes, ma'am," Les said with a salute.

Max couldn't speak. He heard Rocky and Gizmo barking with excitement, but he couldn't focus on their words. Trembling all over, he let Les clip a leash to his collar, then obediently jumped down to the floor of the truck. He tried to press his front paw down—but his bandages wouldn't let him.

So Max half walked, half hopped toward the back of the truck. Carefully, he climbed down the metal stairs to the dusty road.

The asphalt was hot beneath Max's paws, and he closed his eyes against the sudden glare of the sun. The smells and sounds of people surrounded him, an over-whelming cloud of humanity.

Max slowly opened his eyes, letting them adjust to the brightness. Les handed his leash to Dr. Lynn, who gently tugged him forward.

Max looked around him. More men in tan uniforms like Les's lined either side of the street. They stood in front of orange-and-white barricades, just like the ones Dr. Lynn had left as a trail. Behind them were the people, all trying to get a glimpse of Max. Through their legs, he could see the endless city of tents, canvas homes of many shapes and sizes set up in rows and circles, makeshift places to live until it was safe for the humans to return to their real homes.

Though the soldiers stood completely still, their hands held behind their backs, the people behind the barricades clung to one another, talking endlessly, pointing at Max. Some shouted, their tones angry, but others cried out reassuring words.

"That's the dog that saved us, Mommy!" a little girl shouted.

"How is he safe?" a man yelled. "Are we sure he's safe?"

"You saw it on the news," another man said. "These are the dogs that aren't infectious. They helped that scientist find a cure."

Lights flashed, and Max closed his eyes once more. Cameras. People were taking pictures and videos of him. Behind him, he heard people shouting to Rocky and Gizmo, who were outside the truck now, barking at the crowd.

"Yeah, that's right," Rocky yipped. "We're your heroes!"

Max tried to look back at his friends, but with all the flashes and waving arms and the sea of moving faces, he felt overwhelmed. He trembled, anxious.

Dr. Lynn rubbed between Max's ears. "It's okay, Max. I'm right here with you."

And then the noise of the crowd no longer mattered, because he smelled his pack leaders.

Charlie and Emma were here. And not just in his dreams.

Opening his eyes wide, he saw them only a few yards away. Just as he'd dreamed, they knelt on the ground, side by side, waiting for him. They were as skinny as he remembered, but so much time had passed that they seemed larger now, more grown-up. Their parents stood behind them, their hands on the children's shoulders.

Max whimpered at the sight of his human family. So many emotions flooded through him at once that he felt wobbly, unstable, as though his legs were going to give out at any moment.

Charlie wiped away tears with the back of his fist, and Emma reached up to clutch her mother's hand, and they looked at Max with such longing that he finally knew for certain that he'd been right.

They hadn't left him because they'd wanted to.

They loved him. *They loved him.*

Despite his injured foot, Max bounded forward, tugging the leash from Dr. Lynn's hands and letting it drag behind him on the hot desert road.

"Max!" the two children cried in unison.

Then he was in their arms as they practically tackled him. He wriggled every which way, his tail slapping, his tongue lashing out to lick them and make sure they knew how much he loved them.

Charlie stuck his head into Max's fur, sobbing. "We missed you, boy. You're the best dog ever."

Emma ruffled the fur on his neck, laughing as Max licked all over her face. "You're the smartest, greatest dog in the world."

"I came for you," Max barked. "I never gave up. So many animals told me I'd never see you again, but I knew I'd find you."

Though they couldn't know what he was saying, somehow his pack leaders—his human family—knew exactly what he meant.

"We know," Charlie said, hugging Max tight.

"We love you," Emma said, cradling his head.

Past the soldiers, some of the people watching started to cry. Happy tears, Max hoped. They smiled and said "awww," and some of them had to turn away, watching these two children reunited with their pet.

Watching as Max finally achieved what he'd set out to do all those months ago, when he'd escaped his kennel and begun this dangerous journey.

"Mom, look!" Emma cried, letting go of Max with one arm so that she could point. "Those are his friends!"

Max craned his neck to see Ben and Cassie walking side by side, each holding a leash. At the end of those leashes were Rocky and Gizmo.

"Hey!" Max barked at them, his tail flying. "Here they are! These are my pack leaders! Come meet them!"

Rocky and Gizmo barked and lunged forward. Cassie pretended Gizmo was carrying her along, holding on to her hat as though it might fly away, and the people laughed. Even some of the soldiers seemed unable to contain their smiles.

Dr. Lynn's assistants let go of their leashes, and Rocky and Gizmo leaped at Charlie and Emma, wiggling with glee. Charlie grinned as he sat down, letting Rocky climb into his lap and lick his arms. Emma rolled Gizmo onto her belly and rubbed her all over.

"Oh, buddy, you weren't kidding," Rocky yipped.

"Your pack leaders are the best!" Gizmo barked.

Max sat down, his tongue hanging free as he watched his new family meet his original one. He felt warm deep inside, and not just from the desert heat. It was a comforting warmth, like lying at the edge of his pack leaders' beds, watching over them as they slept.

Charlie and Emma's parents stood behind their children, arms around each other.

"I still can't believe he managed to get all this way," their mother said.

"It's quite the story," Cassie said. "The media will be lining up for interviews."

Charlie and Emma's dad ran his hand through his hair. "You're right. I didn't think of that. That's . . . going to be something new to deal with."

Cassie reached out and shook the parents' hands, saying, "Nice to meet you at last. I'm Cassie Stone, one of Dr. Sadler's assistants from the Praxis project." She cleared her throat. "Or former assistant, I guess. She no longer wants anything to do with the company except to make sure this virus goes away forever."

Max looked behind him to see Dr. Lynn—or Dr. Sadler, as the humans kept calling her—talking earnestly with Ben. They both had their arms crossed.

"Have you found out where the other owners are?" the children's mother asked.

Cassie nodded. "Well, we've found one, anyway. Dr. Walters was Rocky's owner. You know him, right? He was your vet?"

"That's right," the dad said.

"He relocated to Florida during the evacuation, and he plans to stay there," Cassie said. "We're going to fly Rocky there, and then the terrier we've nicknamed Jane will stay with us, in case we need to do more tests."

Max stiffened. Even though Rocky, Gizmo, Charlie, and Emma still played together while the crush of people from the tent city looked on, Max no longer felt happy.

These humans didn't know Max could understand them.

They weren't just reuniting Max with his human family. They wanted to separate him from Rocky and Gizmo—his dog family.

Max's head spun, making him woozy. The warmth inside him gave way to an icy chill.

He had a choice to make, one he'd never expected.

He could go home with Charlie and Emma, back to the farm, what he'd wanted and chased after all these many months.

Or he could keep the promise he'd made to Rocky and Gizmo, the two small dogs who'd been by his side as they'd crawled through muck and raced beneath blazing skies. Who'd been brave in the face of every deadly obstacle.

The cloud of darkness in his dreams hadn't been a storm or whatever else he'd imagined it to be. It was always at his heels, Max realized, because it was a dark, terrible choice he was meant to make.

He couldn't outrun it any longer. It was time to pick a path and take a leap of faith.

Still trembling, Max hung his head low and tucked his tail.

He had made his choice.

CHAPTER 24

THE CHOICE

Max looked at the humans around him, one by one, and then he did something he never thought he'd have to do.

He growled at them.

Charlie noticed it first, being the closest to him. Still petting Rocky, he scrunched up his brows and looked at Max.

"What's wrong, boy?" he asked.

Cassie turned from the children's parents and held her hand out to Max. "It's all right. Do you want your kids to pet you again?"

Max snapped his jaws at her, and she pulled away, her eyes wide with surprise.

Baring his teeth, Max raised his hackles and backed

away from her. "I'm sorry," he barked loudly toward Charlie, knowing his pack leader couldn't understand what he was saying. "I don't want to do this. I'm so sorry."

"What's wrong with that dog?" a man shouted from the huddle of people behind the orange-and-white barriers.

"That creature is sick!" a woman cried. "It isn't cured at all! It's gone rabid!"

A commotion rose as panic roiled through the crowd of people. The soldiers yelled at everyone to calm down.

Rocky noticed Max's change in manner before Gizmo. He leaped out of Charlie's lap, leaving the little boy sitting on the road, confused.

"Max, buddy," Rocky said as he trotted close. "What are you doing? These people are being nice!"

Max backed even farther away from his human family. "We have to make them let us go," he said. "They're going to ship you away, and the doctors are going to take Gizmo. They want to split us up."

From Emma's lap, Gizmo's ears perked up. She leaped away from the children, darted between Cassie's legs, and ran to Rocky and Max.

"They want to separate us?" Gizmo asked. "But why? You said your pack leaders would love us. They were petting us so wonderfully...."

Max had to force himself to appear threatening, even though the looks of betrayal on Charlie's and

Emma's faces made him want to curl up on the ground and whimper.

"They don't know," Max said. "They don't realize we're a family, too. I promised you both that we would be together forever."

"But what about your pack leaders?" Rocky asked.

"The people were saying the three of us can't stay together. So I had to make a choice," Max said. "And I chose you."

The murmur of the crowd grew louder and louder. Someone screamed, and wood crunched as one of the barricades was smashed. The soldiers did their best, but the people in the city of tents had spent too long in the heat. Max could smell the fear and anger coming off them. They were becoming a pack, as wild as any group of animals out in the forests and swamps and deserts.

"Mom, what's happening?" Charlie asked, panicked.

"I don't know," his mother answered.

Ben had been talking to Dr. Lynn, who stood in the road, watching the animals, seeming just as surprised as the others. Now he grabbed the end of Max's leash, trying to drag him forward.

"No!" Rocky yelped. He leaped at the man, biting his pant leg and tugging on it as hard as he could.

Ben shook his leg, shouting, "Let go!"

A bottle flew from the crowd, soaring over the people and landing on the road next to Max, Rocky, and

Gizmo. It shattered into thousands of gleaming crystal shards.

Emma screamed in surprise, and her father pulled her close. Cassie flinched as bits of glass flew in her direction. Seeing that the dogs had gone still, she reached down and grabbed both Gizmo's and Rocky's leashes.

"This way," she said as she started back toward the trucks. "Don't get stubborn on us now."

Gizmo flattened her ears and dove at Rocky, who still clung as hard as he could to Ben's pant leg. She nibbled at Rocky's collar and it flew off, freeing him from the leash.

"How did she learn to do that?" Ben asked.

Before anyone could stop her, the tiny terrier leaped over the broken glass and landed on Max's shoulders. Just as with Rocky, she chewed at the collar around his neck until she managed to unfasten it.

Cassie dropped the end of Gizmo's leash and held up her hands. "I get it," she said. "You don't want to be dragged around."

Rocky let go of Ben, leaving drool on his khaki pants. He and Gizmo huddled on either side of Max, joining their growls to his.

Both of Dr. Lynn's assistants raised their hands as they closed in on the three dogs. Charlie and Emma's dad came over to help corral the three pets. The commotion in the crowd began to calm down, as some of the soldiers marched toward the dogs, too.

"What do we do?" Rocky said with a whine.

"What we always do," Max said. "Run."

"To where?" Gizmo asked.

"To anywhere," he said. "All that matters is that we're together."

With one last mournful look at Charlie and Emma, who were hugging their mom, Max turned away from the approaching humans and ran down the road on his three good legs.

Rocky and Gizmo did not hesitate to follow. They raced between the lines of soldiers and the onlookers, past Dr. Lynn, back toward the truck they'd ridden in.

Dr. Lynn's assistants, and Charlie and Emma's dad, and the soldiers all shouted at the dogs, calling for them to stop, to heel, to be good dogs. Les ran after them, begging Max to come back.

But even with his injured foot, Max was too fast for the humans, especially now that he didn't have a leash trailing behind him. Reaching the back of the truck, he, Rocky, and Gizmo ducked and raced under it, where humans wouldn't be able to follow.

Panting for breath, they huddled in the shade beneath the vehicle. It smelled of oil and gasoline, and Max's stomach twisted with nausea and hunger. He realized he hadn't been fed or given water yet, that his body still ached all over from fleeing the coyote and wolf packs.

The shadows of human feet surrounded the truck on all sides, and heads peeked underneath to see the three dogs huddling there. Max, Rocky, and Gizmo growled at the humans, snapping their jaws, doing their best impression of animals gone feral.

"I'm a mean dog," Rocky said, though Max could hear the sad whimper behind his barks. "I'm a mean dog, ya hear? You don't want to mess with me."

"Me, too," Gizmo yipped. "I'm...I'm a bad dog!"

Human voices rose louder, some calling for the dogs to crawl out to safety. Others insisted this meant something had gone wrong with Dr. Lynn's cure. More air horns blasted as the soldiers shouted at the tent-city residents to go back to their makeshift homes, that there was nothing to be seen here.

"I hate this," Gizmo whimpered. "Max, you don't need to run away from Charlie and Emma for me. Please, go back to your pack leaders."

Max tucked his tail. "I wish I could, but I can't leave you two alone. You came all this way to find my humans. You deserve your own family."

"Everything will be all right," Rocky said, nuzzling Gizmo's side.

Hands reached under the truck, but none were able to grab the dogs. Someone had a looped piece of rope at the end of a long pole, but the three dogs easily avoided being lassoed and dragged out.

"How will we get out of here?" Rocky asked.

Max didn't have an answer.

And then, the truck above them bounced, and Max

heard someone stomping up the metal steps that led into the canvas-covered back.

"Listen to me!" Dr. Lynn's voice cried out, enhanced like Samson's back at the mall. "These animals are not dangerous. The cure is real, and it is coming soon. These three dogs are more intelligent than you know— they can understand human speech."

The shouting gave way to intrigued murmurs.

"They are frightened," Dr. Lynn went on. "Because they have bonded in a way none of us could have expected. And now they fear being separated."

"She knows," Max whispered.

An electronic squeal echoed, followed by Dr. Lynn saying, "For the sake of restoring our world, so that we can all go home, please no more shouting, no more flashbulbs, no more throwing bottles. Let me talk to these three."

"They're just dumb dogs!" someone cried out.

"I assure you," the scientist said, anger in her voice, "they are not."

The microphone Dr. Lynn had been speaking through crackled and went silent. The truck bounced once more as she descended the steps, knelt down, and looked underneath at the dogs. Smiling, she beckoned them with her hand.

"Do we trust her?" Gizmo asked.

"We trust her," Max said.

Crawling forward with Rocky and Gizmo at his side,

Max emerged from beneath the truck. Dr. Lynn's words must have sunk in, because the people behind the barricades stood still, watching quietly. Standing behind the doctor were her assistants, Les, and Max's human family.

Cassie clutched her baseball cap in both hands, twisting it anxiously. "So was it me?" she asked. "I mean, I knew they could understand what I was saying, but I didn't know they'd care. I thought they'd just want to be back with their human families."

Dr. Lynn sat up on her knees, holding out her hand to let Max, Rocky, and Gizmo inhale her reassuring scent.

"You remember Mortimer?" she asked Ben and Cassie.

"Of course," Ben said. "Hard to forget an elephant who never forgets. Literally."

Scratching behind Max's ears, Dr. Lynn said, "He was always so lonely, yet he found no solace with the other Praxis test subjects. He longed to be with others like himself, who were as smart as he had become." Simultaneously scratching Rocky and Gizmo beneath their chins, she added, "These three found a way to fill that need in one another. They're not just smart; they're emotionally complex in a way we've never seen in dogs. Whatever they went through to get here has bonded them deeply, well beyond a typical canine pack. They really are a family now." She stood up and wiped the dust off her knees. "It would be cruel to split them up."

Charlie and Emma tugged at their parents' shirts.

"Mom!" Charlie said. "Dad! We have to take them all home together."

"I don't know if that's a good idea," their father said. "With everything we have to do to get the farm up and running again, having two new dogs to take care of could be a hassle."

"That's right. It might be best if the doctors took them," their mother said.

"No!" Emma cried. She came forward and flung herself at the animals, hugging Max around his neck with one arm while pulling Rocky and Gizmo in close with the other. "They have to come with us. Max came all this way to find us; we can't just ship his friends away."

Charlie stared up at his parents with pleading eyes. "Please let them come home. We'll take care of them. We'll do all the work, we promise!"

The children's parents looked at each other, eyebrows raised.

"They are cute," the mom said.

"And they're not too big," the dad said. "How much dog food could one Dachshund eat?"

Max wagged his tail, amused.

"If it helps at all," Dr. Lynn said, "my own home is not too far from yours. I would be happy to set up a laboratory nearby so that I can help take care of the dogs while we continue our work."

Charlie and Emma's parents leaned into each other, whispering softly. The assembled crowd watched, silently.

"Do you think they're going to say yes?" Gizmo asked, trembling in anticipation.

"As long as they don't find out how much kibble Rocky eats, they might," Max said.

Rocky growled playfully. "Hey!"

From somewhere, a woman yelled, "Just say yes, already!"

A murmur of laughter ran through the crowd. Smiling, the dad ruffled Charlie's head and said, "Looks like we have some new members of the family."

Dr. Lynn gazed down warmly at the three dogs.

"That is, as long as that's all right with you," she said to them.

"It is!" Max barked, leaping up onto his three good legs. "Oh, it definitely is!"

Cassie clapped her hands. "I think that's his way of saying yes."

And as the crowd applauded and cheered, all four members of Max's human family knelt down to pet him and Rocky and Gizmo.

The darkness Max had felt looming over him all throughout his long journey was gone, burned away under the hot desert sun.

His families, new and old, could finally be together.

TWO YEARS LATER

◆

Max awoke to the trilling of birds.

It was midmorning, and he lay on the front porch of his family's home. Blinking open his eyes, he peered up to see three small brown sparrows perched side by side under the overhanging roof. They sang a chipper song, not the least bit concerned that they'd woken him up.

Fresh-cut grass filled his nostrils, and he heard mooing and oinking from the cows and pigs. Farmhands whistled as they shifted hay bales in the barn, and the motor of one of the big tillers hummed out back.

"Uncle Max, Uncle Max!" a young voice barked.

Max braced himself as the pattering of tiny paws came up the porch stairs. Seconds later, four tan-and-black puppies barreled into his side, slobbering him with licks. Startled, the sparrows cheeped and flew off.

"Wake up!" squealed the tiniest of the puppies.

They were little things, their features a clear mix of Dachshund and Yorkshire Terrier. Their faces were similar to Gizmo's, except for the floppy ears that dangled like their father's. They had wispy tufts of fur above their eyes and noses and long, low bodies that weren't quite as sausage-shaped as Rocky's. Their black, brown, and white fur was mostly sleek, though it curled up at the ends of their tails and ears, like their mother's.

Charlie and Emma had found out that Dachshund and Yorkshire Terrier crossbreeds were called Dorkies, so that's what they called the four puppies.

The largest of the puppies, a boy the children had named Milo, spun in an excited circle in front of Max's snout.

"C'mon, c'mon, c'mon," he yowled at the porch ceiling. "It's time for TV!"

His brother, Blue, tackled the bigger puppy, nipping at his ears. "I wanted to tell him!"

Max's tail thumped against the porch as he watched the brothers wrestle through half-closed eyes.

The tiniest puppy, Chloe, stood in front of Max's nose. "Uncle Max!" she squealed. "I know you're awake; your tail is wagging!"

Her sister, Lola, lay nearby, her head resting on her

paws. She swished her hindquarters back and forth slowly, preparing to jump on Max.

Before Lola could leap, Max rolled over onto his side, then pushed himself up on all fours. The puppies yipped in surprise. "You don't think I'd miss TV time, do you?" he said to them.

"Yay!" Milo said. "Follow me!"

The puppies bounded ahead, tumbling over one another in their eagerness to get to the door. Milo yanked on the rope that had been connected to the door handle, and the other three shoved the door open. Together, the four little Dorkies and Max walked onto the shiny wooden floor of the foyer, and then into the living room.

Max jumped up on the couch and lay down while Milo, Blue, and Chloe curled up against his belly. Lola climbed onto the coffee table, sniffed at the remote control, and then pressed a button. The big TV blinked on to the dogs' favorite new program.

The half-hour show featured heartwarming stories of humans being reunited with their pets as they returned to the homes they'd been forced to flee.

Max never missed an episode, and the puppies always made sure to join him. Sometimes Charlie and Emma watched, too.

He didn't know most of the animals on the show, though he was always happy to see dogs, cats, and other pets cradled in the arms of their pack leaders.

But sometimes, the show featured an animal Max knew. Those were the best episodes.

It was how he saw the cats Panda and Possum reunited with a tall blond man who hugged them close as they purred in his arms.

Belle was there, too, happily helping her family as they worked to clean up the wreckage of their mansion. The owners of a beachside inn were surprised to find their Saint Bernard, Georgie—the former Mudlurker—at the mansion, too, having befriended Belle. It was enough to make them relocate back to Baton Rouge.

The Dalmatian firedogs, whom Max had met on the riverboat *Flower of the South*, were hailed as heroes for having watched out for a whole city's worth of pets. They were filmed sitting proudly on the back of a fire truck alongside smiling human firefighters.

The German Shepherds named Julep and Dixie were found walking back from the Praxis laboratories. These days, they watched over their town once more with the other canine police. Max wondered if they'd managed to make it to the labs and gone through the second half of the Praxis process, or if they'd given up and headed home.

Then there was the feature on the town of DeQuincy. Humans had found the tiny train abandoned in the desert, near animal tracks leading all the way back to the small town. In DeQuincy itself, the pets that had been left behind had bonded with wild animals—Spots with

Stripes the skunk, the puppies and kittens fast friends with a precocious raccoon Max knew was Tiffany the Silver Bandit.

Spots was at long last reunited with his pack leaders, the old man and woman who owned the train museum. He was also reunited with Dots, who'd been saved by Dr. Lynn's team after he made it past the wall. The footage of the two brothers bounding at each other as though they were young puppies again made Max's tail wag uncontrollably. He was even happier when the narrator of the show announced that Spots's human family had adopted his best friend, a skunk, as a pet, despite trepidations about her smell.

And there were many more stories of reunions still to be told.

Of course, life wasn't as simple as that. Other TV programs showed towns and cities ravaged by storms and neglect, overrun with all manner of creatures. Wild animals had become brazen, refusing to leave the towns they'd claimed as their own. Exotic beasts had escaped from zoos. People reported hearing music at night from a junkyard in Baton Rouge. A city of dogs seemed strangely organized against returning humans, and it was proving impossible to clear out a mall that was now full of mice.

Then there were the animals who'd never heard Max's message of hope, who hadn't known that the humans still loved their abandoned pets. They'd gone feral, afraid of humans, even while other pets leaped with joy at the sight of their returning pack leaders. Kind humans worked to rehabilitate these lost pets, to teach them to trust people again. But it would take time.

It was a new, wild world, one the humans were still trying to reclaim two years later. Though vaccinations had been given to all the people and medication had been released into the air to destroy the Praxis virus dormant in all the animals, normal was still slow to return. Two winters had passed before the birds had even started to migrate back. It was still a novelty to see a flying V of ducks in the clouds or to spot a hawk circling the sky for prey.

But despite the world still trying to sort itself out, on the farm it was almost as if nothing had ever changed. Except, of course, for the additions of Rocky, Gizmo, and the puppies.

And Dr. Lynn.

She was staying in a guest room on the second floor of the farmhouse. She'd returned to find her home destroyed by vandals, angry at her part in unleashing the Praxis virus. A new home and laboratory were being built for her on the land that once belonged to Rocky's pack leader, who decided to stay in Florida after learning his home had been claimed by fire.

But Dr. Lynn didn't mind staying at Max's home. Charlie and Emma called her Grandma Lynn, and the whole family accepted her as one of their own. Sometimes Max saw her looking at a photograph of herself and Madame Curie, sadness in her eyes. He hoped that being with his family, she didn't feel so lonely.

Dr. Lynn had done lots of interesting experiments with the dogs since they'd come home. They had even learned how to communicate with humans. She had a big board with words, pictures, and letters on it. That was how Jane's name became Gizmo again, after the terrier nosed at the letters she thought seemed right.

It was also how Max found out what had become of Dolph.

Dr. Lynn rubbed the sides of his neck after he pointed at the picture of the wolf on the board and then whimpered.

"Don't you worry about him, my friend," she said. "We found a new home for him at a wildlife preserve far from here. He keeps to himself now, howling at any wolf that comes near him. But he doesn't try to come after you. I think, maybe, he has chosen to let you be."

Max thought of the wolf sometimes. Dolph had been so desperate to prove himself in front of his pack that he had chased Max across the country. Now, Dolph had no pack. Unlike Max's journey, the wolf's had left him without a family, alone with his anger in a strange new place.

It seemed a sad life. But Max knew Dolph had chosen it for himself. He'd let his hatred consume him. Not all wolves were like that, not by a long shot. Max hoped that one day Dolph could forget Max completely and find some peace. But he did not know if that was something the scarred former pack leader would ever be able to do.

Music blared from the TV, and the puppies squirmed against Max's chest and belly as the credits scrolled across the screen. Another episode of the reunion show had come and gone.

"Did you see anyone from your adventures?" Blue asked.

"Not today," Max said. "But there's always tomorrow."

Little Chloe leaped to the floor, then jumped up and down. "Time to play! It's playtime!"

"Let's go find Mommy and Daddy!" Lola said as she bounded after her sister.

Max climbed down from the couch, stretching before he followed the energetic little fur balls into the kitchen, where they were racing around Charlie and Emma's mother's legs.

Then Milo swatted the back door, making strange, guttural barking sounds.

From any other dog, the barks would have been excited gibberish.

But to humans—and to Max, Rocky, and Gizmo—the noises sounded almost as if the puppy was saying in human words, "*Open, please.*"

The mother, who had been washing dishes, dried her hands on a towel and then carefully made her way over the yipping puppies to open the door.

"*Thank you!*" Lola said in human tones.

The kids' mother laughed. "You're welcome," she said as they disappeared outside. "You keep an eye on them," she told Max.

Max wagged his tail and barked in reply, though unlike the puppies, he couldn't make his barks sound like people words.

The speaking trick was unusual. The Dorkies had figured it out all by themselves, listening to human words and mimicking their sounds. Of course, dogs didn't have the vocal cords or mouths to truly speak like people, but that didn't stop the brothers and sisters from trying.

Dr. Lynn had told Max that the puppies were unique. Not just smart like him and Rocky and Gizmo, but intelligent in a way that shouldn't have been possible.

"I wonder sometimes if you three are the last dogs," she'd said to Max one day. "And if our pack of Dorkies are a new species entirely. Maybe something good and wonderful has come from Praxis, after all."

Max knew that his nephews and nieces were special. Even though, watching them leap at mosquitoes and fall on their bottoms just like the small animals back at the train museum, he couldn't help but see them as simply the energetic little puppies they were.

"They giving you trouble, big guy?" Rocky asked.

The Dachshund lay next to Gizmo in the doghouse they shared outside, just off the back porch. A large, half-eaten bowl of kibble sat before them.

"Only as much as their parents ever did," Max said as he padded toward them. "How are you two?"

Gizmo climbed to her feet and came to nuzzle Max's side. "I'm wonderful," she said. "Maybe a little worn out from chasing these four all morning." She wagged her tail. "But it's a nice tired."

The puppies had raced into the field behind the house. Blue howled, "Come and play with us, Mommy and Daddy!"

Rocky groaned and flopped onto his side. In the past two years, he'd returned to his slightly plump state.

"I'm not sure I'm up for it," he said.

Gizmo nosed him until Rocky finally rolled onto his feet.

"You need to work off all that kibble," Max said, with a wag of his tail.

"Yeah, yeah, big guy," Rocky said, waddling out of the doghouse toward his children. "Can't blame a dog for wanting to relax."

"I bet I'll get to them first!" Gizmo said.

"No way," Max said.

But before he could move, Gizmo darted forward, running like the wind.

"Aw, no head starts!" Rocky yowled.

He and Max barked happily as they raced after her. A cool breeze rose off the distant trees, carrying with it the smell of rodents hiding in the brush and dandelion seeds dancing in the air.

"Four plus four!" Milo yipped as he chased after his brown-furred sisters.

"Eight!" Chloe barked back.

"Three plus three!" Milo cried.

"Nine!" Lola yipped, then quickly said, "No, no, it's six. Six!"

"I have no idea what those crazy pups are talking about," Rocky said.

"It's something Dr. Lynn has been teaching them," Gizmo said. "They say it's arithmetic, whatever that is. They've been practicing all week!"

Across the field, Max saw Charlie and Emma tossing a ball back and forth.

Max changed course, heading toward the two children. Rocky, Gizmo, and their four little Dorkies followed.

More than once, in his dreams, Max had seen Charlie and Emma playing in the distance, always disappearing before he could reach them.

But now, they stood still, the ball forgotten as they waited to embrace their new family of dogs.

Max tumbled into their open arms, the kids squealing with laughter, the puppies swarming over everybody as they wiggled in excitement, Rocky and Gizmo barking in delight.

Max had found not just one family on his long journey, but two.

And he'd brought them home.

ACKNOWLEDGMENTS

And so we've reached... *Journey's End.*

Little, Brown Books for Young Readers has been faithful and wonderful throughout the life of our series. Thank you to the entire team who worked on the books, led by series editors Pam Garfinkel and Julie Scheina. So far, this has been the best publishing experience of my writing career.

Of course I also have to thank the team at the Inkhouse for once again letting me play with our cast of dogs. Ruth Katcher was there every step of the way to help polish my words and keep me going, and Michael Stearns and Ted Malawer gave the book a great foundation for me to build upon with their top-notch storytelling skills.

Allen Douglas, the series illustrator, always amazes me with how he captures the scenes from the book so perfectly. Thank you also to the always enthusiastic Andrew Bates, who used his incredible talent to narrate the audiobook versions of the series produced by the fine folks at ListenUp Audiobooks.

I can't fail to mention all of you guys, too, readers of all ages who have shared in this story with me. Thank you for picking up our books and for following the perilous journey of three very brave, very smart dogs all the way to the end. I hope you enjoyed how the story of Max, Rocky, and Gizmo ended just as much as I loved writing it for you!